# Branded

## By

## Emma Garriott

Copyright © 2017. All rights reserved.

No part of this publication may be reproduced, stored in a retrieval system or transmitted in any way by any means, electronic, mechanical, photocopy, recording or otherwise, without the prior permission of the author except as provided by USA copyright law.

All characters appearing in this work are fictitious. Any resemblance to real persons, living or dead, is purely coincidental.

The opinions expressed by the author are not necessarily those of Revival Waves of Glory Books & Publishing.

Published by Revival Waves of Glory Books & Publishing

PO Box 596 | Litchfield, Illinois 62056 USA

www.revivalwavesofgloryministries.com

Revival Waves of Glory Books & Publishing is committed to excellence in the publishing industry.

Book design Copyright © 2017 by Revival Waves of Glory Books & Publishing. All rights reserved.

Published in the United States of America

Paperback: 978-1546529194

Hardcover: 978-1-365-94282-2

# Branded

By

Emma Garriott

# Table of Contents

Dedication .................................................................................. 1
My First Battle .......................................................................... 3
Justice and Mercy ..................................................................... 7
The Curse of Mercy ................................................................ 15
Angel of Mercy ....................................................................... 25
Garcel's Story ......................................................................... 39
The Riddles of History ........................................................... 45
Worthless Scum ...................................................................... 53
Discovered .............................................................................. 59
Raliph's Boldness ................................................................... 65
Mercy's Folly .......................................................................... 71
Raliph and Garcel ................................................................... 81
Women Silenced .................................................................... 95
Larcos Has Come ................................................................... 99
Mercy, Hold Me Up! ............................................................ 105
One of Them? ....................................................................... 111
Raliph and Adann ................................................................. 123
Adann's Secret ...................................................................... 127
Many Sunsets ........................................................................ 137
Nadia ..................................................................................... 141
Raliph's Surprise .................................................................. 153
The Heart of Sunfare ............................................................ 159
Garcel's Courage .................................................................. 167
Courage or Folly? ................................................................. 173
Doing Something .................................................................. 179

| | |
|---|---|
| Nadia's Choice | 197 |
| Raliph's Despair | 199 |
| Raliph's Valor | 207 |
| Raliph's Convictions | 215 |
| The Darkest Street in Whitestone | 223 |
| To Bear the Mark of Ellar | 225 |
| Mercy's Doubts | 231 |
| Mercy's Strength | 237 |
| Mercy's Bitterness | 243 |
| Mercy's Darkest Hour | 251 |
| What Mercy Cannot Change | 253 |
| Mercy and Shatam | 255 |
| Raliph's Secrets | 261 |
| Raliph's Plan | 271 |
| Raliph's Facade | 277 |
| A Forbidden Devotion | 281 |
| Raliph's Story | 291 |
| Farewell to the Dim Marshes | 297 |
| A Marking in Black | 301 |
| A Mighty Prince's Greatest Battle | 305 |
| A Different Sort of Legacy | 311 |
| The Merits of a Good Deed | 315 |
| A Darker War | 317 |
| A Bitter Victory | 325 |
| The End of a Love Story | 329 |
| The End of Nadia's Strength | 333 |

# DEDICATION

To Dad. Thanks for being my biggest support since the beginning.

# MY FIRST BATTLE

**Mercy**

I was fifteen. It was a small battle defending a town which I do not even remember the name of. Since I was ten, my royal father had encouraged me to train in archery so I could fight to defend Tarlen from the ruthless rebels we have battled for hundreds of years. All three of my brothers were there under my mother's request whose constant worry and hesitation toward letting me go into my first battle was annoying all of us.

I get to be like my royal father, Justice, Garcel, and Adann; my three brothers who have all been fighting in the war since they were teenagers. I thought. My sword strapped to my side and my quiver over my shoulder. I was with the archers and had to stay there under direct orders of my mother.

"If there are any more safety precautions in this ordeal, we might as well not even call it a battle at all," complained Garcel.

Mother would just get a funny look on her face and bite her lip.

Regardless, I was still there, on the battlefield, watching the rebels come over the hill as I readied an arrow to the string. They looked vile. Like a dirty hoard of animals charging at us in a chaotic frenzy. Some were not even dressed; some were covered in armor head to toe. Many had long unkempt hair and all of them moved like slinking urfanes ashamed to be seen in the light of day. For a moment, I almost felt sorry for the creatures. How in the name of Ellar has the rebel army survived this many years? I wondered. There must be thousands of them if this sorry lot was an example of their military.

But then, they struck, I watched, amazed to see our orderly lines fall back. But only for a moment until Garcel led a cavalry charge and took the head of one of the leaders, throwing it into the crowd of degenerates. I was not scared. I was proud of my brother who feared nothing and could change the tone of the battle in an instant. I killed several of the swine from my place with the archers but I was getting bored. I longed for the rebel ranks to get closer to me so I could give them a taste of my steel. Adann glanced back at me from his place with the infantry and winked at me. I knew it was my moment.

Jumping away from the archers, I spied a dead horse to give me leverage to see the enemy better. Scared and excited but more excited than scared, I climbed on top of the dead horse so I could see the wild faces of our enemy. With quick precise hits, I took down three swordsmen with my arrows. I saw a soldier nearing the horse of my eldest brother, Justice, who was fighting about twenty feet from me where the battle was thicker. I took my aim as I knew so well to do and my enemy spied me. His eyes widened into huge white dinner plates. "Mercy!" he cried.

I froze. People talk about freezing in battle but I was of royal blood. Nothing should make me lose my cool in the middle of a fight. I stared at the soldier. He looked young. His wild eyes changed in my mind from savage to lost. What is happening to me? He approached me and I fought to shoot the arrow from my bow but it won't go. No matter what I do. As if some power beyond my knowledge was keeping the arrow from being released. A spell. I was under a spell. My eyes widened in terror.

"Justice!" I shrieked.

Garcel, from his place leading the charge saw me, frozen in my place. He turned his horse around leaving a trail of pursuing arrows behind him. With his huge sword, he smashed the skull of the boy who called my name and then grabbed me by my shoulder and carried me away from the battle.

"What is wrong with you?" he bellowed at me, sweat pouring down his face.

Tears welled up in my eyes. "It wasn't my fault!" I cried. "Something happened. I couldn't move. A spell or something."

He rolled his eyes.

"He called my name."

Back at the palace in Whitestone Garcel told the story of my humiliation on the battlefield red in the face with anger. I felt silly trying to explain that I must have been under some sort of spell.

"You can't see the enemy as people. That's what you did, Mercy," said Adann. "It makes sense if he called your name, you would see him differently."

Blushing, I remember that I did start seeing that brute differently.

"It can happen to anyone in their first battle," said the king. "We will try again and next time, don't be so ambitious."

I nodded, breathing a sigh of relief.

"No," the queen stood up from her throne beside the king. "You say you felt you were under a spell…"

"Yes…but that's just how it felt. I'm sure Adann's right."

"You might have been."

Everyone in the throne room stared at her.

"Before you were born, I prayed to Ellar to make you special…" she bit her lip. "Merciful and good."

"You did this to me?" I cried my face turning red, now from anger.

"It would seem," she said hesitating. "That Ellar gave you the power of mercy, even in battle."

"You fiend!" I shrieked. "Now, I'm handicapped from ever fighting in battle again. Did you ever stop to think what I wanted? We all know you have stupid ideas about the war but why did you have to project them onto me? I hate you!"

From that day on, my life was ruined. I would watch my brothers and father go off and fight against the rebels and I was stuck at home with nothing to do but embroidery and knitting. Justice stopped going into battle as much and stayed home to govern, trying to teach me how to judge cases like he would but all I wanted to do was fight. Father barely spoke to me and I blamed Mother. She made me like this. The worst part of it all was I could still remember the look in that boy's eyes and remember how Garcel had smashed his skull when he came to save me.

My family became separated. Justice was close to Mother and would try to be close with me. Garcel was close to Father and Adann followed Garcel around. I rarely spoke to anyone but Justice now. I felt separated like a freak with no means of redeeming myself. All that mattered in my family was the war, fighting it and ending it. Having glory stories told about us. Now, all hope of that was lost for me. And it was all my royal mother's fault.

That was the end of my story as anybody interesting, ever.

# JUSTICE AND MERCY

Shields, swords, and metal armor glistened in the sunlight; my eyes ached from the glare of the battalions of mighty Tarlen soldiers riding away. My face pressed against the glass of my window while I watched soldier after soldier ride out of the gates and over the bridge to Fardmore. I was not with them. Sighing, I backed away from my window and sat down on my bed.

The rebels were led by Larcos; the mere mention of him is the epitome of cruelty. Attacking glorious Tarlen cities, he ravaged them for all their riches, took slaves from the greatest of families, and killed thousands. Under threat of death or enslavement, he forced the simple farmers of Tarlen, who would usually pay homage and tax to the king, to be in allegiance with him.

City by city, his army desolated the land. Killing, enslaving, and robbing the subjects of the king. The Cansten rebels wreaked havoc everywhere they went. With the terrible but mysterious god, Morglin, on their side, the rebels devastated Tarlen changing it from a mighty nation into a divided land. The rebels were nothing but trouble and I wanted nothing more than to destroy every one of them. But all I can remember is that horrible day when a rebel solider called my name.

The curse of my name. I, Princess Mercy, one of the greatest archers in Tarlen, was stuck at home with nothing to do but knit and waste the hours away waiting for my confounded brothers to return with all their glorious trophies and mighty tales. My name. My irritating name. How I abhorred it. Mercy. Of all things! Before I was born, my mother pleaded to the god, Ellar. The god who had deserted Tarlen. Blessed with his ear, she asked him to make me merciful. Why she would do that no one can say. So the day I was born, I was named Mercy and since that day if any man, woman, or child pleads mercy from me nothing in my power can stop me from granting it, no matter how much I abhor them. I lie back on my pillows and stare at the ceiling. Paintings of mighty wars, the history of Tarlen documented on my roof; mighty men and women fighting for the right cause; kings on their powerful steeds with their sons at their sides driving their blades into the enemy. The broken blades of the enemy on the ground. Blood. The dying, the dead. The victorious Tarlen king with his sons at his sides. How I wished to be painted on the roof. But I never could because I had to be merciful because my mother, without consulting me, got Ellar to give me the curse of mercy, crippling me for life!

The castle and city were in the hands of my eldest brother, Justice, so I decided to descend from my room and go complain to him.

As the eldest of the royal family, Justice was heir to the throne to inherit the kingdom of Tarlen. Beloved by all and respected, he was to the point of making the rest of us look bad. If ever Mother needed a 'good example' for the right behavior, she would use Justice. It drove Garcel, Adann and I crazy but it was impossible to be angry with him. He had a way of making us feel good about ourselves. He had a way of bringing out the good in us we might not have seen. I'd often wondered if he had the same sort of curse that I had. Never in my mind could I recall a time Justice was not fair and just. If any pleaded to his sense of fairness, Justice would certainly execute it to the best that he knew how. No decision he made could be questioned because it was so wise and fair. He remained the hope of Tarlen in the midst of war and plague.

I found him practicing swordsmanship with his instructor. He smiled at me when I appeared. "Ah, Mercy, it is impossible to resist smiling at the sight of your beautiful dark curly head." He kissed my forehead tenderly. "Dare I hope you are seeking me out?

Or is there some other purpose you hold for your venturing here?"

"I merely came hoping to find you unoccupied so as to keep me company during this lonely hour when our brothers have left," I replied. I had lost all my previous irritation at the sight of him.

Justice sheathed his blade. "Any excuse to stop this gruesome practice would suffice, but if I were to be riding in the wild fields with the wind behind me and the hills before me, at the bidding of my fair sister, well, happily would I return to be in your presence for as long as you could desire my sorry person."

A smile played at my lips again. Justice could always do that to me, make me smile.

He put on his intricately embroidered coat. He looked fine in the deep blue color. "Tell me; is your presence here for a purpose, or merely a whim?" He asked taking my hand and placing it on his arm. He always spoke eloquently like the prince that he was. Whenever he did, I found myself checking my normally rude and coarse tongue.

"Both. I fear I have become angered toward Garcel and Adann for forbidding me to use my archery skills against the rebels," I sighed. "So I sought you out hoping to be lifted from my sorry mood."

Justice waited in case I had more to say. When he was sure I had finished speaking he began. "The war is not what you think, Mercy." His low soft tone drew me in with interest. "Gory scenes of blood and bones strewn over our once peaceful forest glades, our cities, our villages; these are not sights to be envied."

I bite my lip in irritation; Justice has never quite believed that I was under a spell when I froze that day two years ago but merely got a case of bad battle nerves. "It is not the sights that I desire. You know I have seen it once before. But I long for the opportunity to use this skill which I have attained for the good of Tarlen."

Justice waited again, walking in silence through the marbled hall of the castle. "You have many skills and gifts, Mercy. Your skill in archery is by no means small but you mustn't demote the others you possess. Perhaps, while our brothers are away, you may have more chances to work and improve your other skills and gifts for the good of Tarlen."

I knew I should listen to Justice. He was never wrong. But I cared little for my other skills and 'gifts', particularly the one regarding my name.

"You may find your other abilities to be of more value in the end."

"You are treating me as a child, Justice, as though you were our royal mother," I said.

"I apologize, dear Mercy. I was merely making a request. For the love of your beloved brother who is so fond of you, consider what I have said."

I could not be mad at him. "In that light, perhaps, I will consider it."

Justice embraced me. "You are an angel, Mercy. A beautiful angel."

---

Dinner was dull for Justice came in late and I never speak to mother unless I have to. He had been judging a dispute between two landlords. When he entered, he looked upset.

"What happened, Justice?" Queen Laria exclaimed. "Your sad countenance, I fear, adds to the disparity of this table."

Justice bowed. "I apologize, Queen Mother. I'm afraid I'm allowing my sorrow over the sorry state of our kingdom and people intrude my countenance." He slumped down beside me and sighed.

"What's wrong with the kingdom?" I whispered when the queen wasn't listening.

Justice sighed again. "The greed and oppression practiced in Tarlen is corrupting it, degrading it to a dirty heap of waste, the foul stench choking the inhabitants. The plague which is sweeping the poor families of our nation, the very plague which can be easily cured by merely good food and water is killing many even in the cities." He glanced around nervously and continued in a hushed tone, "More young boys have disappeared."

My heart sank. I felt sick. 'Disappeared' meant only one thing, joined the rebel army. I sighed. Now my countenance matched Justice's. What was Tarlen coming to?

---

I was awoken in the middle of the night by a loud knock on the door. I stumbled out of bed, put my robe on and opened the door.

"Justice?" I said, surprised. "What are you doing at my door at this hour?"

He breathed hard. His cloak was on and he was fully clad in armor. "The distress signal has been seen from Bellorn. I'm leaving tonight with some troops to try to save the city."

"But Garcel and Adann have already left to fight the rebels at Fardmore."

"It must have been a decoy; the major attack is on Bellorn. They need reinforcements."

"Will you be alright?" Feeling protective, I placed my hand on his shoulder, wishing I did not have to give him up.

He held my hand there with his for comfort. "I don't know how it will all fare but I will take care of myself and the troops and aim to return as soon as I can."

I nodded biting my lip. I knew he was afraid.

"Pray to Ellar for me," he whispered. I embraced him. Then he turned to leave.

I closed my eyes allowing tears to escape. I was scared for him. I never feared when Garcel or Adann left, only Justice.

I thought of what he'd asked me to do. No one ever prayed to Ellar. Not since Morglin came and raised the rebel army against us. Not since a plague began to ravage the poor inhabitants of Tarlen. Not since Ellar abandoned us. Queen Laria and Justice were the only people I had ever heard of who prayed to Ellar or even mentioned him. *'Perhaps though, I might make an exception for Justice,'* I thought as I watched Justice disappear from my view down the shadowy stone hallway.

---

Time passed slowly for the next few days. Embroidering, I sat by my window where I could watch for him. I wanted to make something for Justice when he returned from Bellorn. He'd always loved golden embroidery.

When the sun began to set on the fifth day, I saw a slow party of battle wearied and wounded soldiers trudge over the drawbridge. On a stretcher lay a man, torn and bloodied… I raced down to meet them. I only had to see their faces to know who the man on the stretcher was. Justice.

They put him down at my feet. I fell to my knees by his side. "Justice," I wept. He had been stabbed deep in the side and shot in the shoulder by an arrow. He was barely breathing, blood covered his body. I knew there was no hope for him.

"Mercy," he smiled. "Remember what I said…before I left…"

I nodded; my face red from weeping.

"Bare my chest."

I stared at him surprised.

"Bare my…ow…heart! You need to see…"

I obeyed and pushed the crimson torn tunic away from his chest and looked. A brand. Gilded in golden letters it read, *"Ellar's"*.

He tried to smile. "I'm marked…"

The Queen appeared at his side. She also saw his mark. Tears filled her eyes when she realized his impending death.

Confused, I stared at his chest as breath slowly left him. His eyes focused on me as though he were trying to give me something or bind me to a promise. I stared back into his eyes biting my lip, tears streaking my face. "Whatever it is," I whisper, "I will try to find out what you are saying."

My solemn promise seemed to relieve him of some great burden. He smiled as he released his last breath.

"No!" I shrieked with every ounce of my being. I embraced his lifeless body. My mother pulled me away from the body and held me while I wept. "No, no, no," I whimpered into her shoulder. The golden gilded letters flashed over my eyes as his final words echoed in the chambers of my mind. What did he want me to know? What were those letters? What does he want from me?

# THE CURSE OF MERCY

Garcel and Adann returned from Fardmore. When The Queen told them the news of Justice's death and his final words to them, they left immediately for Bellorn with many troops. In utter rage. I hoped they'd find some rebels, if merely to vent their anger on. I wished desperately I could go with them. I was angry too.

I spent my days weeping over Justice until the days melded together and they felt like a lifetime of grief. I wept over the many gifts he had given to me. I finished embroidering his coat and hid it among our childhood collections in a secret place adjoining my room only Justice and I had known about. I could not eat. No one could really. The whole kingdom of Tarlen went into mourning for him. He had been the hope of Tarlen. Now, he was dead.

My maid tried hard to make me eat. I tried to as well, but I could not. All I wanted to do was lie on my bed and weep or stare out my window and pine for him. I wondered much about the mark on his heart and what he had tried to say before he died but it was beyond my grasp.

Garcel and Adann returned on their horses dragging a man behind them in chains. On his shoulder, I saw the mark of a Cansten rebel. His shirt was torn and his blond curly hair was unkempt and tainted with blood. Other than that, he didn't look too bad. His build was decent, though not as muscular as most rebels. Possibly, they were bringing him back as a slave. I heard Garcel and Adann were bringing him to the throne room. Curious, I went to discover why Garcel and Adann had brought him.

"Why have you taken this prisoner here?" the King, my father, asked.

"He's weak enough to give us information on the next rebel

attack. We intend to extract the information from him in the dungeons," Garcel replied.

Mother kept her face lowered. Unwilling to look up. I could tell she was disappointed about the whole concept of torturing a prisoner. I sure didn't care. He was a rebel.

The prisoner was silent. I watched his eyes scan the room. He didn't seem entirely aware of his surroundings. When he realized I was watching him, he lowered his eyes and stared at his chained hands.

"You intend to torture this man," said Mother sadly, disapproval clearly marked in her tone.

"Only until he tells us what we ask, then we'll kill him quickly," said Garcel rolling his eyes at her.

"Justice never tortured anyone," Mother whispered.

"Justice could get anyone to tell him whatever he wanted them to!" Garcel's eyes flashed at the mention of his brother. "As we do not have that gift, we shall have to degrade ourselves to dirtier methods." He motioned for Adann to follow him and they left with the prisoner being dragged behind them by soldiers.

Mother fell back onto her chair and sighed. I slipped away. Inside, I was glad they were torturing the Cansten wretch. Death would be too good for the animal.

---

Three weeks passed and nothing seemed to change. I pined over Justice and skipped eating for days in a row. I had no friends or family to fill his void. I had taken to staring out my window, or walking the halls of the palace, sometimes going into Justice and my old hideout hidden in the wall; it was where I could best keep Justice's memory alive. At night, I would slip into my closet and pass into the little door made for a young child. The hideout had a steep path which would lead all the way down to the dungeon if one wished to go. It had once been part of the palace before a king decided to make the halls more majestic and hid that passageway in stone. Justice had been the first to discover it when I was only three years old. He swore me to secrecy and we made many memories there. The passageway was perfect for hide-and-seek, though Justice forbade me to go all the way down to the dungeon.

One night, I couldn't sleep so I decided to go down those stairs. I slipped into my robe and lit a candle. I crawled into the hideout and down the broken stone stairs. I could stand up straight when I was descending the stairs though it was only narrow enough for one person to walk. My footsteps echoed in the dark passageway. It felt exciting to me to explore the secret hall again. Perhaps, I almost felt a semblance of joy since I'd seen Justice's eyes fade into death.

Though I did not mean to, I reached the bottom of the passageway. I heard voices through the wall. Someone shrieking.

"Ahh! No! Please! Mercy!"

Oh no, I felt that hated power on me. It took control of me and forced me nearer. I saw a breach in the wall. Unthinking and unable to stop myself even if I did, I crawled through.

The voices went on.

"Shut up you miserable worm!" Whoever the speaker was kicked the wailing man then slashed him with a whip. It tore the man's flesh; I could hear it. More pitiful shrieks.

I edged in closer. I knew I was in the dungeons but who was the prisoner?

I peered through the bars. A man, a big jailer was dragging another man to a grate. The prisoner was naked but he was so covered in blood one would hardly know it. Then the jailer chained the victim onto the grate with crackling flames underneath it. The man did not fight, only whimpered either from lack of strength or spirit. When the jailer finished chaining him face first onto the iron bars, he fanned the flames. More cries.

Horror overwhelmed me. I staggered into the light of the flames from the grate. The jailer did not see me. But the prisoner did.

"Please," he begged. "Whatever you are. A man or a god. Have mercy on me and kill me."

The confused jailer pulled out his whip to make him be quiet.

He cried out and wept. "If you are Morglin take me as your victim and kill me however you choose," he choked. His voice growing hoarse and dry. "Or Ellar, if you exist, strike me dead in this moment."

"You're losing your mind!" The jailer shrieked. "Be silent or I'll cut your tongue out."

"Please…have mercy," he whimpered. His body shook like he was weeping.

I had no choice. The power was at its strongest. I had to save him. A strange delight crosses my face when I decide how to do it.

In a soft low tone, my voice echoed off the dungeon walls. I had a power in my voice from Ellar. If I were granting mercy, I could make the listener do all manner of things. I learned that accidently when I was watching my mother help a sick man. Too bad it only worked when I was under Ellar's power.

"In the stillness of the darkness. As the land falls asleep. Go now. Join them. Into the world of dreams...

Moonbeams shine down and stars tell silently. That night time has come now and you must go to sleep."

The jailer staggered back in surprise. Then fell down on the stone floor. Snoring broke out as I finished the song.

As soon as I heard it, I rushed into the light. The bars were open because the jailer was in the cell. I knelt down and took the keys from the jailer's belt and unlocked the captive's chains as he moaned on the grate. I rolled him off the iron bars with little care for I was in a rush and it was hot. I put the keys back onto the jailer's belt. With that accomplished, I spied a bottle hiding behind some torture instruments.

I smiled slyly. "That will explain the prisoner's disappearance." I took the bottle and placed it beside the snoring jailer. His open mouth was repulsive with a long thick tongue protruding out of it and drooling saliva dripping down his chin. Putrid creature.

I turned back to the poor man lying face flat on the cold earth. In the dim light, I could still easily see his black seared back. His body was marred with marks I did not wish to envision as one on the torture instruments for a long time. I knelt down to him and pushed him over to his back. He looked up at me with half crazed fear in his eyes.

"Can you walk?" I asked him.

His eyes flickered to his legs. He bit his lip in pain. "They're broken," he croaked. "Please," he pleaded. "I am in misery. You must have a knife… a blade of some sort. Please kill me. Have mercy on me and…and end my life. I…beg of you to kill me."

My heart felt as though it had been pierced by a million spears. What could drag a man so low to beg his rescuer to kill him? New strength came over me and I picked up his limp form. I had always prided myself on being strong.

His body was like sticky fire to my hands.

"What are you doing?" he whispered. His voice all but lost.

"Getting you out of here."

He went limp entirely onto me as I threw him over my

shoulder. The hardest part of getting him out of the dungeon was not ascending the stairs but pushing him through the breach in the wall. First, I climbed through then I tried to yank him through. So much moaning and groaning ensued that I was worried we would wake the jailer and I would be caught. But the spell was stronger than I thought. He was heavy but by my strength and the power from my name, I could ascend the passageway.

He didn't say anything. Probably because his throat had grown so dry he couldn't. His body was hot and wet and dry blood covered me from it. I did not realize the extent until I reached my hideout and saw all the blood stains he'd left on my nicest robe. Completely ruined.

I set him down on the ground and dusted myself off. He watched me in silence as I scurried about finding things to make him more comfortable. I propped him up with some pillows. With every movement I made him do, he winced. I took the cup of water I kept by my bedside and brought it to him in the hideout. I pressed it to his lips. He pursed them shut but he was no match for me. I forced his mouth open and poured the water down his throat. He coughed weakly and swallowed.

"So what is that supposed to do to me?" he asked when I'd released him. I stared at him in surprise.

"Is it a brew to make me go mad? For that is entirely unnecessary. Or is it poison to sting and burn my body and make me cough up blood?"

Dramatic? "It's water," I reply.

"That's worse," he moaned. "Then I shall live longer to endure whatever plans you have devised for this unearthly wretch." He sighed, exhausted. "I had hoped to die of thirst."

"You will not die," I said strongly, bringing in a basin of water and a cloth. The man needed cooling down and to be cleaned off to avoid infection of wounds. His one leg looked like it could be rotting.

"Then my fears are confirmed. What terrible tortures do you have in store for me? Though, I admit I'd rather be the victim of a captor as beautiful as you rather than that pig-faced jailer."

Oh dear, what could I say to this panicky man to calm him down and get him to shut up. I knelt down to him. I could read fear in his crazed eyes. I ran my fingers through his dirty hair to soothe him. He was nearly mad with fear. I wrung out the cloth into the bowl. "I'm not going to hurt you," I said softly. "I'm merely trying to cool you down from your fever."

He heaved a few breaths with effort. "You're helping me?"

I smiled and laid the cloth onto his scalded skin. Most of it was bloodied or blackened or both. I watched him relax a little. Through his parched lips he croaked, "Thank you."

I rinsed the cloth and continued down onto his neck. I was shocked, however, when I reached his heart. As I washed away the char, grime and blood, I saw a marking on his breast. Like a brand done by iron. It read, "Worthless Scum."

The prisoner noticed I had paused there. "That's what they did first to break my pride and remind me what I was while they tortured me."

"Who are you?" I asked. He somewhat resembled the prisoner Garcel and Adann had brought in three weeks ago. But they had told mother they had killed him within three days.

"Worthless Scum, if you can't read my brand," he replied, bitterly.

"What's your name?" I persisted.

"Raliph," he heaved a breath. "Look, you aren't saving anyone worth the trouble. Just kill me and end my misery. I've been tortured beyond resistance and pride. Just end my life and I thank you."

I bit my lip. "Stop asking to die. You will not die at my hand. So be silent!"

Ralph sighed. "I apologize. Worthless scum like me should only speak when ordered to."

I rolled my eyes at him. This man was not built to be a soldier, theatre was his missed calling.

I keep working. When I was a child and had a better relationship with my mother, she would teach me healing. I actually saved a man's life once but I don't remember his name because I was thirteen but mother was proud of me and that's all I remembered. Now, despite all the curses I throw at her, I'm grateful for this skill if only because it is interesting to watch someone get better and know I did it.

"I need to clean your leg. I might be able to save it but it will hurt excruciatingly," I said in an even tone. "I'm going to sing and make you fall into a deep sleep so you won't feel the pain," I said hoping it would actually work the way I described it. This was only the third time I had ever put someone to sleep with my powers. It would probably be better if I had some sort of strong alcohol to numb his pain and wait until he passed out from it but I don't have enough in my room and our family would not leave their wines out where I could steal them because servants are notorious drunks and would take them.

With much effort, Raliph shifted his head to look at me from his position on his stomach. "I cannot stop you from doing anything. But I will not sleep. My agony is too great."

I bit my lip sending out a silent prayer to whoever might be listening. "You will sleep."

He groaned.

I began to sing. His body relaxed a little. He breathed deeply in even breaths. Elated, I finish my song and get to work.

I worked late into the night. While I worked, I realized Raliph indeed had been the prisoner brought in three weeks ago. His hair and his body was the same though he had been disfigured. Garcel and Adann told Mother they'd killed him ten days ago. For some strange reason, I felt anger towards them boil up inside me. I did understand though, they had to take their anger out somehow, what better way than on a Cansten rebel nobody cares about. Still I was surprised they could be so cruel. This torture had nothing to do with getting the information and everything to do with satisfying a dirty desire for hate-induced bloodshed and sick entertainment. I felt dirty simply from witnessing that ugly side of my brothers they never showed to me. Shuddering, I tried to stay on task.

The darkest hour of the night passed as I finished my final task of popping his dislocated shoulders into their places. He must have been strung up at some point by his arms. I stung that huge gaping wound on his leg with hard alcohol I had recently been drinking and hidden here since Justice's death. Probably a better use for it when I thought about it. After stitching it up, I took a couple swigs of it. It was incredibly strong and I was tired. That was about all I remembered after that point.

# ANGEL OF MERCY

I awoke with him staring at me. His looked at me, puzzled. He probably had forgotten where he was.

"Am I dreaming?" he asked.

I sat up, yawned and shook my head. All the blood rushed to my head and I almost fell down again.

"Who are you?"

"Mercy," I replied simply.

He sighed. "I dreamt...ah..." he winced, "that an angel of mercy came to save me from the dungeons of Morglin. Am I...still there?"

My heart tugged at his name for me. Only Justice would call me an angel. A rebel had no such right. "Never call me angel again!" I said, vehement. "Only my brother can call me that. My brother..." I trailed off, the hollowness settling into my heart again.

He shrunk back, oblivious to my grief. "Sorry."

I sighed. "You are in no dream, Raliph. My name is Mercy. You are in a secret hideout adjoining my quarters."

He was silent for a moment. Processing everything. His eyes widened in fear. "No! Please Your Highness, I beg of you, kill me." He began to weep. "I can bear no more. Your brothers have already taken all strength from me." He moaned. "Kill me please! Torture me no more."

I could not afford to allow him to make so much noise so I covered his mouth.

"Now," I began. "Listen carefully. My name is Mercy and I am the princess."

He whimpered.

"Last night, I found you in your cell being tortured. You cried out to me for mercy," I paused. Unsure whether to tell him the secret of my name. "What I am about to tell you, you must never reveal to anyone. Understand?"

He nodded slightly.

"My name has a power over me that I cannot control. I am under the power of Ellar by the petitions of my mother to be subject to my name. When you called my name and its application Ellar's power came over me and I had no choice but to save you. Even now I am still working under his power."

He made a noise from his throat.

"You may speak quietly," I consented uncovering his mouth.

"So I am...ow...at the mercy of Your Highness who hates me, but can only help me because of a spell on you from a powerful but indifferent god."

"That is the truth."

He sighed. "Then I shall do my best to cause your highness the least amount of inconvenience." He sounded bitter. I wondered what went on in his head before I told him the secret of my name. He couldn't have expected me to actually care about him.

He winced and moaned in pain. I put my cool hand on his shoulder trying to comfort him. His skin was still burning. I dabbed it gently with the newly rinsed cloth. He breathed heavily. Sweat was beading all over his body wherever blood wasn't. I traced the W on his brand at his breast. He closed his eyes and bit his lip.

"My shame is complete," he whispered. "Here I lay, helpless in the hands of my enemy. Naked and torn. Not an inch of me whole.

Branded Worthless Scum, and broken. This, before the most beautiful person in the ranks of my enemies." He groaned. "Are you sure your brothers didn't plan for this in order to humiliate me further?"

I was speechless.

"I thought…ow…I had no pride left. Perhaps I still maintained a fraction still. I now know that jailer was right, I am a maggot. A worm, not a man. A pitiful creature meant for nothing better than to be squashed under a man's foot and thrown amongst deplorable and putrid waste until I got into something even worse."

I bit my lip. He looked up and met my eyes. Pleading me with his eyes he stared. Why? What was he asking me for? What did he want? Tears spilled down his cheeks and kept coming but still his eyes pleaded.

"I would love nothing better than to be killed in this moment and hung, naked in the streets of Whitestone for all to see," he whispered. "Birds will devour my flesh, slowly…ever so slowly. While I dangle, dead, the putrid scum I am, never to walk Tarlen again." He sighed heavily. "Could you do that for me?"

I shook my head.

"Please!" he shrieked. "Kill me!" He tried to tense his body but he could not move a muscle. "Satisfy every cruel act upon me after I am dead and gone. Feed me to an Urfane for all I care! No one to tell you that you are…are unkind for it was I…I who asked you to…" his eyes began to glaze over his body went completely limp. "Please. I implore you. Please…"

I stared, shocked and traumatized. Speechless and trembling. What were these strange feelings come over me? Terror of the suffering of another. I breathed deeply and shakily. An unwanted tear spilled down my cheek. Could I truly have pity for a rebel? This bloody mess before me. Did I care? The tear fell down and splattered on his face.

"No," he whispered. "I'm so sorry. I have made the most beautiful and divine woman cry. Forgive me..." his hoarse voice spoke softly. His gentle green eyes stared up at me, repentant as if he had committed the greatest crime known in Tarlen.

"I am not bloodthirsty, Raliph," I said wondering if it was really true. "I do not want to see you suffer or be in pain. I do not want to put you to anymore humiliation."

His eyes fell. "I don't know what to do with that."

"What do you mean?"

He sighed. "I wish you were cruel, or bloodthirsty, or merely in a rage for...if you were...I would know what to say. You are too good to belong in Tarlen. Too good to touch the vile skin of this rancid insect."

Tears filled my eyes and flowed freely down my face. No. He was wrong there was more cruelty in me than in my brothers. Only a spell kept me by his side. Only mercy. I am not Mercy. But maybe I almost want to be.

"Please...don't cry. I'm so sorry," he croaked. "Forgive me. I cannot bear the sight of such beautiful tears. Too good for my tainted eyes to behold. Too perfect for this foul pest to watch."

"No." I said quietly. "I am no better than you. There is no such beauty in me as you seem to see. Rest now. Breathe. I will not cry."

He sighed deeply.

He watched me in silence while I puttered around in my hideout trying to keep myself busy sorting cloths.

"I hate myself," he said.

"Doesn't everyone?"

"Not as much as I hate myself right now."

I did not reply. I did not wish to hear him wax eloquent on my qualities of goodness which I knew I did not have and he wax eloquent on his own pitiable state. It was understandable for a man to be so low, but it was hard to listen to. There is something about intense suffering that makes me want to cover my ears, even when it is not my fault. Perhaps, because if I kept my ears open I would realize how very little I do to stop it. That was how I felt that day. All the time just wanting to cover my ears and eyes and pretend my family and I were innocent of perpetuating the hate that brought this man to suffer so deeply.

Perhaps it was the unfounded expression of compassion on my face as I sat in silence beside him, or just the fact that I was a human being with a pair of ears but he began to tell a story.

"After they branded me and forced me to kill that soldier," he whispered. "I was young…ten, eleven. My father…ah…was a Tarlen soldier. He was killed by the rebels."

It seemed strange to me that he would join an army which killed his father.

"Mother…was deathly ill. Natalia, Sunfare, and Deulis were too young to help…" he paused to remember. "A man knocked on our door…wanted to speak to me in private…from the rebel army. He showed me his mark. Ow!" He cried out. He had tried to shift but he was in no shape to do so. "I told him to go…he wouldn't. He promised me that if I served Larcos, my family…they'd be taken care of. I followed him."

I listened in silence. My mind took in the information and ran it around my ever busy brain.

"They held me down…" he closed his eyes as though he could see the scene. "They branded me with iron…told me I could never go back now as a Tarlen citizen. They said if I was found I'd be tortured, enslaved or killed." He chuckled. "I guess I found that out for myself."

My heart tugged again.

"Then they took my sister...Sunfare..." Tears welled up in his eyes unexpectedly.

"...put a knife to her throat...held down a Tarlen soldier..." a sob escaped his lips. "Said if I didn't kill him...they'd kill her. I killed him." He stopped. "Since that day, Morglin has haunted my every dream," he broke off and wept.

I longed to comfort him but my touch would only hurt him and I was his enemy.

"I do what they tell me...so I don't get whipped and my family lives..." He bit his lip trying to stop crying. "...I get whipped anyway...pushed around...I'm weak..." He stopped and drew a few shuddered breaths. "I was going to a village to enlist a few young boys but I was stopped...my mark was seen..." his voice was hollow now. Stripped of all emotion. "They beat me...then took me down to the darkness," he sighed. "The result is what you see."

"I'm sorry, Raliph," I said, and I meant it.

"There's nothing you have to be sorry for." He closed his eyes and breathed heavily. "You've been nothing but good to me. Unwillingly, of course, but still good. No one would be good to me just for the sake of it. I'm not worth it."

I almost roll my eyes at him. I'm fed up with his degrading himself constantly.

I went to the small door leading into my closet. "I will get you some broth. Lie quietly until I return."

He nodded slightly. About all he could do. I turned away. I felt sorry for him, but sorry for myself for getting into such a mess at the same time. Honestly I wished I wasn't under the power of my name and then again I was glad I was. Part of me wished I was doing what I was doing willingly without the power of Ellar. That was the same part of me that apologized to him for having such a terrible life.

"It's not my fault he has a continual streak of misfortune. Not my fault he was tortured." I sighed and changed my clothes into a clean nightdress and hung a clean robe beside my bed. I had a plan to get him some broth and raise no questions towards my unwillingness to leave my room.

"Why are you doing this Mercy? I mean, you know why, but why are you enjoying this?"

I crawled into the covers. My stomach growled. I sure was hungry. It had been a long night and the sights I had seen and the words I had heard were enough to make me ill. My face was probably white already. This would be easy.

I collapsed onto my pillows with Justice's face in my memory. It was less pillows because Raliph was lying on half of them. I hoped my maid wouldn't notice.

"Lusilla!" I cried trying to sound ill. I was glad I had been through the shock that I had so I needed no powder to discolor my face.

Lusilla, my maid, entered in a hurry. She curtsied. "My lady."

"I have taken ill," I began forcing my voice to sound croaky. "Fetch me some broth and some fruit."

Lusilla curtsied and left.

I smirked. If I made it clear I was ill to Lusilla no one would question my decision to remain in my room and to see no one. That way I could fully care for Raliph and get food for him which would be needed to make him better.

Lusilla returned with a bowl of broth and a piece of fruit as I had instructed. "Leave me alone and inform anyone I am not to be disturbed."

"Yes, your Highness." She curtsied and left.

The moment the door closed. I jumped out of my bed and carefully took the tray into my hideout. I closed the doors behind me. I smiled at my deception. When I entered the candle was still burning brightly and Raliph lay exactly where I had left him. He smiled weakly when I'd entered.

I knelt down next to him with the bowl of broth on the ground beside me. I lifted him up to lean on my shoulder. He moaned at the movement. I drew a spoonful of broth and put it to his lips. He drank it willingly. He drank the entire bowl. When he was finished I laid him down again. He tried not to groan when I did.

"Thank you, Mercy," he said softly.

I couldn't help but smile at him. Despite the fact that the sight of him was enough to give me nightmares I was almost enjoying being around him.

"Have you eaten?" he asked.

I pulled the fruit out of my robe pocket,

"You're wearing your night robe," he commented.

I blushed. "I had to pretend I was ill so no one will question my choice to remain in my bedroom and request broth and tea."

"You're clever."

I shrugged.

"You should rest, you were up all night."

"There's nothing wrong with me."

"There will always be something wrong with me, but people sleep anyway."

I giggled. He smiled weakly. I almost forgot his hideous appearance. I noticed nothing had happened to his teeth. They were nice. He was getting tired, now that he had eaten. I crept back to my room to let him sleep.

The sun shone through my bedroom window on an angle that indicated I had slept for a few hours. I called Lusilla and asked for some soup and tea. I sighed thinking that I'd have to share my food for the next while with Raliph.

I ate some soup then brought it to Raliph. He was still sleeping. His face was peaceful. I smiled wondering what he'd say when he woke up. I lit another candle for some more light. The wound on his leg was smarting and there was a slice in the center of his lip that made me shudder. His eyes flickered open to stare up at me.

"I have some soup and tea for you."

"What time is it?"

"Around two o'clock." I lifted him up and rested his head on my shoulder.

"So tell me about you powers," he says.

I smiled. "I never meant to get these powers. My mother is a devoted servant of Ellar and she wanted a few things for me that I didn't particularly wish for myself."

A half smile broke his face.

"You think it's funny don't you? You realize I can't even participate in battles or judge cases or anything useful because of it."

"It is an ironic predicament for a royal to be in," he said. "You are so rich and pretty but you're stuck in my company because of your eccentric mother. You wear brilliant diamonds around your neck but instead of being courted by some knight you're stuck in a tiny hideout caring for an enemy soldier.

My hand flew to my necklace. I had forgotten to take it off. Not a convincing get-up if I'm feigning illness. I take it off quickly and then stare at it, for some odd unearthly moment.

My father had always given me expensive jewelry to make up for the fact he was always fighting and never at home. I'd wear what he'd give me but I never cared about them. They just felt like excuses to me.

"You can have my diamonds if you want them," I said. There must have been some bitterness in my voice for I caught a curious light in Raliph's eyes.

I shrugged. "My father, King Twallor gives them to me to make up for his absence." I sighed. "The war has always meant more to him than his family."

"He taxes the life out of Tarlen," said Raliph.

"And Larcos steals and burns everything from everyone who won't join his army and believe in his politics," I said quickly, rising to my father's defense.

Raliph tried to shift, and grimaced. "I don't care about anyone's politics. It's all the same to me."

"You...you don't want Larcos to win the war?"

"If we don't I'm a dead man. But he's not an honorable man worth fighting for. If your father provided food for my sisters and mother when they needed it, I'd fight for him."

I listened thoughtfully. It occurred to me I was hearing the convictions of many underprivileged people in the kingdom of Tarlen. I fingered around with my necklace. I had an idea.

"I'll be back," I told him and left the hideout.

I crawled into bed. "Lusilla!" I called making my voice sound hoarse again.

She appeared. "Yes, your Highness."

Has anyone desired to speak to me yet today?"

"Your mother and brothers."

"Good, send them in."

Lusilla left and brought Queen Laria and the princes Garcel and Adann. The Queen wore a high collared ebony dress. No embroidery or precious gems to adorn her person. I always wondered why father had married her; she wasn't exceptionally beautiful and had terrible fashion sense. When I saw Garcel and Adann I tried my best to smile at them but their faces looked as marred as Raliph's to me.

"Mercy, how sorrowful we were when we heard of your illness, we..." Adann began.

"We have news for you," said Garcel, cutting his brother off.

I watched my mother back away from my bedside where I lay. I tried to make out her expression.

"You can fight in the war!" Garcel continued. "Our lead archer was shot in our last battle. We all agreed as long as you remained an archer and stayed out of the fray instead of hand to hand combat and..." Garcel went on and on. I barely heard him. I felt sick. Kill more people. Possibly young boys who were trying to save their families from starvation. My brothers wanted me to fight now. Now that it was the last thing I wanted to do. Justice's description of the war flashed through my mind and I felt worse.

"What is it, Mercy?" Mother asked.

"I...I don't want to fight."

"What?" said Garcel. "You must be very ill. Don't you want to avenge Justice's blood?"

My heart tore. *'Not the way you did, Garcel,'* I thought. "I want to honor Justice's wishes. He didn't want me to fight in the war so I won't."

"What's gotten into you?" said Garcel.

"Garcel," the Queen said sternly. "Your sister has given you her answer."

Garcel sneered at her but shrunk back.

"I'm sorry Garcel, Adann," I said. "May I speak to mother alone?"

Growling Garcel left the room followed by Adann. Queen Laria sat down on my bed beside me. "What is it, Mercy?" She searched my eyes. "Does this have anything to do with Justice?"

I coughed to keep up my charade, and began in a hoarse voice. "Our last day together he told me to put my other gifts and skills to practice." I pulled my necklace out from underneath my nightgown. "And I was thinking, I could help the kingdom…" cough, "by selling my jewelry to buy land and build a shelter for boys who have lost one or both of their parents by the war or plague. They can work to support their families by working a farm adjoining the city."

I watched my mother's face light in surprise.

"The rebel army enlists many young boys. If I could give those boys a safe place to be where they and their families wouldn't be at risk it could help stop the war, less young boys would have to turn to the rebels." I finished with a smile. "What do you think?"

Queen Laria searched my face. I could tell she knew I wasn't telling her the whole truth. "I think it is very clever. Can you afford it?"

"I have six diamond necklaces and five others of precious gems. They in themselves are worth a fortune. That's not even including my bracelets. In all they are enough to feed and clothe both armies for two years if I wanted to."

"And you are willing to give these up for such a cause?"

"I care little for the jewelry." I lowered my eyes. "It will be put to better use this way."

Gently Mother placed her hands on my face and raised it up to look at her. "Is it possible, my child that the blessing I prayed over you is coming to fruition in your heart as well as your actions?"

I shrugged not wishing to talk about it. "I'm just trying to do as Justice would have wanted.

# GARCEL'S STORY

Garcel was always suspicious of me about everything no matter what I did so I wasn't at all surprised when he snuck me this letter with his side of the story in it.

'It is not rare when you and Justice share a secret but it certainly is when you and Laria do. I am tolerant enough that you never talk to me about anything happening in your life whether personal or not but this time it went too far. Strange things were happening in the castle and I did not get to be a historically excellent military strategist by minding my own business. My entirely incapacitated prisoner went missing mysteriously and his guard was found passed out beside an empty rum bottle. Suspiciously perfect if you ask me. But that wasn't the only strange thing happening in the palace over those couple days. You got sick. Fake sick, like the sort of sick you would be on a day of writing, history and mathematics and recover the next day in time for fencing lessons. Your face was pale but I remember when you used to scare yourself on purpose so you could terrify the queen into letting you out of something you didn't want to do. Pretending you were emotionally unstable was your way to avoid going to parties. On the whole you were predictable. You knew how to get what you wanted and I always knew what that was. Pretending to be sick, sucking up to Laria, and not jumping out of bed the moment you heard you could go into battle is not only suspicious but also completely rubbish. I make it a point to understand my family members because royal families are notorious for betraying each other, often to death in order to get the crown so the moment you started to confuse me I went to find out what nonsense you were up to.

I got some flowers for her hoping that will soften her a bit and she'd actually talk to me. She makes no secret that I am her least favorite and would have the littlest to do with me as possible. I ascended the stairs to her chambers at the top tower in the farthest corner from the king's chambers. Understandably, I suppose, as she doesn't want to see all the whores who come in and out of there on a regular basis. I don't remember a time when they were even friends although Justice does. They must have had to be considering how many children they managed to procreate. Rarely are they ever seen together except in the throne room during important meetings. With that in mind, I reached the top stair and prepared to knock on her door when I heard voices inside.

"There is nothing normal about her behavior, witch! You ruined her life and you know it and I will not stand for any more of your sorcery!" It was the king's voice.

"There is nothing magical about Mercy wanting to honor her brother's wishes," insisted the queen. Why, by every sacred thing would those two be talking?

"Justice's wishes, Justice's wishes. Rubbish! How long will you hide behind that excuse? You have done something to her to make her refuse to fight in the war. She never cared what Justice thought about the war before, there is no reason why, whether he is dead or not, that she should care now!"

"You never even cared about Justice in the first place! You'd rather that savage son of yours, your puppet Garcel be king!" Her voice was taut; she must have been close to tears.

"Justice was my firstborn and I loved him greatly. Then you corrupted him. You played your tricks with him and turned him against me! I saw what was on his chest. I'm no fool. You did that, and if I wasn't the compassionate man I am I would have you killed for it. You know the rule yet you disobeyed me anyways."

"He could have got it from anywhere. Don't blame me that you couldn't control your eldest son. You are the king."

Something smashed in the room. "Shut up, woman! If I find out you put your dirty magic into my daughter again I will stage a happy accident for you and no one will regret it in the least, especially now *your* favorite puppet of a son is dead." He stomped his loud boots toward the door. I decided I should disappear before he found out I heard everything.

"You won't win, Twallor. Men who do what you do never win. This is the generation that will end the war despite you and your foolish sons. Mercy will end it and there's nothing you, nor I, will be able to do to stop her."

I stopped to listen just to hear what the king would say.

"One more chance, Laria. Your life is hanging by a thread."

"I'm not afraid. I will start the whisper of change and Mercy will turn it into a shout and you will lose. You have already lost her."

I ran down the stairs my heart pounding. What was happening to my sister? The idea that you were getting hijacked by a sorceress was nonsense even though Laria does have a few limited supernatural strengths. But she must have had some reason to be so confident that you would act in a way so entirely unlike yourself. She spoke of Justice as the key; something happened between you two before his death, they say he died in your arms so some kind of connection must have happened. Perhaps, it was Justice with the magical powers. I smirked to myself at the thought. I am not superstitious and you are the last person in the family who would ever let yourself get manipulated by any power other than yourself. Justice would know something about the ludicrous change in you but he happens to be six feet under and, much as I was curious about whatever was on his chest that Twallor spoke of I had enough humanity in me not to dig up my dead brother. However, not enough to stop me from spying in on Justice's chambers. Justice was the sort of man who liked to record things. When he was a boy he used to write down the terminology of what each of the fencing moves were in the middle of his lessons. But most of us thought that had more to do with how much he hated fencing lessons as opposed to loved writing things down. But my only chance at finding out what was actually happening to my sister was in Justice's mysterious books. He would never throw away a single page that he wrote all his life, but instead hid all the important things somewhere he knew for sure we wouldn't find them. We thought he did that so we wouldn't make fun of him for what he would write about his crushes but perhaps, he was secretly masterminding some plan. That sounded a little too far-fetched but I couldn't leave any stones unturned if I were to solve this puzzle and help you so I tore his chambers apart, every inch of it, finding every single piece of paper in the place. It was an unfortunately boring day as I settled down to learn what Justice had to say about eating stuffed fish, playing urfane hunting, and studying, lots and lots of studying. I learned Mercy and Justice had a secret hideout that he refused to write down where it was. That was one interesting thing about his childhood but most of it was boring study notes or complaining about his three younger siblings.

I was interested however, when I came over a more recent book.

*"I spoke with her again today,"* it read. *"I know she doesn't understand me but I feel like she is getting close. I think I will tell her soon. But she is so obsessed with Garcel, the king and the war that she will never listen to me. I've started to let her see my disappointment in the kingdom and her sensitive soul seems to be affected but I could lose her any day. She could become another Adann and just start following Garcel around. I'm playing with a thin thread that can break any moment. How do I get through to her? How do I convince her of the evilness of this war? This family? If something happens to me, all hope is lost because the fate of Tarlen rests on my shoulders unless Mercy can learn the horrible side of this war. Should I tell her father's secret? Mother refuses to and has forbidden me but if Mercy is allowed back into*

*the war for some reason again I will lose her, just as I lost Adann to Garcel and Garcel to Twallor. This war is not just between us and the rebels it is me and mother against Twallor and Garcel. Mercy and Adann are just casualties unless I can get through to Mercy. Ellar, help me get through to Mercy."*

I felt like I had been struck. So that was how Justice felt about me? The enemy. I was his enemy, competing for the attention of our younger siblings. Slamming the book down I try not to remember the rush of childhood memories with Justice and the comradery we used to have laughing at the antics of our younger siblings. Right before his death I was his enemy. So Justice really did make you change somehow. Right before his death he 'got through to you'. I see. But I am not about to watch everything you loved and cared about come crashing down because Justice was trying to manipulate you. I will see to it that you know that truth about Justice and Laria and you will be free to fight in the war all you want without feeling guilty.

It occurred to me that I was not only ignoring my brother's dying wishes but actively working against him but I was too confused to think of anything but extrapolate you from whatever web Justice and Laria had you caught in. It wasn't until your very cutting words that I realized what I was feeling towards my dead brother, betrayed."

# THE RIDDLES OF HISTORY

Raliph nodded slightly in acknowledgement when I entered my hideout. His ghastly appearance struck me again when I saw his damaged face. The cuts and the scars from past tortures disfigured his once handsome features. He was sweating so I moved the blanket off him and dabbed his face gently with a damp towel down to his neck.

"If you forget to close the door…and I strain my ears…I can hear what you say in the other room."

I blushed.

"I was terrified to hear the voices of your brothers."

"You would've been protected by my mother and myself."

"They destroyed me. Body and mind. How can I think rationally at the sound of their voices?" His eyes were wide in fear.

"I won't let them find you."

He turned his head away. I thought he must have been getting stronger for him to be able to do that.

"Prince Justice was a great man," he whispered, his face still facing the dark wall away from me. "If I were to honor any man, it would be him."

I stared at him surprised. How did Raliph know my brother as anything but the son of the man who wanted to kill him and the brother of the men who almost did? "Why do you say this? What do you know of my brother?"

Raliph moved his head slowly to look at me. "I met him once."

"You did?"

A smile cracked his broken lips. "He was hunting alone a while ago."

"Go on."

He sighed. "I was on a remote forest path and my mark wasn't hidden when he passed by me. He saw my mark, dismounted and drew his sword." He closed his eyes as though he were envisioning the scene. "Being the cowardly worm that I am I fell to my knees and begged for mercy. I knew beyond all shadow of a doubt he was a far stronger man than I and could capture or kill me without trouble. So I pleaded with him to spare me for the sake of my sisters and mother who I was their sole provider…I only cared about my own skin at the time," he chuckled. "I was a pitiful sight I was. Not as bad as now though. I figured I would grovel for a while he'd have some fun with me then perhaps let me go after he was done…" He paused. I listened intently wondering what my brother did.

"He didn't even touch me. He stood nobly above me and said for the sake of Mercy whom he loved, and that which is gilded on his heart… then he lowered his blade from my throat. When I heard it being sheathed I raised my eyes, surprised he had not hit me, mocked me, or kicked me into the dirt. He smiled at me as he mounted. I thought he was the noblest, greatest man to live. He warned me to cover my mark in case I met others who were more anxious to destroy men such as I than he was. Then he left."

I felt like I'd been sent a message from Justice, though a very strange one. "He spared your life for my sake, when I wouldn't have even done so," I mused.

"What is gilded on his heart?" he asked.

"A golden brand," I whispered the pieces slowly coming together. "The word Ellar's on his breast." I stood up.

"Where are you going?"

"To get a book on the history of Tarlen. I need to find out if that marking has appeared before and who Ellar actually is. My explanation isn't making sense anymore."

---

Lusilla brought me a huge stack of books from the palace library. She seemed surprised I wanted to read so much, particularly on history. Growing up I had never been one to read. I enjoyed doing things more than sitting down and reading books. I never had many female friends probably because while they were all reading elegant romance stories I was shooting arrows. Besides, books give me headaches. But today I have nothing to do and have some questions to answer so I carried the stack into my hideout so I could care for Raliph while I read. I also got some more broth and tea for him so he'd continue to get stronger.

I sat down on the floor against the wall next to him and began to read.

Raliph didn't say anything, only stared. He was getting glassy eyed so I fed him some broth and he passed out. I didn't bother to wake him up until about seven. I gave him some tea and while he drank it I told him some of the mysteries I had discovered.

"Tarlen is a kingdom established about four thousand years ago. Ellar led people here, legend has it, and set up a king over the people. For the first thousand years there is little documentation on what happened during that time." I paused to shift. I've been sitting down way too long. "A shadow began to fall over Tarlen and an evil creature they named Morglin began to take over the kingdom. No one knows where he came from or why he does what he does. The shadow continued to fall over every city and village for a thousand years. Many people died of disease or despair. Then Ellar appeared. He gathered an army to battle Morglin and together they marched against him. Morglin had an army of beings which, the legend says, were past victims of his and had fallen under his power. Morglin had distorted them so they never die of old age or disease. They were said to have the appearance of black cloaked and animal clawed men. They were terrors and had the power to spread fear and disease among the cities of Tarlen. Ellar wore pure white as the story goes as he went into battle…" I stopped. "This is confusing, because there are some records of Ellar himself being defeated as a sacrifice for the army."

"Then why do we still pray to Ellar? Is the shadow is still here?" Raliph cut in.

"That's just it! The shadow left the land, Morglin's servants either disappeared or were killed."

"The question is if he was overpowered by Morglin how could he win? Why is his power still at work over you?"

"He must be a spirit or something," I said, truly knowing little on the subject.

"After the battle everyone expected the darkness to return and there to be another war with Morglin, because of Ellar's disappearance but that hasn't happened to this day. Reports of surviving soldiers and their families having a strange golden mark at their hearts went around. The word Ellar's in gilded letters. The bearers claimed it was Ellar's hand who branded it on. The men with this mark were mighty and good. Known for their fairness, mercy, and ability to heal. The women also with this mark were strong and good, renowned in songs and tales. Strangely enough, the royal family never took on this mark." I wiped some sweat off Raliph's forehead. "A king came into power many hundreds of years later who hated the mark and claimed the bearers of it were trying to bring down the kingdom. He reminded the people that Ellar was dead and told them that the mark was merely Morglin's ploy to gain influence back in Tarlen and bring the shadow and plague back."

"Jealously," Raliph muttered.

"The mark became illegal and anyone who wore it was killed. Many hid their marking, others fled Tarlen, and the rest were killed."

"Your brother had this mark?"

"I believe so," I whispered huskily. I cleared my throat. "Soon after that a man named Canstine began to speak against the king for the disease and poverty that was ravaging. When his execution was ordered he fled with a large band of followers with him into the forest. They named themselves after their leader and lived in the depths of the forest. Together, they led raids against the cities that were in complete allegiance with the king. They would take prisoners and steal crops. Kill prominent men and they enlisted anyone who would join in exchange they would pay the soldiers by supporting their starving families. However, after a while many rebels deserted when their families were better and chose to live civilized in Tarlen cities. In order to prevent that, Canstine ordered every enlisted man to be branded the mark of the first letter of his name on their shoulders. Canstine died before he had a chance to overthrow the king. His son succeeded him as leader. Since then, war has ravaged between Tarlen society and the Cansten rebels. Disease and poverty are rampant and no one has any solutions."

Silence. The story seemed pretty bleak.

Raliph heaved a sigh then winced from his broken ribs. "If...Justice hadn't died, he would've stopped the war. For he had Ellar's mark."

"My mother did not marry my father for love..." I mused. "She prays to Ellar and has the power to heal..." the pieces were coming together. "My mother must bear Ellar's mark secretly!" I stood up and left the hideout. I ran up the stairs to my mother's quarters. I found her on her window seat singing softly and sewing a quilt.

"Where is it?" I demanded.

Queen Laria looked up at me, surprised.

"The mark of Ellar. The mark I saw on Justice."

She smiled, put down her sewing and beckoned me nearer. She pulled her collar down so I could see the golden letters. That's why her dresses were always so modest.

"You brought Ellar into the royal family on purpose!" I cried.

She smiled. "You now know my secret."

"Why?"

"Because of you."

I blinked, stunned for a moment. "What…do you mean?"

"The war must stop or Morglin will take over Tarlen forever. You must understand the rebels will not win the war nor will your father. You and Justice have been destined by your father's birth and my prayers to become servants of Ellar and to use your power to stop the war."

"But I don't want to stop the war! I don't want to be destined to do anything! Ellar deserted Tarlen since the war began and he makes me do things I don't like!" I stomped my foot. "All I wanted to do was to defeat the rebels. Now, after Justice's death, I want to protect children from them. I'm only seventeen. I can't stop a war."

"Not alone."

"No!" I turned away. "In my brother's memory, I will embrace my name which you have forced upon me but I will not take up an illegal marking from a god who has only caused trouble for me since the day I was named."

"I didn't name you," she said softly. "I only did what Ellar told me to. He named you and empowered you. Take up his mark as your brother and I have."

"No!" I shrieked. "I will not. I cannot. Stop praying for me!" With that I fled, tears streaming down my face. I plunked myself onto my bed and crawled under the covers. Pulling them over my head, I cried myself to sleep as Justice's face and Mother's pleading eyes pass through my memory. I would not be forced to do anything I didn't want to. I hated the rebels. I hated Raliph. I didn't want the war to stop. I loved the war. As long as more rebels were killed, it was a perfect war.

# WORTHLESS SCUM

"Mercy! No! Aah!"

I woke up to a terrible shrieking. It was coming from the wall. The voice sounded like Raliph. Terror froze my heart. I ran to my closet. The shrieking continued. Agony. But it was more. Deeper than physical pain. Something terrible was going on in the little hideout. I went into my closet and slipped through the door. There, I beheld the worst thing my eyes had ever been forced to take in. Morglin

His form was black and his eyes red. He was ghostlike as a shadow but solid as a man. His hands were like claws to tear flesh apart and stained with blood. He slunk around Raliph's writhing body.

It took me a moment to make out what he was doing. Brands had been burnt all over Raliph's chest and arms. Wretch, Maggot, Hideous, Useless, and Coward. Every time Morglin would remove his claw-like hand, another one would appear. He laughed. Raliph moaned and writhed, shrieked and wailed.

I was frozen in my spot.

Morglin pulled Raliph up by his hair and whispered something into his ear. Raliph groaned but his voice was growing weak. He was losing his will against the creature. Morglin placed his claws on Raliph's head. Raliph cried out in his misery. His shrieks were heartrending. He writhed but Morglin would not let him go. Slowly, Raliph stopped writhing and only wept softly.

Morglin moved his hands and I saw Victim in crimson on his forehead.

Raliph caught sight of me and with his tear filled eyes implored me. Morglin was tormenting him. I understood what was meant now when they would say Morglin would torture his victims in the worst ways. He was destroying Raliph's heart and his body.

"Now, my victim," Morglin hissed into his ear. His voice was terrible and filled with anticipation for what he was going to do next. Raliph groaned at his words. "I'm taking you down to your worst nightmare. The dungeon chambers in the palace."

Raliph cried out.

Morglin traced Worthless Scum on his breast with his claw and Raliph shrieked and writhed in pain. The mark was darker now and bleeding. Morglin laughed.

"There you will be tormented under my skilled hands until there's nothing left in you but a hollow shell and bleeding skin. You will lose yourself into an unending nightmare of torture and death. You will be mine, Worthless Scum." With that he put his hand on Raliph's torn, bleeding, and branded body. Raliph let out a final cry of despair and Hopeless was left. With that finished, Morglin grabbed Raliph's broken arm and began to drag him. His eyes were dull and glassy now and his body grotesque. A sob escaped his lips. Morglin tightened his grip on Raliph's hand.

My mind raced. What could I do?

"Mercy," Raliph mouthed and let his head fall limp to his chest.

My brother's words flashed through my mind. *"Pray to Ellar for me."*

I cleared my throat and began to sing but all I could sing was one word. "Ellar." My body trembled. I repeated it again and again.

Morglin looked up startled. His face was menacing. I shuddered but didn't close my mouth.

Raliph's eyes caught a slight ray of hope. Courage rose up in my heart. I spoke clearer now finding new words to incorporate like help, help, and help.

Fear entered Morglin's eyes. He hissed at me then disappeared.

I slumped back against the wall. Raliph breathed heavily. I knew soon, I'd have to help him but for now I was too weak. I glanced over at him to see how he looked. He wasn't even looking at me. I wondered if perhaps he had finally gone completely mad for his eyes were raised as though he were acknowledging someone but I knew no one was there.

I felt a hand on my shoulder. I looked over, startled, to see a man or so he seemed. In a dark red cloak, hooded, so a shadow was over his face but his eyes and smile I could see. His eyes were a gentle grey and his hands…well, his hands on my shoulder could only be described as a carpenter's hands, rough from working wood, a writer's hands with ink marks on them, dirty like a potter's hands with clay under the fingernails, and soft like a physicians with a healing touch. He was the one Raliph was staring at.

Ellar, or so I assumed, walked purposely to Raliph.

Raliph breathed heavily and cast his eyes over his own body. He blushed deep crimson.

Raliph, piteous and humiliated. Branded everything he was but everything he could not bear. Tortured and destroyed. All that he could even claim his own had been taken and purged from him. The very sight of him brought tears to my eyes.

"Your servant my lord," he raised his eyes to behold Ellar's face.

Ellar knelt down next to him and placed his hands on him. He spread his fingers over Worthless Scum. Raliph cried out at his touch. Ellar kept his hand at Raliph's heart. He cried but it wasn't the sound of despair it merely sounded like normal pain. Like the pain someone would have when having their finger cut off. Ellar's hand remained on Ralph and the marks began to disappear one by one. Now only Victim remained on his forehead.

"Give up everything you've hid behind. You will not be Morglin's victim."

Raliph cried out continuously but the letters began to disappear.

"Ellar, you're hurting him!" I said.

"I'm healing him," Ellar replied. Gently, he removed his hand off Raliph's heart. My breath caught at the sight I saw. Branded in golden letters where Worthless Scum had once been, Ellar's shone on his breast. Raliph's face was peaceful.

"Thank you," he whispered. Ellar gathered Raliph's limp form into his arms. The movement didn't even seen to hurt him. I was jealous. Ellar held him near and Raliph began to breathe evenly.

I ventured nearer.

Ellar was very focused on his task as he bent over Raliph. Somehow or other, he produced a cup and held it to Raliph's lips. He drank it willingly.

"Is he alright?" I asked drawing closer.

"It is my intention," Ellar replied, his voice soft and low. It reminded me of a rough cloth, warm and durable but one would have to be pretty cold to consider touching such material. It was hard to describe him. Clearly, he wasn't a spirit but he was too imposing to be a man.

"What did you do to him?"

Ellar put the cup down next to him and continued to comfort Raliph with his touch.

"What did you do to him?" I repeated.

"I healed him."

"How?"

Ellar smiled, almost in amusement. "I took his brands, gave him mine."

"What are you?" I didn't dare touch him.

"Ellar."

"A spirit, a man, a god, a beast?"

"Many things."

I sighed. His evasiveness is getting on my nerves.

"I have a question for you," he began slowly.

I listened. At that moment, I realized how powerful the being before me really was. I wondered what could possibly possess me to ask him such questions. He could strike me dead in a moment.

"Will you take up my name?"

I remembered the letters on my brother's breast. The well concealed gilded mark on my mother. I glanced at Raliph's chest. The word shone in gold on the scarred and torn body. I thought of the law. The reason why no one was allowed to bear such a mark. It occurred to me that this being could very well be someone else entirely than he claimed.

I thought of Raliph's words before he had been branded. Servant. I didn't want to be anyone's servant. I was already subject to my name, I didn't want to be subject to the one who gave it to me. I wanted to be myself. To fight the rebels, not save them. To be brave and strong and fight for Tarlen. I knew if I took Ellar's name, I would be someone else entirely. Something I didn't want to be. Raliph had nothing to live for. He was the lowest of the scum in Tarlen. Of course, he needed help. But I, well I was a princess. If I were to be marked those would be the words on my heart. I didn't want Ellar's mark. I didn't want Ellar. I wanted to live!

I bit my lip and shook my head. "No, Ellar, I can't…"

Ellar turned back to Raliph, he held him awhile in silence. Finally he spoke, "You are a noble princess as you reminded yourself. But if Morglin were to brand you, you would find other things appear." His soft voice haunted the depths of my guarded heart. "But it is your choice who you choose. You may choose the path of your brothers or mine."

"My brothers?"

"They are Morglin's servants, doing what he wants them to."

I stared at him, confused.

"You will fight to have control of yourself but really it is Morglin who will control you."

I backed away. No! I didn't agree. Morglin had no power over me and neither would Ellar.

As though he could hear my thoughts, he glanced over at me with sad eyes. "I will ask you again someday."

I looked down at Raliph. He was sleeping now. Ellar laid him down on his bed in the hideout. Then he stood up.

I backed away a bit when he faced me. "He will be entirely well in three days."

I nodded.

"I shall leave you now." He turned to leave. "Call upon me. If you need me again."

I bowed respectfully.

He left. I don't know how but he did. I felt like I'd awoken from a dream when the crimson robed figure disappeared or went back into one. I wondered why his robe was red. I knelt down to the slumbering Raliph. I touched his new mark in gold. Tears filled my eyes when I remembered Ellar's plea. Why did I feel so hollow? I wept.

# DISCOVERED

"Good morning, Mercy," I heard softly in my ear. A gentle hand moved a tendril of hair from my face. I stirred. "How are you feeling?"

I opened my eyes. Yawning, I sat up and looked around. A lamp burning low on the floor, a chest of memories of Justice and I, and Ralph lying propped up by pillows in his usual place in the corner. I realized, I had cried myself to sleep accidently. I rubbed my eyes.

"Are you well after that terrifying night?"

I searched his face. Something in his voice startled me. What was it? He seemed genuinely concerned about me. He wasn't moaning his own tragedies.

"Is everything alright, Your Highness?"

He wasn't going to stop asking until I answered. I nodded. "Are you alright, Ralph? You had the worst night of us two."

He smiled. "I've never been better. Look, I can move my arms!"

I caught his smile. "He said you'd be better in three days."

His brows furrowed. "Three days isn't very long."

"You don't want to get well?"

"No, it's not that," he shook his head. "It's just…"

"Just?"

"I have nowhere to go. I don't want to go back to the camp; they probably think I'm dead and wouldn't care anyways. But I have to take care of my family…" He paused. "For the first time in my life, I am exactly where I want to be."

"In the palace?" I was confused.

"No, with you."

I blushed and stood up quickly. "I have some things I need to do today."

He watched me quietly.

"Will you be alright on your own?"

"Yes."

"I'll get you some water and a book."

"I can't read very well, Mercy, so don't bother. I stopped learning when I was seven." He said. "Did I offend you?"

"No, I'm merely unaccustomed to Cansten rebels enjoying my company." I slipped away.

As I passed through my closet, I pulled out my soft purple dress. It was more white than purple but I still liked to call it purple. Then, I gathered up my satchel. Taking a deep breath, I approached my jewelry box. Hesitantly, I reached down and took out two bracelets and three necklaces. Swallowing hard, I put them in my satchel. I closed my eyes and envisioned the ten year old Raliph being branded. I reminded myself that this would be the way I fight the rebels. Though, if I thought about it, it was truly only Larcos I was opposing.

I didn't want my family to know where I was going or what I was doing so I snuck down the stairs to the kitchen and escaped up through the cellar. Behind the palace, the city of Whitestone lay. Whitestone is essentially, exactly its name. In the starlight through the streets, every stone the light of the even hits shines a pure white. It is the city of royalty. My home and I loved Whitestone with all my heart.

I knew of an architect who lived on the wall protecting the city. I pulled my cloak over my head to hide my face. If word of my project leaked out to anyone, particularly my brothers and father, it could mean disaster.

I returned to my room after dark. Humming cheerfully. I had to break into the kitchen through the cellar because the palace doors had all locked but I'd done that before with Garcel when we were children. I was satisfied with what I had accomplished. I had bought a large piece of land inside the city. Laid out plans for the building with Charmot the architect. I even hired a builder. My orphanage project was working perfectly. Both Charmot and Tanyar, the chief builder, had promised not to mention that I was behind this. The financer of this project was only to be known as the Compassionate Angel. I named my alias after all the strange things Justice would call me. He had some funny ideas of what I was going to be when I grew up.

I took my cloak off and let it fall to the floor. I thought to visit Raliph before I went to bed. I stepped toward my closet. The door was ajar. Taking a deep breath, I tried not to panic. I walked coolly to my closet. Pushing past my clothes, I saw the hidden door had been opened. I heard a harsh voice inside.

Two men were in my hideout. Raliph, lying on the floor, bashed up and bloodied. And Garcel, standing over him, kicking him and taunting him. Raliph didn't even cry out. He noticed me enter but looked away quickly.

Garcel picked him up by his hair and hit him against the wall. "What's wrong with your legs, Scum?" He laughed cruelly. I felt terrified of my own brother.

"Stop it, you beast!" I shrieked for I could not watch any longer.

Garcel dropped Raliph onto the floor. Turning, he glared at me. "So this is your illness for the past two days?" He kicked at Raliph as he moaned on the ground.

"So this is the reason you spent so much time in the palace for two weeks, you liar!" I shot back. "You did not kill him the third day! I saw what you did to him!" My face was flushed in my fury. "If you tell on me, I'll tell mother what you did to him. Down to the last whipping."

Garcel sneered at me. He knelt down on the floor by Raliph. "He called your name, didn't he?"

"Yes," I admitted, wishing once again that I had not been forced to do the good that I had done.

That was all Garcel needed. He drew his knife and stabbed Raliph. The knife went deep into his stomach. Raliph moaned. I screamed.

Garcel pulled the knife out and stood up, satisfied. "You'll get over it, Mercy. If you ever want to fight the savages."

"You monster!" I screamed. "I hate you!" I ran to Raliph who was groaning in pain on the floor.

"What's the matter with you, Mercy? What's gotten into you?" Garcel grabbed my wrist and pushed me against the wall. I tried to break free to help Raliph but he held me firm. "You act like you want to help the maggot. As if you liked your name."

"Well, maybe I do!"

Garcel loosened his hold and stared at me surprised.

"Maybe I don't want to be cruel like you! All your pride, stubbornness, and brutality! Maybe Mercy isn't so bad. Being somewhat decent among wicked men like you. Maybe I do like my name!" I breathed hard, pulling away from him. "I used to want to be like you! So strong and brave, I thought!" I glared up at his dark thunderous eyes, wild with wrathful passion. "Now, I know that you are a brutal, cruel and heartless man with no regard for anyone but yourself. And I would rather die…" I caught my breath. "Than ever be like you."

Garcel dropped my wrist.

"I hate you, Garcel, for what you have done to Raliph. For all your brutality. And I will hate you until the day I die."

Garcel backed away.

"I fear greatly for the sake of Tarlen because I know you will be the worst king ever to reign." I paused. "If Justice were alive, he would be ashamed to call you his brother."

"Mercy." Garcel regained his voice. "You are harsh."

"There is no way to be harsh enough to you except do to you what you did to Raliph."

"I see this Cansten worm means more to you than your own family," said Garcel, his voice hard and hollow.

"He means more than you do. Now, I know what you are."

Garcel turned away from me. "You have done your worst. I shall leave you and keep my face from you from this day forward. Goodbye, Mercy." He paused before he slipped away. "But I loved Justice. And I love you."

"Leave!"

Garcel disappeared and I fell to my knees and wept. I touched Raliph's bloody face and looked at his wound in his stomach. My breath caught. He was lying in a pool of his own blood; crimson exuding from him. His face was pale.

"I…will not…be a cause," he coughed, "of enmity…between you and…and your brother."

"I hate him."

"No!" his voice rasped. "Mercy."

I nodded silently.

He heaved a few more breaths then lost consciousness.

I cried over him, confused and heartbroken. He had lost too much blood to live but I was unwilling to let him die. I cared too much about him. Too much to let him die.

My mind went back to the night before. *"Call to me…"* Ellar's words rang in my memory.

"I cannot do this. I'm scared and alone. I am at a loss. I just don't know. I cannot heal or help anymore. Ellar please come and heal once more. Ellar please come and heal once more."

# RALIPH'S BOLDNESS

Once again, I woke up on the floor in my hideout. My mind raced to the still form before me. Blood stained his body and the blankets which lay about him. I put my hand on his heart. It was still beating. His body was warm. The blood was only leftover from his beating and wound the previous night. I got some water and proceeded to clean him up. When I reached the dagger wound on his stomach, I saw it had disappeared. Not even a scar.

I washed his face and chest and was about to turn him over to his stomach so I could wash and bandage his back when he stirred.

He opened his eyes and looked at me. "I didn't die."

"No."

He smiled. "I'm glad."

"Me too."

"After your display last night, I believe you," he said bringing his hand up. He gently touched my cheek. "You called Ellar. That's why I didn't die."

I nodded. "How are you feeling now?"

"I struggle to find something wrong with me. The only thing I can complain about it that I must leave you soon."

The realization hit me and I realized I was sad. "Will I ever see you again?"

"If I may dare." He sat up and took my hand. "I ask you to come with me and be my wife."

My eyes widened and my heart leapt.

"I know you have only seen me as a virtually unearthly creature, torn and destroyed like an old worthless rag. But I have been told before that I am good-looking." He paused. "But then, you are a princess and I am a rebel with two illegal markings. I do not know where I will go or who I will be. I have everything to fear. As a princess, you have nothing to fear. But…if I could somehow convince you to, you will always be loved and cherished…"

"Raliph…" I said, finally regaining my composure. "There are things I must do as a princess. I cannot run away with a rebel whether I thought he were handsome or not."

Raliph let go of my hand and slumped back. "I know." He sighed. "But do you love me?"

"Does it matter?"

"It does to me. No one has ever loved me but my family, even they are up to question."

I thought for a moment. "I love you, Raliph. Whether as a friend or as you think you do me."

"You do not believe me."

"You have not been under normal circumstances for the duration of your knowing me."

"I wasn't alive until I met Ellar and you."

I stood up. "You need to eat."

"I offended you."

"No, merely surprised me. I do not normally speak of such things. Nor think of them either. You merely surprised me."

He smirked. "I do that, don't I?"

"Yes."

I spent most of that day preparing for Raliph's departure. I snuck into the kitchen and raided the cellar for bread and cheese. The servants were used to escapades like that from the royal family. Garcel and Adann would often do that even now that Garcel was twenty three and Adann twenty. The royal family was not known for their maturity.

I found some clothes from Adann's closet and took them. Making sure they were the commonest so he would not miss them. Then I packed his food, one change of clothes, and some rope all in a wool blanket. I took a small bracelet and put it in the inner pocket of my brother's grey wool cloak that I had stolen.

Finally, I found my spare knife and the extra sword I owned which had always been too big for me. My father had given that to me.

Raliph smiled enthusiastically when he saw I had some travelling clothes for him.

"I hope I remembered everything," I said as I dropped all my findings on the floor."

"I've travelled with nothing but the clothes on my back for three days. I'll be more than prepared."

"You leave tomorrow morning early," I said. "In the meantime…" I ran to my room to get a sack of things. "Let's have a farewell party."

I pulled the things out of the sack. Things I had raided from the kitchen. A basket of fruit, a choice leg of crall, a delicacy in Tarlen; some roasted seeds and baked merbis, a yellow root vegetable grown in the wetlands of Tarlen.

Raliph saw all I had brought and beamed.

"I have to get one more thing." I left to get a bottle of wine and two glasses. When I returned, he was fully dressed in Adann's clothes and on his feet.

"Aren't you a little young?" he asked when he saw what I had brought.

"I'm seventeen."

"That's not that old."

I laughed. "It's a party, Raliph!" I sat down on the floor and began to pour the wine.

"To celebrate the fact you will never have to see me again," said Raliph quietly and took his glass.

I frowned. "No, to celebrate my friend's health."

Raliph shrugged. "I'd rather have two broken legs and be with you than be well and far away."

I sighed inwardly. "That is tomorrow." I took a sip of wine then bit into a piece of fruit.

Raliph helped himself to some crall. He raised his glass. "To you, Princess Mercy. May you continue to be the compassionate asset to Tarlen and one day find Ellar."

I lowered my eyes. Raliph's words hit me hard. It wasn't fair how he could evoke emotion in me with everything he said. I had always considered myself to be one not easily carried away emotionally. But with Raliph around, I had broken down three times in the past four days.

"I'm sorry; I said something wrong again, didn't I?"

I smiled. "It's fine. I guess I'm feeling sad too…for tomorrow."

Raliph beamed.

I raised my glass. "To you, Raliph. May you be strong and brave as you fight to right what has been wronged."

The glasses clinked and our eyes met.

"I love you, Mercy," he whispered.

I lowered my eyes to my lap.

"That I cannot apologize for."

Our party lasted until late. Because we both managed to get slightly drunk, we found ourselves behaving more idiotic than usual. I laughed hysterically when he tripped over a blanket and landed face flat on the floor. And he roared with hilarity when I bit into a piece of fruit and the juice squirted all over my face.

When our feast was done and antics nearly exhausted, I stood up to leave. "You must get an early start tomorrow. Goodnight."

Raliph stood up, surprisingly steadily, and bowed. "Your Highness."

As though it were completely thoughtless and uncontrolled, he took my hand and kissed it. I backed away and knocked my head against the low roof of my hideout. Disjointedly, I fumbled through my wardrobe and shut the door behind me. Knowing in my heart it would be the last time I would see Raliph.

Confused and slightly intoxicated, I stumbled and fell onto my bed. My head collapsed onto my pillow. I knew I would regret my behavior with a headache the next morning.

Half asleep, I felt a hand gently caress my cheek. I felt a soft kiss planted on my forehead. "I love you, Princess Mercy," he whispered.

A small piece of paper was placed in my open hand as it lay over my duvet. He moved a tendril of hair off my eyes. A teardrop fell onto my cheek.

"Whatever happens, it has been an honor knowing you."

His footsteps faded and my room was silent again. I jumped out of bed the moment I was sure he was gone. I ran to the window knowing that would be his escape route. A stealthy form slinked up a wall using a rope to grapple, then over. I continued watching when he appeared on the outside of the wall striding through the fields beyond the city. When he reached the forest beyond the fields, he turned back and looked. Regret pierced my heart. I really wanted to follow him. I unfolded the piece of paper he had left me. This was all I had left of my forbidden Cansten friend. Or was he my lover? I touched my forehead where he'd kissed it.

"Goodbye, Raliph. I'm sorry I didn't come with you."

I lit a lamp and sat down to read the messily printed note.

*Deer Mercy, I thot you wer an angel when I firs met you and I beleev that still. I know your frendship with me has been bittersweet becuz of your greef for your brother, but to me, it has been nothing but a pleshur and honor knowing you.*

*Now I am gone, pleese do not forget me. Peraps, find it in your heart to care for me the way I do you.*

*I know that I love you and I always will.*

*Yours Raliph*

# MERCY'S FOLLY

Months passed and my orphanage plans were proceeding as I had hoped. I bought a large piece of farmland just outside the city that the boys could cultivate, sell the produce, and send that to help their families. It was a perfect way to thwart Larcos and cheat him out of more victims. The boys could get educations and learn to be upstanding citizens of Tarlen, far from the grasp of Larcos and the fear his mention ensues. I also bought a strip of houses in Whitestone in case the boy's families were being pressured and threatened by Larcos, they could move into the city where they would be safe. It was working out perfectly. My contribution to fight Larcos.

Tomorrow, I would put out notices all throughout Tarlen and begin accepting boys. I was practically bursting with excitement.

The King was currently with the sixteenth and tenth divisions near a minor city near Belstrom, holding off a rebel attack. Adann was at Fardstone with four other divisions, guarding it and the outskirting land. They needed to protect the crops for the city that year. The rest of the main captains were spread out all throughout Tarlen from the opposite edge of the great forest to the edge of the Marshlands. As it was harvest season there were many raids from the rebels and Larcos would try his best to bring the Tarlen cities to poverty.

Presently, there were only the normal guards of Whitestone protecting the city and Garcel in charge of the castle but that was okay because the rebels were so tied up elsewhere, we feared no attack. Tomorrow, the third division was due to arrive.

I hadn't spoken to Garcel since our fight in my hideout and had no intention of it in the future. He himself had taken to avoiding me so I rarely had a chance to show him the extent of my disdain.

The only communication I got from him was a stupid letter that I skimmed through and forgot about the next day. Then I tore it up. Then I burned it.

I kept Raliph's note in a locket around my neck. It was the only jewelry I wore now unless the King was around.

No one found out that I was the financer of my odd project as I had taken extra care to secure. Whenever anyone asked about it, the builders were commanded to reply a Compassionate Angel. I coined the name in memory of Justice.

I often heard my father growl about how the money used for the project this mysterious person was financing could feed and clothe his army for a year. I thought it best to hold my tongue. The irony that he was technically paying for it did strike me as entertaining several times.

The project was the talk of the kingdom and everyone wanted to know who the Compassionate Angel was. I would always hide a smile when I heard people gossip about it in the streets.

I would walk the streets of Whitestone frequently now. I never used to before. I would dress in common clothes and shadow my face with a hood so I would not arouse attention. I would sneak out through the cellar into the kitchen and return late. Lusilla tolerated my odd behavior without question. She was a palace maid and that meant she would have to expect odd behavior and be prepared with a good lie to explain it away to anyone of importance who asked.

Today, I had just visited the workplace to watch the final bed carried in. I went to a designer paper shop and gave them my plan for what I wanted the notices to look like. My architect promised to prepare several messengers to carry the notices throughout Tarlen.

Tomorrow, things would be set in motion that no one would be able to stop and I was enthralled. It was impossible for me to return home now that I was so excited so I decided to take a walk in the fields outside the city before the gates closed.

The wind blew my hood off my face and I let it catch my shadowy hair. I laughed, happy. Nothing could stop me now!

Heart brimming with joy, I set off in a run through the fields. I stopped when I reached the edge of the forest. The same place Raliph had turned and looked one last time at Whitestone. I always wondered if he had seen me watching at my window. I wasn't allowed to go into the forest but I peered in anyways.

"Mercy, what are you doing here?"

I jumped. It was Garcel. I glared at him. "Taking a walk."

"Not here." He took my arm and pulled me back through the fields towards Whitestone.

"Let go of me!" I shrieked, trying to yank away.

"There are rebel bandits in the forest. You'd fetch a pretty price. How many times has father forbidden you to go past the walls of Whitestone?"

"Father doesn't care about anything but the war!" I wrenched myself out of his grasp. "And you're no better."

He caught me again. "Whether he cares or not, I do! I lost one sibling to the rebels, I won't lose two!"

"Let go of me, you brute!"

Garcel snatched my other arm and forced me to face him. "Look Mercy, I don't care what you call me or what you think of me. Somebody's got to watch out for you and it might as well be me." His jaw was tight and his eyes were like stone. "Compassionate Angel."

I stared at him, startled. "How did you know?"

"I've been watching you since you fooled Laria and Adann about being ill, didn't you read my letter."

My blood boiled. My face was red with rage in fury at my cruel brother. "How dare you!"

Garcel continued dragging me back to Whitestone while I kicked and screamed. People finishing their day's work would stare at us as we passed by. I didn't care.

"Tell me, Mercy, when will you stop wasting your money, or should I say father's money, on commoners and saving rebels and try to save Tarlen from the enemy ravaging our land?"

"Tell me, Garcel, when you are going to stop burning in your hate towards the rebels because of Justice's death, being father's cruel puppet, selling yourself to Morglin with all your brutality, and do something that will actually help?"

"Do you have any sense of justice, Mercy? You save the very men who killed our brother!"

"After you mutilate them!" I shrieked.

"Shh, Mercy, stop making a scene."

"I'll make a scene if I want to, Garcel! I hate you! I hate you! I hate you! And everything you are!"

Garcel forced me through the gates.

"You will be the worst king ever to rule in Tarlen! You're cruel, selfish, vengeful…"

"Enough, Mercy!" said Garcel and he pushed me into a wall in a back alley. "Like I said, I don't care what you think or what you say. Just stay away from the forest."

With that, he dragged me through the streets to the palace and up the stairs to my room, as I shrieked at him the whole while.

He slammed the door and locked me in. I screamed insults at him and banged on the solid wooden door. He ordered no one to open the door until Father came home. I hated my brother.

As soon as he left, I decided I'd show him. I ran to my window and smiled. He couldn't control me that easily. It was dangerous to climb down from my window but it would be worth it. I pulled my cloak over my shoulders then my hood over my face. Bravely, I stepped onto my window sill. I straddled over the edge, one leg dangling outside, and the other still in the safety of my room. Cautiously, I fumbled at some vines, my hands shaking, and crawled down the wall using the vines as handholds.

The sun's light was fading behind the forest beyond Whitestone. It didn't matter. I wasn't scared of the dark.

Reaching the bottom, my feet stepped down onto a flower bush with prickles. It hurt. My ankles bled. Slipping through the city, I passed through the gate before it closed that night. I decided to stay out all night just to get Garcel furious. Remembering that knife he drove into Raliph's gut, I clenched my fists. How I hated that brute.

I set my pace through the fields instead of the wide path leading to the forest. I didn't want Garcel recognizing my cloak and come after me.

My breath caught at the beautiful sight of the sunset as it disappeared under the trees then I disappeared into them. *'I'll go a little into the forest so no one will discover me and make me go home,'* I thought.

The shadows grew deep and the old gnarled trees swayed. Nervousness crept up on me. Faint rustles in the distance sent goose-bumps all over my skin. I took a deep breath trying to calm myself but my imagination went wild.

There was a famed creature that ravaged through Tarlen known as the Urfane. Stealthy creatures with powerful claws and terrible teeth. The biggest predator in Tarlen. Wearing a white coat but somehow invisible. Preying upon any living creature, they would weaken their victims with poison from their claws and teeth then tear the heart out while their prey lay alive, helpless, and in agony. If somehow, they escape the gory practice of having their heart wrenched free from their body an Urfane's victim dies slowly as the poison makes its way to the heart and stops it. Superstitious people claimed Urfanes were Morglin's demons. I closed my eyes trying to shake off those images. No good.

I longed to go back home but my stubbornness would not allow it. I stumbled and backed into a tree. Sliding my back down on the trunk, I slumped down and curled up. I buried my head in my lap.

"What do we have here, Shatal?"

"Something to break the monotony of a spy job."

I jumped up, startled, to see the speakers. They were two tough men, both tall, with evil glints in their eyes. They were half naked except for the leather straps holding a battle-axe on their backs. Each had two swords and a dagger strapped at their belts. On each of their left shoulders, a strip of ornamented leather was bound around them. I knew what it was hiding. The illegal mark of a rebel. My heart seized in fear.

I turned to run but one of them grabbed me. I screamed but that was soon muffled by his hand.

"Not bad," the other man commented, his eyes looking over me like I was an object or his prey that he'd caught.

They dragged me deeper into the forest where no one could heard me scream. Then my captor removed his hand from my mouth.

"You dare touch me and I will see to it you both have the ugliest deaths since the kingdom of Tarlen began!" I said.

They laughed.

"And who are you to talk so bravely?"

I shook my hood off and let my black hair catch the shadowy

light of the forest. "Her Royal Highness, the Princess Mercy."

Their jaws dropped.

"Look at her. She is!"

"I demand you release me at once or have every soldier in Tarlen to pay."

They laughed.

The man holding my arm leered over me. Glancing over me from my ankles to my dark flowing hair, he chuckled. "Larcos has been trying to catch you alive for years. We'll be captains!" he exclaimed. "Tie her up and let's bring her back to the camp. Larcos will return when he's done pestering the king."

Pushed to the ground and held down struggling, they procured some rope and began to bind my wrists.

"Ow!" I cried, exaggerating.

"Don't hurt her, it'll be our heads," one warned. "Remember what happened to the last man who played with Larcos's last prize."

"What?" I asked, suddenly curious.

"Stabbed ten times by Larcos's dagger and left to die in his own blood."

I wished I hadn't asked.

They tied me up and the leering man, Shatal his name was, threw me over his shoulder and they trekked through the forest. I exercised my biting tongue on them until they gagged me. My mind struggled to find a way out of my predicament. I knew that whatever Larcos wanted regarding myself, I wouldn't like it.

My captors were hard, cruel men. By appearance, they looked much like Raliph. Long hair which fell to their shoulders. Tall and powerful men with muscles used to hard work and hard battles. Many scars covered their arms and a few on their faces.

Gagged and struggling they informed me, laughing harshly, of all the terrible ways to kill a Tarlen soldier; what torture instruments Larcos liked to use best on his prisoners and all the ways they planned on eradicating the rest of my family.

I'd squirm and moan and they'd laugh. Being around the rebel beasts made me wonder if Raliph had ever been like them.

Along the way, we met a few other rebels on the secret Cansten paths. They'd laugh and congratulate my captors on their accomplishment. One promised to take the four day trip and bring the news to Larcos…for a small price.

After six days of being dragged, jostled, yanked, gagged, bound, and mocked, Shatal announced the end of the journey.

My head throbbed and my wrists and ankles were bleeding from the ropes. I felt sick and achy from being thrown over the shoulders of two savages. In all honesty, I was so grateful that I was done being toted around on the backs of two beasts that I didn't care I was being forced into the camp of my enemies.

My eyes scanned the camp my father had longed to see for so long. It was in a clearing surrounded in trees and a steep decline led down to it. Brown and deep green tents were set up in the clearing; their colors I assumed were to blend in with the surroundings. Shatal carried me through the tents. Past men lying on the ground around a fire pit, passed out. Past fanned flames, melting iron and blacksmithing instruments. Slaves in chains worked the metal and were whipped or hollered at by rebels driving them. Past young boys being trained by huge, tough trainers. I shuddered hearing their harsh voices and loud threats directed towards the poor boys. Past a small grouping of tents where cruel men were laughing at one of their fellows, strung up by the feet upside down. They had blindfolded him and were mocking him and beating him with sticks. They stumbled about like drunkards.

"Pretty place, isn't it?" Yaris, my other captor, chuckled in my ear as he took me off Shatal's back.

They dropped me on the ground and dragged me through the dirt. A young girl slipping past caught my eyes as they hauled me, still bound, to somewhere I did not know where. Her clothes were torn and the drunks I had seen before caught her and dragged her, weeping, to their circle of tents. Terror in her eyes, they grabbed her, laughing harshly, I closed my eyes unable to bear any more.

Finally, they threw me into a tent still bound and gagged. "You'll wait here until Larcos comes for you!"

Their harsh laughter faded and I was alone.

# RALIPH AND GARCEL

**Raliph**

I heard of Mercy's capture from a messenger bringing the news to Larcos. Terrified for her, I left immediately for the palace.

When I reached it, I uncovered my mark and begged to see the prince. They looked at me strangely but let me in. They took my weapons and tied my hands. I let them because I knew if I showed any resistance, they would think I was a challenger and beat me. They hit me a few times but not as much as I had expected. Pushing me roughly into the throne room, they told me to wait and left, shutting the door behind them.

I stood alone for a few minutes then I heard footsteps approaching.

Garcel entered; in his hand he held a whip. My palms went cold and my knees knocked at the sight of him. That man knew how to create fear in me. He slammed the door and I was alone with him.

"When I heard a rebel was here to see me, I could only guess who it was," he said striding towards me, whip in hand.

I fell to my knees before him. "Your Royal Highness." I stared at the ground.

"Tell me, Raliph." He paced around me. "What kind of fool are you to put your head in the Urfane's mouth?"

"Just a common fool, Your Highness," I replied, still staring at the ground.

"Oh no, you don't give yourself enough credit." He raised me up by my hair and said in my ear, "You are the most extraordinary fool I have ever met." He released me and I fell back on my knees.

"You confuse me, Raliph." He paced around me again. "All I have known of you is a pitiful worm who begs and whines like a dying rat. Now you appear before me, alone, willing to fall helplessly into my hands. Knowing you will get far more than what you ran away from. Any man like that is clearly brave but you kneel before me like a man receiving his death sentence." He cracked his whip behind me.

"I know Your Highness intends to harm me and I expected it by coming here but you must hear me out before you do. It concerns one we both love."

"Because of you, she hates me!" Garcel roared, all restraint lost. Laying a stripe across my back, he cried in rage. Knocking me to the ground, he whipped me again. I bit my lip and dug my fingers into my palms for the pain.

"Your Highness, please…"

"Silence!"

With all the strength the powerful man possessed, he beat me. Slicing my back with his whip, my blood trickled down onto the royal carpet.

"Your sister has been kidnapped by rebels!" I cried.

He stepped back. Reaching for a chair, he stumbled back unsteadily. "What?"

"Two days ago, she was kidnapped by rebels."

He reached for a chair for balance. The whip clattered on the floor when it fell from his hand. "My sister…"

I painfully got up to my knees from my position prostrated on the floor. Meeting his eyes bravely, I watched him. My enemy.

His eyes were wide and crazed, wretched tears filled them. "Tell me where she is, please…I'll…I'll release you. Give you money! Whatever you want…"

"It's impossible to tell you, it is hidden in the forest and those who find it never return to tell the tale. You need a guide to take you there safely," I said slowly.

"What will happen to her?"

"She will be held until Larcos returns. Then, he will decide what to do with her," I paused. My back burned in the searing pain from Garcel's whip. "But it will not be good. Larcos is a cruel man."

"Have you come to gloat over my agony?" He asked his voice hollow like it was the day Mercy had sworn her hatred on him.

I found myself feeling sorry for him. "Let me lead you. Let me help you save her. She saved me and I owe it to her. Then, you may take me prisoner and do to me whatever you wish."

Garcel pulled me up to my feet. "I must trust the man who would kill me in my sleep to save my sister who hates me?"

I squared my shoulders. "You need never fear me, Your Highness. I just want to help Mercy."

Garcel walked to the door. "Guards!" he bellowed.

Five men appeared.

"Round up as many soldiers as we can spare and report them to me!"

The men jumped to obey Garcel's orders.

Garcel turned back to me. "For the love of my sister, you will lead me to her. Swear to me that you will not betray me!"

"I swear on the golden mark on my breast and that which I have in my heart for the Princess Mercy, I am not a traitor."

About ten soldiers appeared and lined up.

"Is this all we can spare?" demanded Garcel.

"We need them to guard the gates."

Garcel growled under his breath. "You have been chosen to go on a secret mission to rescue our beloved Princess Mercy," he addressed them. "Raliph will guide us to the rebel hideout where she is being held."

"Your Highness..." a timid soldier spoke up.

Garcel nodded.

"The castle needs every man we can spare..."

"And we wouldn't really make a difference anyways on this mission," another added.

"We are not trained for this sort of mission..."

"So, we respectfully request to be dismissed."

"I'm sure Larcos will set an affordable ransom on her..."

Garcel ground his teeth.

"The odds are vast against us. Ten to a thousand."

"Besides, how do we know this rebel won't betray us?"

"Cowards!" Garcel shrieked. "None of you love your princess enough to take a risk but this Cansten rebel?" He slapped the face of the first speaker. "I'll deal with you cowards later! Pack our two best horses for the journey! Bring our best weapons! We'll go alone!"

The trembling soldiers stumbled over each other to obey his orders.

I was feeling faint from my beating. Garcel threw me a towel to clean the blood off me.

"Come!" he beckoned me to follow him. I obeyed. One thing Garcel possessed was the ability to strike enough fear into men's hearts so they obey him and I was no different.

His hair was dark like Mercy's and his eyes the same green but his face did not hold the same expression of compassion as Mercy's did; it was angry and cruel. When in the presence of this man, the best things to do are either grovel or run.

He led me to his private chambers where he fed me and ordered his servants to clean me up and arm me. After we were both prepared to leave, he led me down to the stables where two magnificent horses stood saddled and packed for the journey. Not a man was in sight.

Garcel chuckled. "Funny how a busy stable can get so quiet."

I shuddered at the sound of his voice. My back hurt. Watching him strut about it occurred to me, I could betray him. Rid the kingdom of the monster but I had sworn upon Ellar my savior, and my love for Mercy not to do so. I couldn't turn back.

He mounted and I followed his example. Nodding to me he said, "Lead on."

I urged my horse forward with Garcel's steed at its heels. We said nothing when we entered the forest and for hours afterwards.

"How long is the journey?" asked Garcel after hours of silence.

"Three days on horseback for a man who knows his way well. Five days on foot for a strong man." I turned to look ahead. "I pray to Ellar we reach her before Larcos comes."

Silence. For hours, we urged our horses through the thickets. Any trail to the rebel camp was never worn; we had been trained specifically never to leave a trail. However, this made it difficult to gallop through the woods on horseback. Half the time, we had to go at only a brisk walk so the horses would not lose their footing.

"Raliph," Garcel broke the silence again.

"Your Highness."

"Why aren't you dead?"

"You mean since you stabbed me, Your Highness?"

"I know well you'd cherish the thought of seeing me dangling from the top of one of these trees with a rope around my neck. You hate me just as I hate you so stop with the 'Your Highness' attitude as if you actually respected me," growled Garcel. "And, yes, since I stabbed you. I'm beginning to fear you have several lives."

I smiled slightly to myself. "I fear you more than I hate you," I admitted quietly. "I lived by the prayers of your sister and the grace of Ellar."

"Ellar…" muttered Garcel. "One of Mercy's favorite topics."

"Really?" I said surprised. Mercy had seemed somewhat opposed to Ellar.

"Yes, she likes to tell me I'm selling myself to Morglin with all my cruelty and that Ellar will have to save me but I deserve Morglin's enslavement anyways so Ellar probably wouldn't even try to save me." He chuckled bitterly. "She says I'll make the worst king ever to rule Tarlen, that I'm a cruel, selfish, vengeful monster."

"Not the mildest of princesses," I said.

"No, never has been."

"I'm sorry."

Garcel looked at me in surprise. "For what?"

"For causing a breach between you and your sister. I know I am the reason she hates you."

He lowered his eyes to stare at the perfectly clipped brown mane of his mount. His lips played a bitter smile. I hated that smile; I had seen it many times in the torture chamber. I breathed heavily trying to remind myself not to panic in this man's presence.

"Harsh as she is, she is right." He threw back his head and

laughed.

I stared at him, shocked and terrified.

"Every word of it!" He cried and laughed his deep harsh laugh again. "You know that better than her. I'm a selfish, cruel, tyrant sold to every dark power existing. I'll lead Tarlen to ruins." He laughed harder.

The prince was going insane. I'd never seen him before like this. I didn't know what to do.

He breathed heavily. "That is why I will die saving Mercy."

"Your Highness…"

"Don't call me 'Your Highness', fool!" he barked.

I bowed my head and tried not to remember that voice. The same tone that ordered me to be branded Worthless Scum, whipped, burnt, and poisoned.

He saw my face. "But I don't need to tell you what I am, Raliph. You know firsthand. But…" His eyes filled suddenly with tears. "I loved my brother, Justice. And I love Mercy…"

Despite myself, I could not keep my heart from aching to see the prince sink so low. "I believe you."

I awoke to the sight of an Urfane drooling on my face. He saw my eyes open and attacked my body with ferocity. His teeth dug into my shoulder and I cried out in pain. Rolling over, I tried to get the creature off me but another jumped upon my back. He punctured my leg deep with his claws. "Aah!"

I tried to reach for my dagger at my waist but the other one stepped on my arm. I felt my back being clawed until it tore. The poison in their claws and teeth weakened me. Unable to fight now, they rolled me over onto my bleeding back. They snarled at my face. I managed to draw my dagger but in my weakened state, I could not use it. Powerless now, I dropped it on the forest floor. My captors roared over me in victory and prepared to tear out my heart as the vile creatures liked to do with their prey; one stood on my legs to keep me from thrashing and the other stepped onto my chest. Its wild eyes met mine in a furious hunger. They dulled. It collapsed onto me. Someone moved it off and I saw the other one lying in a bloody heap at my feet.

"I'm surprised you've lived this long since you can't even fight an Urfane," Garcel mocked.

I groaned. "I can fight an Urfane, sure. But two, when I'm half asleep, is a little more difficult!"

Garcel knelt down and poured a sharp poison into my wounds to counteract the Urfane's poison. I hoped the wounds had not been left too long for the poison to be killed. I cried out when the cruel cure burned my body. But I lay still until Garcel had finished giving me my medicine and bandaging the wounds.

"Thanks," I muttered. Now the pain was subsiding, I felt embarrassed that I needed my enemy to save my life.

"Can you ride?" he asked.

I sat up. "I've been worse than this before."

"I know. But you certainly weren't riding."

I sighed looking at the dead creatures on the ground, bleeding and grotesque. "I have a way getting beaten up by anyone and anything that comes by."

Garcel pulled me up to my feet. "Saving my sister is probably the bravest thing you've done."

"The *only* brave thing I've done."

Garcel laughed but not cruelly. I forgot how scared I was of him and smiled. "I am pathetic."

He shook his head. "No, a man who can stand up to me,

especially after I almost killed him twice and go against his own leaders, I couldn't call pathetic."

"My lord, did you just compliment me?"

Garcel shrugged. "Barely."

I laughed as I mounted my horse. "Then, I shall have to return the favor."

"Don't!" he shook his head. "If anything, mock me. I am not a good man."

I glanced over at the solid prince mounting up onto his saddle. Straight and strong, he sat. Strangely enough, I felt a tinge of admiration for him. The royal family always had something about them. Was it in the way they carried themselves, the way they fought, the way they spoke? I could not understand it. But I had never seen such love for a sister than in Garcel for Mercy.

Urging our horses forward, we galloped through the trees until the forest grew too thick again to do so. I had been through this route a hundred times when returning from battle, bringing a boy or a good prisoner, spying, or hunting. The day was waning and the shadows of the trees were lengthening. Night was coming upon us but I was not afraid of it. The only fear I held was that we may meet other rebels along this road. I told Garcel to pull his hood over his face and pretend him and I were friends. When we stopped for the night, I was pleased with our progress. We had covered many miles. I built a fire and caught a few small forest animals. They were tough but we were hungry.

I leant against a tree to rest. It quivered in the wind. The night felt eerie but I was used to the deep forest in the dark. I watched the flames of the fire flicker up to the starlit sky. It blazed and devoured the firewood Garcel threw on it. I knew I was safe from Urfanes tonight. They hated fires. I let my pain-ridden body relax with that thought.

"When the horses are rested, we must leave again," said Garcel, staring into the flames. "How are your wounds?"

"Not bad." I still felt faint from the counteracting poisons but that was the least of my worries.

"Do you think she'll be alright?" Garcel asked looking up at my face through the rising flickers of fire.

"Only if we get there before Larcos does."

"What is it like there?"

"I don't think you want to know, it's a savage place…"

"Like the palace torture chamber?"

I lowered my eyes. "Must you speak of that?"

"I am trying to understand you."

I sighed. "I am a man not worth mentioning. A man who nobody wants or needs except to vent on. A man who has stood for nothing and lived for nothing. A coward, a fool, a victim, but…" I paused. "I must retain some worth upon myself for I am Ellar's."

Across the fire, my enemy stared in silence. I felt his eyes on the brand at my breast.

"Ellar's," he whispered. "Is Mercy, Ellar's?"

"I don't know. When he asked her, she said no."

"What does it mean to be Ellar's?"

I thought for a moment trying to know the words to describe it. "To fear less, to be protected from the power of Morglin, to belong to someone, to be cared about…" I thought again. "The mark you branded on me was replaced by this at his touch. Morglin branded many such things on me as well." I chuckled when I glanced at Garcel's face when I mentioned meeting Morglin. "Yes, I met Morglin. He had a few words with me. He told me a few things about myself. Ellar didn't deny them, he replaced them." I met

Garcel's eyes bravely. "Now, all I am is Ellar's."

Garcel nodded thoughtfully. "I wish I could lose my past, the brand it has burnt onto me, and who I am now which I detest…" he paused. "And solely be one who belongs to good."

"Ask him," I said, leant back and soon fell asleep.

When I awoke, I knew something was different. I sat up quickly. Two men were talking. I recognized the cloak of one of them to be Garcel's. The other wore a long grey robe. They were about twenty yards away and were talking earnestly. I felt the presence of Ellar. I heard his voice and watched his hand come out of his cloak and onto Garcel. Behind his back, Garcel clenched his fists. It hurt, I knew. I remembered. When Ellar took his hand off, Garcel fell to his knees before him.

The poison in my body caught up with me and my eyes blurred. I fell back onto the ground and passed out.

"Time to go, Raliph." Garcel awoke me. It was still dark but the fire was almost out. I raised my head despite my dizziness. He pulled me up with his arm.

"How are we going to get her away?" asked Garcel while he packed his horse.

"Larcos's important prisoners are brought to a tent at the end of the camp. There are two guards posted at the door facing the forest and the door facing the camp. We go by the back and kill or bribe the guards."

"They can be bribed?"

"All Cansten rebels can be bribed," I said and swung up into my saddle. Garcel must have saddled it while I was still asleep. I wanted to ask him about his meeting with Ellar but didn't dare. Garcel was too much of an intimidating man to inquire about such personal things.

We rode in silence for a while.

"I asked him," he said.

I smiled. "I'm glad..." I paused. "Your Highness."

Garcel smirked.

We travelled on. Our horses were well rested and bore us well that day. In my mind, I formed a plan to get us through the guards. We could use the horses as decoys to distract the guards so we could take them out without causing a stir. That was one plan among many. I wondered if Garcel was forming multiple plans in his mind too while we rode.

The day passed as we passed through the trees. Nothing exceptional happened that day. The horses got spooked a few times from forest animals; we met some rebels coming and going from the camp. They eyed Garcel suspiciously because his clothing was rich and his weapons costly. If they asked questions, I would explain that we had just robbed a rich Tarlen captain. They naturally assumed, as Garcel was a stronger build than I, he had beaten me in a fight and had taken all the spoil from our accomplishment. Of course, they would laugh and those who knew me would laugh harder at the thought. It was no secret that I was a whimpering weakling. The way of the rebels was a harsh one. Biggest and strongest get the spoil. But however powerful they were, they'd better do what Larcos tells them or they'd be dead or worse.

Larcos had the strongest arm, the vastest of ambitions, the most dangerous blade, the most terrifying of tempers, the fastest horse, the most beautiful women, and the cleverest mind. No one would dare challenge him. It occurred to me that Garcel could. Garcel was reckless, powerful, dangerous, skilled, tall, and brave. He was a great man. I was not.

The horses slowed to a walk. The sun was beginning to fall. Garcel reined his horse up next to mine.

"He woke me up last night and asked me if I wanted to ask him something."

I smiled. "I can see him doing that."

"He is good."

"Yes, he is."

"My sister needs to know him. You must help her."

Garcel's tone unsettled me. I felt like he was trying to make me swear an oath. "Why me?"

"Because something is going to happen to me there. I don't know whether I'll be captured or killed. I need someone to take care of her. I can't anymore…" Garcel took my arm in his steely grip. "Swear to me you'll keep her safe! Swear to me you'll show her Ellar!"

Tears filled his eyes. I tried to shake off his gaze but he held me fast. My arm whitened in his grip.

"I swear," I whispered. "I don't know why you choose me to do this but I will."

Garcel let go of my arm and wiped his eyes. "You are a worthy man. A good friend."

"Friend?!" I said, startled.

Garcel smiled. "If you can."

"If I can…" I paused. Was it possible to be friends with this man after all he'd done to me? How the very sound of his voice filled my heart with terror. Friend…

"I'm sorry for all I did to you."

I stared at him, stunned. "Your Highness, I…"

He waited.

"I do not know what to say." My heart was beating ten times faster than it should and twice as loud at that.

"Just take my hand in friendship and forgive me." He put his hand out to me.

I took it and he shook it firmly.

He smiled. "Thank you."

I led the prince around the edge of the camp and around to the back. We hid in the shadow of the trees. My hope was to spirit the princess into the darkness of the forest before anyone noticed her absence.

I glanced beside me at Garcel as he took in all the horrors of the camp but his eyes showed no terror, only determination.

Two guards were posted at the door of the tent specially made for Larcos' prized prisoners. They stared alertly, standing straight as posts, into the dark woods we were hidden in.

"We'll have to use our horses to distract them then move in," I whispered.

Garcel gripped my arm again in his powerful grip. "Get her out of there. Whatever you do. Do not look back if anything happens to me. Promise?"

I nodded gravely and tried not to allow faintness to overtake me.

"Say the word so I may be sure."

"I promise, Your Highness."

# WOMEN SILENCED

**Mercy**

I was thrown into a pitch-black tent, bound hand and foot. Guards were posted around my new prison and they began to talk amongst themselves. They would laugh harshly when they spoke of Larcos and all the terrible things they predicted he would do to me. I think they were purposely trying to scare me. It worked. I curled up tightly in my ropes and cried into my knees.

It was terrifying in that place and I wished with all my heart I had not been so stubborn and just obeyed my brother. He had been right though I still hated to admit it. Now, I was paying for my folly. I cried more.

The men laughed harshly outside. I closed my eyes and listened to the sounds of the night around me. The screams of prisoners, the grinding and hammering of metal, the drunken laughter of rebels, the cries for mercy from voices probably as young as eight years old. Boys were being branded and forced to kill. This was war. And I was the prey of it. If Larcos knew of the work I was doing to save those boys, there would be no telling what he would do.

What about the orphanage? Would Mother save it in my absence? I had given up all hope of ever going home again. How I detested the terrible place I was in. I cried harder until I was too exhausted to make a sound.

I awoke feeling more uncomfortable than ever in my life. An old woman came in with a basin of water and a change of clothes. She put them down on a table I had hit my head on last night. She looked at me trembling me. Then she cut the ropes on my wrists and ankles. She did not speak only motioned for me to wash and dress.

I did so and she brought me something to eat. It was some small comfort to be clean. I felt a bit better and the food made me feel alive again. The guards had grown tired of mocking me and were talking about other things. I began to hope that maybe a ransom would be paid for me and I would be able to return home unharmed.

I sat down on a chair I had not seen last night and wondered what to do.

The old woman came in again. Keeping her grey head down, she began to spread fine carpets on the floor. I stood up to help her.

"What is your name?" I asked, longing to talk to someone.

She shook her head and kept her eyes on the ground. Welts were on her face and arms.

I stepped nearer to her. "No, please speak to me. I'm scared and alone and need someone to talk to."

The old woman finally looked up at me. She opened her mouth and I saw. She did not have a tongue! I was horrified.

"I'm so sorry! So sorry."

She raised her hand and touched my face. It was wrinkled but it was human. Tears filled her eyes. She turned away. I heard the guards mocking her as she left.

"Old woman, can't you talk? What's wrong with you, ugly old woman?" One struck her.

Angry, I walked to the door of my tent. I threw the flap open. "Stop it you brutes!" I cried. "Are you really so low as to hit a defenseless woman?"

They stared at me, shocked. The woman kept her head down.

"To feel good about yourselves, you must harm someone who

can't even fight you?"

I felt satisfied when I saw their faces. They had gotten a taste of royalty's sharp tongue.

One finally cleared his throat. "Watch your words or you'll end up like her."

"Someone has to stand up to you brutes! Leave her be!"

Growling, they let her go and bit their tongues. I held my head up high and turned back to my tent. They didn't try to scare me after that.

I tried to keep myself occupied for the next few days. I found out the old woman's name was Meta. She was once the wife of a wealthy Tarlen lord before they were captured. Her husband was killed and she was forced into slavery. This was the case for many of the people in this camp. Girls mostly. The men would fight over them, use them, then, when they got older, beat them and make them work harder. I had taken to going through the camp with a guard and saw these things firsthand. Surprisingly, I had a lot of freedom; because no one could hurt me for fear of their own tongues, I could help many of those young girls and women without anyone stopping me. At night from my tent, I would sing songs of hope for them. Because I knew no other source of hope in that terrible place, I would sing of Ellar.

"He sees your tears

He's heard your cries

He'll come to save you

So whisper a prayer

Tonight, tonight

To Ellar, Ellar

He'll prove himself true

In the darkness

In the fear

In despair

He is near

He won't forget us now

So pray in the night

For Ellar, Ellar

To come and save us somehow."

Still there was the looming fate which lay heavy on my heart. It was spat at me by cruel men when I helped their victims. "You wait until Larcos comes. You wait!" Then they would laugh.

I knew I could stand up to a rebel soldier but I wondered if I could to their leader. He would come and soon.

I had been there four days now. I lay alone in my tent. My songs of hope were exhausted after my mind could think of no more. Unwilling tears fell down my face. Between all my songs for others, I had no hope for myself. But I was still not willing to give him myself. Not yet.

"I'm alone and I'm terrified

I have no hope to stand on but lies

So Ellar, Ellar, please try

To save me, save me

Save me."

# LARCOS HAS COME

"Larcos has come!" I heard the shout go out. My heart dropped to the pit of my stomach and fear seized my body.

They brought me to my tent and there I was bedecked in fine clothes, jewels, and perfumes.

The rebels built a huge fire about ten yards away from my tent door. They passed the drinks around and hollered insults and taunts at me from outside. Cheers broke out loudly when Larcos appeared, walking through the crowd. They parted to let him pass. He was seven feet tall and his shadow from the firelight made him seem twice that height. The crowd of inebriated brutes cried out praises to their leader as he passed them by. Around his waist, he wore a jeweled belt which held up his sword and girdle. His shirt was made of the fine cloths that only royalty wore. My anger was incensed when I recognized my mother's embroidery on it. He wore many necklaces and had one ear pierced with a fine diamond earring hanging from it. His dark curly hair fell to his shoulders and his eyes were blue and cold like ice, glittering in the firelight. When he reached the door of my tent, he pulled off his shirt and necklaces and tossed them into the mob. The men cheered but were soon fighting over the finery and jewels they had just attained.

"See to it that we are not disturbed under any circumstances," he ordered the guards.

"Yes, my Lord."

His tall build blocked the door as his looming figure entered the tent. He looked over me with a lustful eye that reminded me of a wild animal.

He bowed mockingly. "So, we meet at last, my beautiful

princess." He took my hand and prepared to bring it to his lips.

I yanked it away. "I demand you release me at once or you'll have my father, The King Twallor of Tarlen and his whole army at your throat.

He laughed. "Really, princess, you think that will work?" He chuckled. "Besides, we have been nothing but good to you."

"Then keep it that way and release me." I crossed my arms and turned my back to him.

"Ah, Princess," he began in a slower, softer tone. He stepped nearer to me. I kept my back turned to him. "I am not an unreasonable man."

He touched my hair. The crawlies went through my body at his touch. Skillfully, he brought his hand to my cheek and then slid it down to my shoulder. He faced me now. "I merely want to make a proposition." He put his other hand on my shoulder and drew me closer to him. I exerted all my strength and pushed him away. He wasn't expecting that.

"Keep your hands to yourself, you cad! I am a princess!" I tossed my hair and looked him square in the eyes. "If you wish to speak to a princess, you shall have to do it past arms' reach."

Larcos laughed. "Very well, I'll play your game." He sat down comfortably on the only chair in the tent. "But you may find you'll be playing *my* game in the end."

I hated his cruel tone and laugh. I turned away so I wouldn't have to look at him. He was good-looking to be sure and could be polite if he wished but he embodied cruelty when I looked at him. I knew he wanted nothing more than someone either to stroke his ego or fall under his power. I hoped to do neither.

"As you know, Princess Mercy, I intend to take over the kingdom. To do that, I must either marry into kingship or overthrow the present aristocracy…"

I could only guess what his 'proposition' was.

"I have sent messengers to your brothers to come to a certain spot with ransom money for your safe return." He grinned wickedly. "I have an ambush waiting for them to kill them and their guards. Then, I shall collect the money anyways."

My face went white. I knew my brothers wouldn't fall for such a trick but if they knew my life was at stake, well...

He read the fear in my eyes with pleasure and continued, "Then, I shall marry you and kill your father. I shall be king and two warring people shall become united in peace."

"Not the way you'll rule it!"

"I'm better than your father, Princess, you know that as well as I!" He stood up, angry all of a sudden. "Your father enslaves my troops to work in the mountains beyond the Marshlands till their deaths for your jewelry and his excesses!"

I stepped back in shock. "No!"

"He's a terrible father; he doesn't even care about you at all. He just buys you over with the blood of my men so you'll close your eyes to his dirty deeds. You think he and the other rulers don't have the power to wipe out this entire camp? All the rebels if they want to? Of course they do. They've only allowed us to continue for so long because they can justify the slave labor in the eyes of the public. It's all a front just to pay for you rulers' excesses. A game of chess giving us just enough to continue but never enough to win. Don't you see, you naïve girl, I'm only trying to free Tarlen of your father's nightmarish rule. I save poor families and starving children! I fight the real oppressor, the monsters of Tarlen, your father and his cronies. I am Tarlen's deliverance. Think of it, you know your father's military strength, and you've seen mine. Do the math."

I couldn't believe it. I wouldn't. No one had ever told me this. I never thought that was where my jewelry came from. I always thought father killed the rebels not chained them to rock and made them labor until their anticipated deaths. He must have been lying. Did the king, my father, really do this? Did Garcel and Adann know? Did Justice know?

"Your brother, Garcel, heir to the throne. Cruel to the core. Pushes anyone around, anyone he can. He's your father's favorite because he helps him with his foul practices of greed. King Garcel! What's Tarlen coming to?" He spat on the ground. "As for Adann, he's your brother's puppet. Does everything he asks him to and follows him around like a dog…"

I found my courage reminding myself what I'd seen those dark days in that camp. "So, my land is to be ruled by a man who cuts women's tongues out and whips ten-year-old boys instead! By Ellar, what sort of fool do you take me for?"

Larcos grabbed me and pulled me into him. Holding tightly to my shoulders, he hissed into my ear. "You will play my game now. Those men outside are waiting for me to release you to them. You know Meta, she was sweet and pretty, just like you, until my men got to her. If you agree to my generous proposal, you will be protected. You will find me a faithful and generous husband and a good king." He pushed me to the door and opened the flap. I saw the drunken monsters laugh and holler when they saw me. "Either take my offer or you deal with me then you deal with them." His voice sent chills of fear through my spine. I glanced at the crowd then at his cruel glittering eyes. Smiling wickedly, he closed the flap and began to stroke my hair again.

"Like commander like soldier. The reason your men are Urfanes is because you are!" I tried to pull away but he was prepared.

"Then you will stay here, a no-good slave like the rest to be used and beaten. Your brothers and father will die, your mother too. And I will be king alone with you," he yanked my hair back and gripped my neck in cold icy strength, "serving me, my every whim, at my beck and call."

"Stop terrorizing my sister! If you wish to kill me, fight me yourself!" I recognized the voice of my brother Garcel. He came in through the back of the tent with his sword drawn.

Larcos let go of me and drew his sword.

I ran to his side.

"Mercy, get out of here!" he said. The challenge of the battle wild in his eyes.

"My brother, you should not do this for me," I whispered.

"Do you love me, Mercy?" he asked me earnestly. "Like you did Justice?"

Tears filled my eyes. "Yes, Garcel, I'm so sorry."

He pushed me at the back door of the tent. I fell through and landed in somebody's arms. A guard!

"Come," he whispered in my ear. "Before they realize you're gone."

Raliph? It sounded like Raliph. I recovered myself and turned to see the face. It was Raliph! He took my hand and pulled me into the dark forest.

"Wait! We should go back! Help Garcel!"

Raliph didn't stop. He dragged me further.

"Raliph, Garcel!"

"Garcel ordered me to get you out of here," he said evenly. "So, I will do as I'm told."

"He's my brother!" I cried.

He covered my mouth. "Your brother made me promise, whatever happens to him that I would keep you safe. For once in your life, do what your brother tells you," he said then released me.

I began to cry. "Raliph, my brother's back there. He'll die."

"Mercy, there's nothing we can do."

# MERCY, HOLD ME UP!

He led me by the hand farther into the forest, along paths I did not recognize. I wept more the farther we got from Garcel. My brother had chosen to give up his life for me. For my stupidity, he would die. I loved my brother. I loved him so much. I knew that and despite all those terrible things I'd said to him, he loved me. More than anything else, I wished I could take back all the terrible things I said to him. If only I could go back a week. I just wanted to go back and do everything all over again. It wasn't right! It is I who should die! The fool that I am. But now, he was to die for me.

I turned to Raliph. Tears were in his eyes.

"Are you alright?" I asked.

"I wish I could've helped him," he wiped his eyes. "Garcel..." he bit his lip. "Garcel was the bravest, strongest, and most honorable man ever to live."

I stared at him, shocked. "Raliph, what happened?"

Raliph led me quietly through the forest while he told me about his strange adventures with my brother. It made me happy to remember Garcel. It was hard to imagine Garcel and Raliph talking together in regular tones.

When he neared the end of his story, the sun was beginning to rise. I glanced over at his face. He was white.

"Raliph..."

He gripped at a branch for support. I quickly put my arm around him to keep him up. The poison of the Urfane was still in him. Gently, I let him down onto the soft dirt.

The poison would weaken him, slowly make its way to his heart and stop it. It was a cold way to die. I knew there was no antidote for an Urfane's poison. Unless it is killed within the first hour, there's nothing that can be done. I would lose Raliph slowly. Lose him to agony, to delirium, and to hopelessness.

"I've got to get you out of here," he whispered hoarsely.

I pulled him up and practically carried him down to the trunk of a tree that was hidden from the path. I set his head down on some fallen leaves on the soft earth. I touched his cheek tenderly. It was growing cold. His fingers were cold and lifeless. But his eyes were wide and glancing around wildly.

"I've got to get you home!"

"Don't think about it. Just rest." I laid my hand on his shoulder.

He struggled to sit up. "Rest until I die while you watch me slowly fail? No! Leave me, and let me die alone."

"No, Raliph, I don't know the way. Even if I did, I wouldn't leave you."

"So, we both die?" He fell back down on the dirt in despair.

I touched his face with my soft hand. He was still as handsome as I remembered him. His light curls falling over his face, his troubled eyes closing as he was fading. He was trying so hard to fight it. So brave, so selfless. "You have changed, Raliph," I said softly.

"I'm still lying flat on my back, a weakling, before you," he grunted.

"You saved me from a fate far worse than death and went against your greatest fears to do it."

"What's the use?" he opened his eyes and met mine. "I fail at everything I ever do, Mercy, everything."

I bit my lip. With all my heart, I couldn't let him go. I longed to comfort him but I could not even comfort myself. Taking up his hand, I drew it up close to me. He stretched his cold fingers open and circled them around my neck. He gently stroked my cheek before he fell to the ground again. "I love you," he whispered.

"I love you too, Raliph."

My eyes widened at my own words but not as much as his did. "Mercy, you cannot! There is nothing to love about me."

"But I do..." I paused uncertain if I should continue. "And if you fight and get better, we'll find a way to be together."

"I want to, Mercy, more than anything...but there is no way...I'm done for."

I sighed. A tear fell down from my eyes until it splattered on his cheek. I clutched his hand, unwilling to let it go. As if holding onto it would make the light come into his eyes, color back into his face, or warmth back into his body. "Please, don't. There must be a way..."

I wiped my eyes and met his again. They were rolling back and glazed over but there was some semblance of sanity in them. He caught my glance. "Ellar," he whispered then he fainted.

Ellar, I had forgotten about him. The thought of him gave me hope. Maybe Ellar could save Raliph's life once again...wait! Could I face him again? Face the question? How could I expect Ellar to grant my many requests when never would I grant his? Sighing, I leant back against a large root jutting out of the ground. I gazed at Raliph's paling face. Slowly dying and I could do nothing about it. I could, but would I? Burying my face in my hands, I cried. Why didn't I want Ellar? He had been nothing but good to me. Bearing his mark was illegal to be sure but it could be easily hidden. I was just too proud. Now, I couldn't even bear to ask him to save Raliph, again.

Raliph's chest rose and fell. His mark still glittered in the light though it seemed to dim as his body grew colder. Ellar wanted me to be his just as Raliph was. I wanted to be my own. But I could not save lives on my own. Nor could I heal. Not like Ellar. If Ellar was better than me in everything then why did I want to be my own? My brain hurt from all these thoughts. I glanced at Raliph again; he was moaning and growing delirious. Gripping his hand, I hoped to bring him back but I couldn't. Ellar.

"If you want me, please come

If you still want my heart.

I am lost and away from home

So far, so far,

If you care to have me, I will let you

I'm sorry it took me so long

Ellar, to you, I have decided

I want to belong. Belong."

I stood to my feet and sang with all the strength and power of my voice.

"I wish for the one who I've only ignored

Until the moment I needed him

To come and be a part of my every breath

My every moment."

I paused and sighed.

"Because I know I'm not as great as I thought I was

I need someone stronger to have me

Ellar, here I am once again

But this time, I ask you to take me."

My voice was hoarse. I leant against the tree. Staring at Raliph's troubled face; I whispered the final words, "Ellar, I want to follow you now. And finally take your mark. If you still want me, put your hand on me, and burn it on my heart."

He appeared from behind a tree. Gentle and safe as I remember him. With the same dark red cloak and deep cowl. His face was brilliant as he smiled broadly at me. I forgot myself and ran to him. He opened his arms to hold me. I felt safe. All at once, everything was okay. I wasn't alone. I was happy. I was special. I was loved. All at once, everything was different. Just because he was there and was holding me.

"I want to take your mark too, Ellar." I said. "To follow you."

Wordlessly, he put his hand on me and I felt his power go through me. It was like he was trying to take everything, and could see everything, even if I didn't want him to. That hurt. A lot. But when he drew his hand away, I was glad. I touched the gilded letters at my heart and saw their shine. Meeting his eyes with all the courage I could muster. They saw all. Every part of me. But seemed to still like what he saw. I found myself blushing. For the first time in my life, I felt like a princess.

"Ellar, Raliph's dying," I said. "Please come and heal him."

"I've given him what he needs to be healed. But I will come."

I led him to Raliph's side. He knelt down to him and touched his shoulder.

Raliph's eyes opened, wild in fear. But when they settled on Ellar they calmed. "Ellar, my Lord."

For some reason, the way Raliph spoke and looked at Ellar made me happy. I almost felt like I loved him more because he loved Ellar.

"The poison in your body cannot compete with that engraved on your heart. I am stronger and you must believe that. You are not as other men who lose hope and die. You are strong!" His voice grew louder. "You are stronger than the poison of Morglin servants because you are mine and I am strong." He lowered his voice again. "Believe in me and my power and you will not be weakened and killed by the poison of Morglin."

Raliph smiled slightly. "I believe, Ellar. Help me."

Ellar touched him again then stood and left like a passing shadow.

Raliph slowly sat up. "Mercy, help me," he said struggling. "Put your hand on my heart and pray to Ellar for me. Believe for me, so I can believe."

I obeyed and softly sang some songs I had sung in Larcos' camp. Raliph struggled to get up, fighting hard.

"Hold me, Mercy, help me stand."

I pulled him up to his feet.

"Speak to me, tell me of Ellar. Tell me what he can do."

I began. I told him of what Ellar had done for me and how good and strong he was in my life. He leant heavily on me as we walked. I sang of the great battle he had won. I sang of the love he had for him and I sang of what he was going to do for him.

Slowly, his strength returned.

"Let me walk alone now, Mercy. But do not stop singing."

I released him. He stumbled and leant against a tree for support but soon kept going. His face was twisted in pain. I sang and prayed and we continued on.

The sun had gone down and the stars were out by the time his stride was strong.

"We must reach Adann before Larcos kills him," I told Raliph.

A light of a challenge came into his eyes. "Come!"

# ONE OF THEM?

I was afraid we would meet rebels looking for me along the way but for some odd reason we didn't. When I asked Raliph about it he said, "I know this forest better than most. I doubt if there's a back trail I don't know by heart."

"Why do you know them better than the rest of the rebels?"

Raliph smirked. "The strongest man gets the best plunder. If I stole something and didn't want it stolen from me again, I'd find back ways to get to where I wanted to go with it without running into anyone who would take it."

I laughed. "Smart."

"Smart but cowardly. When you're a weakling, you have to be clever to make up for it."

"You aren't a coward, Raliph."

He shrugged. "Not so much anymore. Not since I met Ellar. There's a lot less to be scared of with him."

We continued. For hours, he kept walking ahead of me. He never stopped for a break. I knew he was trying to save my brother, Adann, but still. My feet didn't want to walk anymore. My energy was running low. And I was hungry. My stomach growled.

"Here!" He tossed me a piece of bread.

Grumbling, I bit into it and sped up to keep pace with him. Why did he have to take such long strides?

I followed him all night and we hid during the day. All throughout that time, surprisingly, he didn't try to take my hand, kiss me, or even speak eloquently to me. Besides leading me through the forest at an exhausting pace and answering a few questions, he virtually ignored me. At night, he would make me keep pace with him and during the day he would let me rest. Though I prided myself on being a strong girl, I was getting exhausted. I couldn't be angry with Raliph for not paying me much attention or considering my well-being. He was trying to save the life of yet another brother of mine that he should hate.

Perhaps, the trek through the forest wasn't so much tiring as it was mundane. Rarely, did Raliph talk to me. Only to order me to eat something, stop, go, or hide somewhere. I enjoyed being with him but I wondered why he was so inattentive and quiet. Was this what he was like under normal circumstances? But we were both tired and would have little to talk about anyways.

Still, it was hard not to imagine what he was like under normal circumstances. Maybe, he was like those terrible guards who beat old women like Meta. Since I'd only seen him in odd circumstances, he very well could be just like all the other terrible rebels. I glanced over at his focused, sweating face. His intense green eyes stared intently at the ground in front of him. I wondered what he was thinking.

He sensed my gaze and looked up at me. "What is it?"

"Just thinking."

"About me," he smiled knowingly.

I blushed.

"Is it good?"

"I don't know."

"'I...'" he climbed over a log and offered his hand to help me over, "Would like to set your mind at ease if I can."

I refused his help and climbed over myself. He chuckled.

"I saw many things I would have rather not seen at the rebel camp and..."

"You're wondering if I'm one of them."

"Yes," I said bluntly.

"Well, you must know at that camp, the men are either showing off or trying to avoid getting whipped or beaten up by those who are stronger than they. Larcos keeps a strict regime set on strength, duty, and obedience. Do what you're told and you'll get food for yourself and family. And if you're strong, you can take whatever you want from your fellow rebels. That includes their skin if your captain isn't watching. That's the code of the rebels."

"But what did you do?"

"I hid in the shadows so no one would beat me up." He smiled at himself. "Didn't work but I tried anyways. I didn't even try to get a slave girl, even an old one just to do my work for me. I just could never afford to be a bully." He circled a large boulder and paused for me to catch up.

I followed him though a bit slower because I was tired. "So, you didn't care about the people who were hurting you were only afraid for your skin?"

"In all truth, yes. Before I met you, I did not know the meaning of kindness and mercy. Only duty and fear." He disappeared behind a tree and turned to see if I was following him. "Larcos does his best to take all emotion out of his soldiers. It's part of his strategy. He'll be hard on his new recruits because he wants to model his soldiers after him. He most easily knows how to deal with brutes."

"Larcos is cruelty in itself."

"But his good quality of duty he ingrains in us so he has few deserters. A duty to our families. If we didn't have that, we'd be a bunch of completely heartless brutes fighting amongst ourselves."

"My father uses greed, fear, and hate to keep his troops in

line." I sighed. "I hate war."

Raliph paused and looked at me with an indiscernible expression. "You have changed."

"I know." I heaved a deep breath and continued. "Raliph?"

"Yes, Mercy?"

"Is there any way to save Meta and the other girls?"

Raliph paused and thought. "A rebel could possibly sneak a few out of the camp and lead them to civilization by back trails. But…"

"But?"

"They would be outcasts in society with no homes or futures."

I sighed. An idea came to me. "Raliph?"

He chuckled. "What is it, Mercy?"

"You know the orphanage I'm building for boys at risk?"

"Yes."

"They could help run it!"

Though I was still tired, the thought of saving Meta and my other friends from the terrible rebel camp made me want to bounce.

Raliph laughed aloud. "Mercy, you are bursting."

"We could teach them about Ellar and how he loves and heals them. In this war torn land, they could use some hope."

Raliph paused. His smile faded. "Mercy, what about your father?"

I had hoped I wouldn't have to think of him. "Something must be done about those mines."

"What?"

I sat down on a rock, head in my hands. "I don't know how but I'll find them. See the place, if it's really so terrible. Then somehow, I'll hatch a plan."

He knelt down beside me and put his hand on mine. Gently, he drew it away from my face. "Mercy, you are turning Tarlen around. You are in danger already."

I shrugged. "I know."

He pulled me up with a strong hand. Chills of excitement went through me when he did not release my hand. I felt like the world was perfect. "Raliph…" I ventured.

"Yes?"

"Could you sneak those girls out of your camp for me…?"

He looked over at my smiling face and pleading eyes. He chuckled. "Anything for you, Mercy."

I squeezed his hand. "I love you, Raliph."

"You really do?" he said.

"You're a lot more attractive when you aren't covered in ugly sores with a rotting leg."

He ducked.

"We need to switch onto the main road," he said. "We may meet both rebels and Tarlen hunters. We're both in danger so we must be silent."

"Why are we switching?"

"Adann will take the main road. We need to catch him before he gets too far."

Suddenly, the reality of Adann's looming fate hit me and I sped up. Raliph led me from tree to tree. I could not understand how he could know the thick woods so well.

"Raliph, what are you going to do about Adann?"

"What about him?"

"If we meet him on the road, you must hide."

"If you wish it."

"You aren't scared?"

"I'm terrified but does that make a difference?"

We continued travelling during the night and hiding during the day. We had been travelling for four days now. I was exhausted. Raliph led me beside the main hunting road Tarlen soldiers and huntsman used. When I asked Raliph about why we were avoiding the main road, he explained that the less we travelled in the open the less likely we were to get caught. As much as I admired his smarts for keeping us safe, he never seemed to have any to make the journey more comfortable.

After several hours on the main forest road, we heard footsteps approaching. Raliph pulled me behind a rock and told me to keep quiet.

I glanced over the rock for a moment to catch a glance of a party of about a hundred men. Hooded and cloaked with swords at their sides that clinked as they marched. The leader of the party put his hand up to call a halt. "Whoever you are," he called. "Come out from behind that rock."

Raliph pushed me down, stood up and approached them. I knew if they were rebels, Raliph could send them off. If they were Tarlen men, it could be an entirely different story for him.

"Bring that man to me," the soft voice commanded.

I recognized the voice. "Adann!" I jumped out from my hiding place.

"Mercy!?" Adann stared at me, shocked.

"Aren't you glad to see me?" I asked for he did not even embrace me.

"Yes…I'm just surprised," he stuttered. "Are you alright?"

"Yes, I am, but we must get back to Whitestone quickly. Larcos is scheming to kill you."

"In a moment." Adann turned his attention to Raliph. "Who are you and why are you with my sister? You seem familiar…"

Raliph bowed. "Your Royal Highness, My name is Raliph. You do not know my name but you will recognize me from the palace dungeons."

Adann's eyes widened. "Arrest that man!" he commanded.

"No!" I cried. "You would not harm my rescuer?"

"Him?" Adann motioned at Raliph. "He can't even rescue himself."

"Let's get out of the forest. I'll explain."

Adann nodded.

We walked back to Whitestone at a tiring pace. I had new strength now though because I had caught Adann in time before Larcos got to him. But we weren't safe yet. Adann and I wouldn't be safe until we were safe inside of Whitestone again. Raliph followed Adann and I. His hands tied behind his back and shoved roughly if he slowed.

"Mercy, Garcel left to rescue you several days ago. Where is he?" Adann asked.

I swallowed hard remembering my parting with my beloved brother. "He…he…"

"He fell into the hands of the rebels," said Raliph for me.

Tears threatened my eyes.

"How?" Adann demanded.

"He…challenged Larcos so I…could escape," I whispered hoarsely.

"And then?"

"I don't know. Raliph made me go so the rebels wouldn't catch us." I broke off and sobbed uncontrollably.

Adann clenched his fists. "My brother…"

"He was a noble prince, Your Highness. A great man," said Raliph.

"It was my fault," I whispered. "I tried to spite him by going into the forest. It was stupid and childish of me…" I swallowed down some more sobs before they escaped my trembling lips. "I'm so sorry…"

Adann turned away. "Garcel was my dearest friend. I loved him. Better than any brother can…" He covered his face in his hands. "First Justice, now Garcel. How am I ever to be a king? I am a weak man. Garcel…" he whispered, "Garcel…

"Your Highness," the captain interrupted. "We must leave these forbidden forest paths."

Adann dropped his hands to his sides. He turned to Raliph and hit him to the ground. "I will deal with you later."

The captain set a quicker pace to return to Whitestone. Both Adann and I were grief stricken as we stumbled along. I fell back to walk with Raliph as his captors shoved him over the dirt and exposed roots of the wild forest road.

"I'll get you out of here," I promised him.

He nodded; his face tense. Blood trickled down his forehead from where Adann had struck him. "Adann has taken the death of your brother hard."

"I'm afraid he'll take it out on you."

"Don't make me think about it. I'm terrified already."

"I will make sure nothing happens to you."

Raliph smiled slightly. "Thank you, Mercy."

I knew I could free him even if worse came to worst. If Adann persisted on keeping him prisoner, I could always tattle to my mother of Adann's past violence to Raliph. Adann always obeyed the Queen Mother. But by the look on Raliph's face, I knew whatever I did I should do it soon for his sake.

I approached Adann. "Let Raliph go, Adann."

He glared at me. "Why?"

"He saved my life! He led me to safety. He's saved yours by reaching you here before you fell into the hands of Larcos."

"We were prepared."

"You have no idea who you're dealing with, Adann. Their numbers are vast and Larcos and his men are animals."

"What is Raliph then?" Adann challenged.

"Raliph is my friend."

"I'd like to know how exactly you met him."

I sighed. "He begged mercy from me."

"You broke him out!" exclaimed Adann, "Mercy, what's wrong with you?"

"What's wrong with me? What's wrong with me? What's wrong with you, Adann?" I shrieked at him, allowing my quick temper to fly. "I saw what you did to Raliph. And even now after he's saved my life and yours, you won't let him go."

"I shall speak with him first," said Adann firmly.

I wasn't about to give in. "If you don't let him go, I'll tell Mother."

He sneered at me. "I shall speak with him first. Then, I'll let him go."

"Fine, as long as it's only words. I saw what you did to him."

"You should know me well enough that was more Garcel than me…"

"You were still part of it!"

He faced me and met my eyes. "I am not bloodthirsty, Mercy. I hold nothing against Raliph at the moment."

I wasn't convinced but I knew it best not to push him. I couldn't risk losing everything if I lost. I didn't want to jeopardize Raliph's fate so I fell back to Raliph.

"He says he'll let you go."

Raliph let out a sigh of relief.

"He says he wants to speak with you first."

"What does that mean?"

"Let's hope, exactly what he said."

We reached Whitestone by nightfall. Mother ran out of the castle to the drawbridge and embraced me and Adann. She scanned the crowd of cloaked figures as they marched through the gate.

"Where's Garcel?" she asked.

I bit my lip and looked down.

"No! Not my son! Garcel!" she cried. Tears spilt down her cheeks. "My son."

I led her into the palace with Adann, Raliph and some guards. She wept mournfully as we passed through the city into the palace.

"What happened?" She asked.

"Do you want to know?"

She heaved a shuddered sigh. "Yes."

"He fell into the hands of the rebels on purpose so I would

have time to get away. He…" I wiped a tear from my cheek, "He challenged Larcos…" I tried to swallow my sobs back but they escaped. I wept until my body could bear no more. "Oh Mother, how cruel I had been to him!" I cried. "But...he did it for me. He…he…" I wiped my eyes and met hers. "My brother died for me."

# RALIPH AND ADANN

I was afraid for Raliph so I snuck over to Adann's quarters where he had taken Raliph. Creeping up to the door, I put my ear to a crack in the door and listened. I could hear my brother's hesitant stride in the silence of the room.

"As you know, my brother, Garcel, was dearer to me than any other in all of Tarlen," Adann began.

I peeked through the keyhole. Raliph stood with his hands tied, in the center of the room, his face down, staring intently at the floor. Adann circled Raliph like an animal circles its prey. They were around the same height though Raliph was of stronger build. Adann looked weak compared to Raliph, almost like a ten year old boy wearing a sword. Raliph was older than Adann by about four years and had much more experience in the art of war than Adann. To me, Adann was a little hot-headed child, spoiled to the bone, shy, and sickly. He was never a noble prince to me, not even now that he is to become king.

"My brother, for some fool reason, followed you to the rebel camp."

Raliph kept his head down and did not say anything.

"It seems strange that *he* should be captured and *you* return safe."

"Safe is not what I'd call this," Raliph interrupted.

"I did not give you permission to speak!"

Raliph stared down at the intricate carpet again. "Your Highness."

"What I am saying, fool, is that my brother could have very well fallen into your trap. You knew my brother would be desperate, you convinced him to trust you and then you betrayed him to Larcos to exact your revenge on him!"

My blood boiled at the lie.

"If you need someone to blame, you may blame me but your brother told me before we approached the camp that his intention was to fall into his enemies' hands to save Mercy."

"You lie," cried Adann and he threw a porcelain vase at Raliph's head. He ducked it and it shattered loudly on the wall.

"Your Highness, if I wanted him dead, wouldn't I want you dead, as well? Mercy knows well that we purposely switched onto the main road in hopes to catch you before you fell into Larcos' trap." Raliph straightened and met Adann's eyes bravely. "Your brother was one of the greatest men to live. I know. I watched him kill two Urfanes to save my life. I saw him bravely approach the Cansten camp. I heard him challenge Larcos to save Mercy. Garcel became my friend, Your Highness. I loved him. Though, I cannot say I know the extent of your grief, I am grieving over his death as well."

Adann turned away. "I don't believe you."

"Believe what you wish," replied Raliph. "I cannot make you believe what I say. You have little reason to do so. But you must understand you are not alone in your grief. That I loved him..." he hesitated, a tremor in his voice. "And that I wish it had been me to die in his place."

Adann turned to face Raliph with tears in his eyes. "As do I." He covered his face with his hand. "Leave me now. You are released."

Raliph took a step nearer to him. "Your Highness..." he stopped unsure how to comfort his enemy.

Adann drew his knife and cut the ropes at Raliph's hands. "Leave me!" he cried and overturned a small table, shattering an oil lamp on the floor that had once been peacefully positioned on the low stand. The oil stained the rich carpet and the glass shards scattered all over the floor. "Leave now!"

Raliph left in silence. He opened the door to see me crouched down at the keyhole. Shutting the door quickly so Adann would not see me he said, "I have been released. I must leave immediately."

I scrambled up. "I'm glad."

I led him down the dark stone hall away from Adann's quarters.

"What are you going to do now?" I asked him when we were far from the royal quarters.

"I can still safely walk the rebel camp. I will go and fulfill Your Highness' wishes and guide some slave-girls from the rebel camp to Whitestone." He paused. "I do not know when we will get to be together even if ever. But we will serve Ellar to save Tarlen. And someday, when I hold you, it will be for good." He bowed and kissed my hand. Then, he disappeared down the stone steps. I watched his shadow fade.

"Raliph!" I called.

"Yes, Mercy," he stopped. I ran down to him. He was in the courtyard.

"When will I see you again?"

He took my hand. "In ten days. At sunset, look to the edge of the forest. I will be there. Meet me."

Then he left.

I leant against the cold rock wall. "May Ellar be with you, Raliph," I whispered. "I love you."

# ADANN'S SECRET

That night, I dressed up in my hood and some common clothes and snuck out to check on my orphanage. I was pleased to see everything was in order and fifty boys were already sleeping in soft beds. I had previously met the headmaster and his wife who I had hired. They were known for many charitable acts and after lengthy conversations with them; they admitted to me they were secret servants of Ellar. However, they had just taken a bad turn financially. I couldn't believe my luck. I met the mistress in the kitchen to find out how everything was working out.

"We need more help," she said holding a cup of tea out to me. I took it and began to sip it slowly.

"Hire some extra help for about ten days. You'll get some hard working women by then but they'll be runaways from great oppression. They will need to know about Ellar. Can you teach them?"

Lillis, that was her name, smiled. "Why don't you teach them?"

"I cannot show my face," I said. "I am already in danger from Larcos; I can't allow my father discovering what I am doing."

"Then disguise yourself. These people need to hear from you. The boys are already asking me about you and for all I knew you were dead."

I nodded. "Alright, I'll wear a wig and a mask over my eyes."

"Thank you," said Lillis, smiling. "Are you alright now?"

I shrugged. "Alright as I can be. My brother died in the rebel camp."

"I'm sorry."

I bit my lip to keep from crying.

"There's nothing wrong with crying."

"I know, it's just I've cried so much since…"

Lillis took my hand gently. "He was a strong man."

I nodded. "I must leave." I drew a jeweled bracelet from my pocket. "Buy some seed for the fields and the boys something special to eat. Keep the rest for yourself and your husband. I will return in two days. Then, I shall meet the boys and you may report to me any problems you may be having."

Lillis curtsied. "We are indebted to you, Your Highness."

I turned to leave. "They must know of Ellar if there is to be any hope for Tarlen. We must teach them. We must help them. If there is ever to be an end to this war and hatred."

I snuck through the cellar to get back to my room. But as I reached the kitchen door, I heard footsteps. I hid under a table. I recognized the hesitant gait of my brother. I watched his feet pass my hiding place. Coming out of my hiding place, I saw him go down into the cellar. Curious, I followed him. His shadow slunk through the streets towards the city wall. The streets glittered white in the moonlight. He stopped when he reached a dark abandoned house. Looking around to make sure no one was watching, he went in. I peeked through the window to see him move a wooden chair from the corner of the room then push aside a material drape to reveal a hole. Glancing behind him again, he climbed into the black tunnel. Silently, I followed him unsure where the tunnel would lead. It led out to the other side of the wall to the bank of the moat. I saw Adann's shape come out from the water onto the bank on the other side. Gathering my courage, I slipped into the ice cold water. Passing by some fields, I followed him as he made his way towards the edge of the forest. He stopped at a small farmhouse near the edge of the forest. The door opened for him and he stepped in and out of sight.

I snuck up to the window to listen to what was going on. What could Adann be doing in a commoner's home? It was very unlike him.

"Adann, I'm so glad you came tonight. Come in." A soft melodious voice enticed him inside.

I wondered if this was one of Larcos' ploys to capture my brother. My hand flew to my dagger and I prepared my mind for the worst.

"Sunfare, it is good to see your face. I am sorry I am wet, it was too late and I had to swim the moat. Where are your sisters?"

"Duelis is sleeping and Natalia is caring for mother."

"Is she ill again?"

"I fear so."

Natalia, Duelis, and Sunfare…where had I heard those names before? Raliph! His sisters! Adann knew Raliph's sisters?

"Sit down, Adann. Do not worry about our problems. You have enough of your own," said Sunfare in a gentle nonintrusive tone.

Adann heaved a deep sigh. "Garcel, my brother died to save my sister from the rebels and my sister has fallen for a seemingly rogue Cansten who claims to have saved her from the rebels. I don't know what to make of any of it."

"It is an odd story indeed. Imagine, a rebel even being allowed to associate with the princess. She never seemed to me to be the type who would condescend to such a level. Who is this rebel who has managed to infiltrate so deeply?" asked Sunfare, her tone light and careless. I assumed she was pumping him for information. Probably a spy.

"His name is Raliph. Some nobody really…" he stopped.

"Sunfare, are you alright?"

"Yes...of course," she said quickly. "I was just thinking what a perfect night it would be for a walk."

Liar, I thought and quickly hid behind the bushes. Adann took her hand and they strolled past me.

"I will be king when my father dies," said Adann in a low voice.

"Adann, that will be wonderful!"

"No, I will make a terrible king, but..." He stopped and took her other hand. "When I am king, I will be free to do as I wish;" He drew her near to his body and kissed her lips. "And then I will make you my wife."

Sunfare stepped back, smiling coyly. "What makes you think I'll accept you?"

Adann caressed her arms and drew her near to him again. "Because you love me."

"I do?" she laughed.

"Of course you do."

I had heard enough. My head was spinning. My brother was the secret lover of the younger sister of my secret lover. And Raliph, being my secret lover, is also on Adann's list of people he most dislikes. And Adann is on Raliph's list of people he most fears. If Sunfare had any idea of what Adann had done to her brother, would she have anything to do with him? I looked up again to see him offer her a bag of money.

"Buy a new dress for yourself," he told her.

"Adann, how thoughtful," she smiled then kissed him on her own initiative.

So that was it. She was pumping him for money. It was obvious she didn't particularly love him. It's easy enough to tell. Her mother was dying, her family poor, and her brother in an army that practically enslaved him. She had taken matters into her own hands. And a prince, showing obvious interest in her, how perfect! But the dark secret of Adann's past cruelty to Raliph could cause even her to hesitate in her schemes.

I crouched lower behind the bushes as I waited for Adann to leave. My intention was to speak to Sunfare. Clearly, Adann was entrapped by this beautiful girl but she was entrapped by poverty and the dark knowledge of the horrors of war.

"Ellar, help me," I whispered.

Adann kissed her then slipped away. She waited until he was out of sight then she clutched the bag of money and ran into her house. She was met by her two sisters who eagerly counted it. I went back to my place at the window.

"This should buy Mother some medicine and the fruit and vegetables that she needs to get better," said Sunfare counting out the coins.

"Natalia, I need your nicest dress to wear the next time he comes by."

"He gave you the money for a dress for yourself, didn't he?"

"Of course he did," replied Sunfare as she took two coins out of the pile. "These will be for my savings. For my own use." She put them into her dress.

"What did he say tonight?" asked Duelis. I assumed she was Duelis because she was the smallest and had younger features.

"He'll be king and he doesn't want to be but he'll marry me when he does."

"Do you want to marry him?" asked Natalia.

Sunfare shrugged. "Why not?"

I knocked on the door. I heard some whispering, coins clinking, and doors shutting. Sunfare opened the door. Her eyes opened wide at the sight of me.

"Your Highness." She curtsied and opened the door wide. "Come in."

I stepped in. I could clearly take in the full beauty of this girl. There was a lot of her brother in her. Her eyes were green like his, her hair was a bit darker than Raliph's, but it had the same curl to it. She was almost as tall as I was and she had shapely hips and waist. Her clothes were simple but her sparkling, shining eyes and gleaming curls made up for her plain attire. She observed me with obvious fear in her brilliant eyes.

"May I get you anything?" she asked.

"No, thank you. I came to discuss a topic which concerns both of us."

Sunfare sat down and burst into tears. "Your Highness, please don't tell on us. We'll both be in so much trouble and I'll probably be killed."

I knelt down to her and touched her shaking shoulder. "Don't worry Sunfare, I won't tell," I promised. "But why are you seeing him?"

She wiped her eyes. "When your brother saw me at the market in Whitestone three months ago, he liked me. I thought it would be a good chance to get my sisters out of the fields; they are worked to the bone there and in so much danger from the Tarlen army if they find out about Raliph. My mother is ill and I thought I could get some money for medication through him. And..." she stopped.

"And get Raliph out of the rebel army," I said.

She looked up at me, surprised. "How did you know?"

"You saw the camp didn't you? When you were little and he was branded. You watched him kill his first man at eleven years old."

Sunfare stood to her feet, pulled a table away from the wall to reveal a small hole in the floor. She pulled out a bag of money from the hole and dropped the coins from her dress into it.

"This is the money to move into the city of Whitestone. Duelis could become a maid and Natalia could care for Mother or perhaps even marry." She wiped her eyes again. "With us safe in Whitestone, Raliph could escape the Canstens and move far away to the outskirts of Tarlen where he could have a decent life away from the war. Away from Larcos and the rest of the brutes who push him around. He doesn't tell me but I know he's pushed around. He's never been a fighter," she sighed. "I've seen the scars from whip marks they gave him. He's practically a slave there."

"I've seen them too," I whispered. "Sunfare, he's hidden so much from you so you wouldn't know how bad it is for him."

"I know he's hidden things from me. Once, he didn't come by for nearly a month. When he did, he was completely different, even Mother noticed it. He refused to tell me why...but there are secrets...in his eyes...he hides them in his eyes..." She sat down and wept on the table.

"Have you told him of Adann?"

'No, he'll worry about me," she wiped her eyes. "He thinks Adann and his brother are spoiled and cruel."

I nodded, wondering whether I should tell her just how bad my brothers were to her precious brother. I glanced over at the girl's serious but still perfect sun-browned face. "You understand your brother well."

She sniffled and smiled a little. That girl was beautiful. "Better than most. Duelis is young and Natalia spends all her extra time caring for Mother."

Any previous anger I could have possibly borne in my heart towards this girl completely vanished. I was filled with an incurable desire to help Sunfare, and at the same time help Raliph and myself as well. "I can move you and your family into Whitestone. I can hire Duelis as a maid and possibly grant a pardon for Raliph."

Sunfare smiled brilliantly at me. Her eyes shone like the sun's purest rays. No wonder Raliph was so handsome, if he was anywhere related to Sunfare he'd have to be. I swallowed my admiration and adopted a stern tone. "But you must promise me something."

"What is it, Your Highness?" She curtsied still smiling like someone from a painting.

"Stop using my brother. Love him or stop seeing him."

She blushed, ashamed and stared down. "He might kill me if I reject him," she said softly. "And I don't know how to love; I live in too harsh a reality to know anything about it."

"You know how to love. You love Raliph more than I ever shall."

A small smile broke her lips. "You're fond of him, aren't you?"

I giggled. "Yes, very much. He is a brave and noble man."

"Did he really save you from the rebel camp?" she asked, her eyes wide.

I nodded. "Hopefully, Larcos never finds out."

"He's in danger, isn't he?"

I sighed. "He always is."

She said nothing for a bit, thinking. Then she giggled. "Isn't it funny that you, a princess, should fall for my brother, a rebel, then your brother, a prince, falls for me?"

"I think it's a mess," I said, unwilling to look at the irony of the situation as anything but disastrous.

Her eyes lowered to the floor again. "I know," she said quietly. "But I never could have even dreamt of anything this strange."

"I was surprised to find you seeing Adann."

"I was surprised when Adann mentioned Raliph as your lover."

I smiled a little. It was somewhat ironic when I thought about it.

Sunfare stood to her feet and walked to the window. "When your brother comes again, I will do what I can to find where he stands in my affections. I will tell you my decision in three days. I am in danger from him if he finds out I am using him."

I nodded soberly. "I will make the appropriate arrangements."

Sunfare faced me and curtsied. "I am in your debt, Your Highness."

I stood up to leave. "One more thing."

"Yes, Your Highness."

"Don't tell Adann your brother is Raliph. Could turn out badly for all of us."

She nodded. "I understood that much."

I left the house and ran quickly back through the fields to Whitestone. Adann had found an incredible, intelligent and resourceful girl, I thought. Too bad he only liked her for her looks.

# MANY SUNSETS

I met the boys. I wore a blond wig and a mask over the top half of my face. I was unrecognizable.

Lillis saw me and laughed when she opened the door. "Come in, we have just finished dinner."

I entered the simple building; because it was new it had next to no decorations. Lillis led me to the dining room where I saw nearly sixty boys looking back at me.

"Boys, this is the Compassionate Angel. She can't show you what she looks like because she's in danger from Larcos and the King."

The boys nodded solemnly.

"But she wanted to meet all of you and tell you a story."

"Adrad," said one boy.

"Sanor," said another.

"Entac."

"Fulan."

I smiled at each of them. When they had all introduced themselves to me, Lillis told them to go sit down in the vast sitting room where I would tell them a story. Most of the boys looked to be under eleven. All of them were thin and dirty. Many of them had probably already been offered a position in the rebel army. Their parents, if they had any, sent them here to save them from the war so they could work and live without fear. I was happy I had saved so many already.

They all sat down facing me. A few of the younger ones curled up as close to me as they could. I smiled at their affection. I wondered though, if they would be so bold if they knew I was the princess.

"Have any of you ever heard of Ellar?"

A few of them nodded vaguely.

"Well, I'm going to tell you a story of Ellar..." I glanced up at Lillis' face as she leant against the doorpost. Her old eyes were sparkling and her lips were turned upward in a smile.

I continued. "There once was a shadow over Tarlen. A creature called Morglin wanted to dominate Tarlen and cover it with darkness. He hated Ellar and hated the people of Tarlen..." I proceeded to tell them the story of how Ellar saved Tarlen from Morglin. The boys listened attentively.

When I finished Lillis said I had to leave but in three days I would return to tell another story about Ellar.

I slipped out, pulled my hood over my face and took my mask off. Joy took over my heart and I laughed. For one of the first times in my life, I had a real purpose. "Thank you, Ellar,'" I whispered. "I'm so glad I met you.

Sunfare told me she wanted to talk to her brother before she made any decision about Adann. I guess I understood but it seemed to me like she was stalling. One thing about Sunfare I found was that she was just too sweet and pretty to be able to say no to her. I think I must have fallen into some sort of trance. She just looked at me with her big green eyes and pleaded with me. How could Adann have fallen into such a trap?

Though I tried to push my feelings of worry and sadness over Raliph in my orphanage, I often found myself staring out my bedroom window towards the forest. At night, I would dress in a nice dress and put on some perfume. I would ready my horse and wait by my window for him to appear. He didn't come. I watched.

I waited. I prayed desperately to Ellar. Ten days passed, eleven, twelve. By thirteen, he still did not appear.

What if he got caught? It was a terribly dangerous mission I had asked him to complete. What if Larcos found out he'd rescued me? There were millions of possibilities. It was dark the fourteenth day. Sunset had passed. I crawled under my covers and cried myself to sleep.

# NADIA

**Raliph**

I stared up at her window in the palace and thought of how much I'd miss her. Sighing, I turned back to the forest. I took my secret paths back to the camp so I wouldn't be found by any Tarlen men or slowed by any rebels coming back from a raid. I was glad I did not meet anyone or anything undesirable on my trek. But five days is a long time to be alone on dark forest paths.

I reached the camp, conveniently at dark. When most of the men were drunk celebrating their spoils of their last battle. I hoped my commander wasn't there or he'd ask me where I'd been over the past month. There were plenty of lies I could give him for my absence. And plenty of scars to prove extenuating circumstances. But it was always such a bother to think of an appropriate lie.

I slowly approached the camp in the darkness. Passing from tree to tree, unsure whether I wanted to make myself known or not. I heard a faint sound of sorrow and followed it to a nearby tree. It was girl curled up in the dirt at the trunk of a tree, crying. She looked up at me in fear and dread as I stood over her. I observed her dress was torn and falling off her shoulders. She had welts all over her arms and legs. She looked to be perhaps a bit older than sixteen.

Slowly, I knelt down to her. "Do you know where Meta is?" I asked her gently.

She stared up at me her eyes wide; probably surprised I hadn't grabbed her and dragged her off somewhere. "She's at the corner of the camp gathering sticks for the fire as ordered, Sir," she replied shakily.

"It's alright, I won't hurt you," I said gently. "Would you like to get out of here?"

"What do you mean?" she ventured, suspicion written on her face.

"Do you know Princess Mercy?"

The girl smiled and nodded enthusiastically. "Yes. Mercy was so good to us," she stopped. "Now she is gone."

"She sent me to find as many as I can and bring you all safely to Whitestone."

The girl stared at me in utter shock.

"Go over to that boulder. I'll return for you." I pointed to a great rock about thirty feet away beyond the camp guard's view. It was vast enough for many people to hide behind it.

The girl obeyed. Disbelief still written on her face but the hope of my offer sounded too good not to take the risk.

I went around the edge of the camp until I found Meta collecting sticks. She was terrified when I first approached her but when I mentioned Mercy she calmed and I spoke to her Mercy's words. Tears ran down her face and she smiled beautifully through her broken teeth. I asked her to find some girls and women and bring them to the boulder. For efficiency's sake and the sake of my own skin, I didn't want to brave the camp that night to deliver such messages myself. Besides, Meta would know those brave enough to take the risk of following me.

I went back to the boulder and hid behind it with the young girl I had just met. She was still terrified of me so I asked her about how she knew Mercy. The mention of Mercy brought a new light into her eyes and she told me a story of how Mercy had pulled her away from a cruel man, brought her to her tent, and sang songs of hope to her until she fell asleep that night. I was impressed by how brave Mercy was when she was helping people.

One by one, more girls and older women joined us. When I noticed the men in the camp were looking around for the girls, I said it was time to go. I led them to a secret path as quickly as possible. I counted sixteen of them. I knew I could not safely bring more than that in one trip. They didn't speak the entire night. Not until I led them to a hiding place under the shadow of a cliff face did they even whisper. Daylight came upon us. I told them to sleep, hidden in the shadow of the cliff. There I left them.

I couldn't find anything particularly tasty but I did catch a few small forest animals which would give us the strength to make it through another night of travelling.

They were grateful when I returned with the food. I had a good chance to look at them when they were altogether, huddled under the shadow of the cliff. They all had welts and bruises. Torn rags covered their thin malnourished bodies. Most of them kept their heads down as though they were ashamed to be alive. I wondered why I had never noticed them before. Some of them recognized me as the spineless Cansten rebel under Caraph's command. They found it difficult to understand why I, of all people, would risk so much to save them.

"Princess Mercy sent me. I love the Princess. We are both servants of Ellar who seek to bring hope and goodness in this war-stricken land," I explained.

"Mercy brought us hope and you are fulfilling it," said a young girl, raising her head up for the first time I had seen. "We were all so sad when she escaped because we feared our hope was lost. But she didn't forget us. Ellar didn't forget us. Just as she had promised."

I smiled. "Ellar never forgets."

I was tired so I leant down against a tree trunk to rest for a while. Meta got a fire going and directed the younger girls about to gather firewood and cook the meat.

"Who do you think he was?" One girl whispered to another while they gathered small sticks off the forest floor.

"I don't know. Someone noble for sure."

"He had the same mark as Raliph."

I perked up my ears to hear their conversation.

"Larcos is scared because whatever he does to him, the golden letters won't disappear."

Now I was alert. I sat up and went to the fire circle. "The man you're talking about, with the mark on his breast like I have. Is he still alive?"

"As far as we know," replied an older woman. "He's being brutally tortured for saving Princess Mercy."

My mind raced. "Meta," I turned to the oldest woman. "Keep them hidden. I'll be back sometime tonight."

"Where are you going?"

"The man you're speaking of is Mercy's brother, Prince Garcel. I cannot return to her knowing I could have saved him but remained too much of a coward to do so."

"Will you return for sure?"

"By the power of Ellar I will," I said hopefully. "But if I do not, in two days travel underneath this cliff face until you reach the town of Harton. It's a four day journey but you will make it." I drew my knife and threw it to the ground. "Use that if you need to."

I turned away. "Pray to Ellar for me." Then I disappeared.

I reached the camp at sunset. Hidden by the darkness and shadows, I slipped from tree to tree down into the camp. I was fully armed with two swords strapped to my belt, my battle-axe behind my back and a dagger in my boot. Walking casually to the smith fires, I pretended I was going to sharpen my axe. From the fires of melting metal, I would hopefully be able to hear what was going on next to me where Larcos tortured his prisoners who did not succumb to his will. No one noticed me while I sharpened my axe and checked my sword blades. It was dark and most men did not work with the fires at this hour. I heard a cry. Loitering nearer, I pretended I was looking for something along the edges of the blacksmithing tents. Listening carefully, I heard harsh voices. I slipped into the shadows behind a tree.

"Where's the whip?!" It was Larcos. "Give me the whip!"

I risked a look from my hiding place and watched the form of the man I feared so much whip a limp form on the ground. Four other men stood nearby. Some were busy running errands for their raging leader. The others fanned coals under a grate. I recognized that torture instrument.

The man was undoubtedly Garcel for I recognized his voice when he cried out in pain. He was lying on the ground with his back exposed. I did not wish to get a close look at what had been done to it. Larcos was raging and whipping Garcel within an inch of his life. Garcel did not move much, they didn't even have him bound. I wondered if they had broken some of his bones.

"Club him, then chain him onto the grate!" Larcos ordered, dropping the whip to the ground and breathing heavily.

"But my lord, we have already broken his arms and legs, he may die if we club him again," one man protested in a shaky voice. I wondered why he was frightened at the thought of killing Garcel.

"I give the orders around here you sniveling cowards! What are you afraid of?" Larcos demanded kicking Garcel's motionless body. "There is no power greater in this camp than me! Not some shining letters on a dying man's chest. Club him, now!" With that, Larcos stormed off to tend to some other diabolical business.

The men obediently took up several thick sticks and began to bring them down onto Garcel's body. He closed his eyes and not a sound escaped his lips. I drew a deep breath and bit my lip. Thinking hard on what to do, I contemplated attacking Garcel's assailants now before they killed him. But what happens if I can't defeat them? I'll get twice the punishment of Garcel. Gathering up all the courage I could, I stepped out of the shadows.

One of the men recognized me for we were under the same captain and motioned me to come help them. They were dragging Garcel to the grate and chaining him on. I took the opportunity Marat, my fellow rebel, gave me to get closer. There were three men. One of them, I knew. All of them were tall and broad. Two of them heaved Garcel and threw him onto the grate, He cried out as the burning metal seared his skin. They then proceeded to chain him up.

"Chain his feet, Raliph," Marat ordered. Once, Marat had taken some things from me by force. Perhaps he still assumed he could bully me.

I approached the grate. The sight of the great prince lying naked, bloodied and broken over a searing hot grate made my blood boil in anger.

I stepped nearer to the man who had just picked up the whip and was about to bring it down on his victim. My dagger was in my hand. Wordlessly, I drove the dagger deep into his side and into his heart. Without a sound, he fell down beside me.

Marat had been too preoccupied chaining Garcel to notice my crime but the other man did. He opened his mouth to warn Marat but I aimed my dagger at his heart and threw it. My aim was true and he fell to the ground.

Marat stood to his feet. Saw the two dead men and looked at me. His eyes widened in fear.

With all the force of my body, I pushed him into the shadows of the forest then I hit him to the ground. I drew my swords and positioned one at his throat, the other at his heart. I knelt down beside him. "How would you most like to die?" I whispered, still not quite sure how I had managed to bring the huge man down so easily.

He trembled and sputtered. "Please, Raliph, I'm sorry I beat you and...took your best swords. P...please, don't kill me. I have a family who need me. Please..." he begged piteously. "Have mercy, Raliph." He coughed for my sword was pressed near to his throat. I loosened it a little. I remembered the time Justice had spared my life when I asked him.

"Swear to me you will not betray me to a soul. Those two men were killed fighting each other, understand?" I pressed my sword closer to his throat.

"I...I swear. By my family and by my sword, I...swear," he choked.

I pulled the blade away from his throat, raised it up and knocked him out with the handle. He went limp, unconscious. I would spare him but I couldn't afford to have him possibly raising an alarm on me. I took the keys of the grate from his belt and went to Garcel. As quickly as I could, in the heat of the fire, I unchained him and lifted him off the burning heat. He moaned but remained completely limp as I drew him up. The metal was hot but my hands were tough and calloused already. I hoisted him over my shoulder and slinked into the forest bearing him into the shadows. Silently, I passed through the trees. Behind me cries of bewilderment sounded.

"The prince is gone! The prince has escaped!"

I kept running until all sounds faded away.

In the darkness, I laid him down in the dirt. I pulled my water skin from my belt and raised his head up to drink. He drank willingly.

"Mercy, where is she?" he asked hoarsely.

"Safe in Whitestone."

"Thank Ellar."

I took my cloak off and wrapped it around his body.

"This is a switch," he whispered. "Burning on a grate like the one...I chained you...ah," he groaned. "Did you enjoy seeing...your torturer tortured?"

"Your Highness..."

"Don't, Your Highness me! Ah," he grimaced. "Do I look high and mighty now?"

I did not answer but pressed the water skin to his lips again. When I drew it away, a groan escaped his lips.

I sighed. "To me, you are noble and lordly and brave," I said quietly, looking at the bold battered face of the prince. He was noble. He was great and good. He was everything a prince should be. "When I saw you, my heart burned in anger against Larcos and his men. Men such as I belong in dungeons with stripes laid on our backs. I am a coward, a selfish coward. You are a noble prince. Brave and honorable. You belong on a throne or leading an army. I belong in chains..."

"You are no coward, Raliph." Garcel heaved a shuddered breath. "You are a better man than I."

I wiped some of the grime and blood off his face with my shirt. His form was so broken; I didn't know how I could move him without causing him to be in more pain. His eyes watched me, whatever I did. His body was hot and feverish. How I wished I knew what Mercy knew to help him, or at least force him to sleep. I knew only what I had been taught when tending to a fellow rebel after a battle. It would be terrible if Garcel died after his rescue.

"Garcel, I'm taking you home to Mercy."

"I'll die on the way," he moaned. "Just kill me now."

Tears arose in my eyes at his words. I remembered begging Mercy that very same thing. Silently I put him over my shoulder as gently as I could, grunting under the weight. With all the strength I could muster, I bore the prince over my shoulder through the darkness. Ellar gave me strength and I reached our camp at about noon the next day.

Meta and the girls were relieved to see me return but shocked to see the bloodied prince I bore over my shoulder.

I laid him down in the shadow of the cliff and asked Nadia, the girl I had first met on my venture, to tend to him. Exhausted, I went to a tree and collapsed.

Nadia seemed to know what she was doing. She ordered some of the women to make broth and focused on her task. She tore a strip off the bottom of her dress to use as a cloth and wet it to clean off the grime and blood off his face. He watched her in silence observing every little thing about her.

"You...were there too," Garcel croaked.

Nadia nodded. "Mercy sent Ralph to save us from Larcos and his men."

Garcel looked over her scars and welts, her torn dress and black eye. "I'm so sorry you had to be there."

Nadia continued to tend him and offered him some more water. "It's war, your Highness. I'm just a spoil from it."

"No!" He protested, clearly struck by Nadia's sad sweet nature. "You are beautiful and noble..." he grimaced and heaved a breath. "And good."

"I am a slave, your Highness. To be beaten and used," said Nadia, her voice soft and filled with pain.

"I am a cruel man with a hard heart. A prince but a slave to myself…" he paused, "worthy of nothing but torture and death."

Without a word, Nadia moved the cloak off his chest and arms. She cleaned the blood and grime off the golden letters at his heart.

"Ellar's," she whispered, touching the golden letters with her soft gentle hand.

"That's what I am," he said quietly. "I don't believe it yet."

"Ellar's." She smiled. "Mercy sang of Ellar. Whenever she sang, we'd try to get as near to her as we could. She always had hope in her voice."

"Hope…in this war?" he groaned.

"Maybe it's in Ellar," whispered Nadia.

"Hope?"

"Yes."

"I used to…hope. Ah," he tried to move but collapsed, limp on the ground. "But after what I've seen from Larcos, my father, myself…don't believe there's hope for Tarlen anymore."

Meta brought Nadia the broth. Nadia gently brought him up and allowed his head to rest on her shoulder. Then she fed him the broth.

"I lost hope five years ago when I was stolen away and my family killed," Nadia began. "Then when Mercy came, she started to give us hope, courage. She said Ellar wouldn't forget us. We weren't forgotten. Maybe it was Mercy, maybe it was Ellar. But we weren't forgotten."

She let his head rest back down on the ground. Garcel watched her every move. He stared at her beat up face and scarred arms. He looked down at his own body. "I don't know why Raliph wants to save me," he said. "Nobody's ever…liked me before." He groaned.

"I was a cruel man to Raliph…"

Nadia remained silent and let him talk.

"I was so angry…at everybody. So, I took it out on him." He sighed. "When I was finished, he looked like I do now."

Though Nadia's expression changed in shock, she did not reply to his confession.

"Why?" he cried.

"Your Highness, there is more to you than you think!" she countered quickly.

"I'm a wretched, cruel animal."

"No," she said sternly. A trace of a smile of hope came over her face. "You are Ellar's."

It was nearing darkness when I awoke from my nap. I glanced over the camp of sleeping figures. Someone was missing. Nadia.

I stood to my feet and looked around for her. My eyes caught some movement in the trees a little ways from the camp. I put my hand on my sword hilt for I saw not one, but two figures moving in the trees. My hand loosened its hold on my sword hilt and I leant back onto a tree when I recognized the crimson cloak of one of the figures. The other I knew to be Nadia.

I sat back down against my tree, satisfied. All was well. Or better.

Nadia returned as quietly as she had left and resumed her care of Garcel.

"Ellar is good, isn't he?" whispered Garcel.

Nadia smiled. "Yes, he is."

We travelled mostly at night. I carried Garcel on my back and Nadia would keep in step with me to keep Garcel company. Her intention was to distract him from his present pain of the journey but no pain inflicted on him could quite match the feeling of humiliation I could only guess Garcel was going through.

The journey was longer than I had hoped because of my burden. The women were also difficult to keep hidden and organized. They were not trained soldiers, they were runaways. I'd have to remind myself of that whenever I found myself growing impatient with them. The women liked to talk. It was a good thing to be sure but not when I was trying to hide all sixteen of them from the rebel army!

It took nine full days to make it to the edge of the forest near Whitestone. We had a few run-ins with rebels. Most of the time, I gave them the slip but a couple times I had to kill a few. The realization of my skills at war and strategy began to come to me. I had never acknowledged before I possessed the kind of strength and intelligence needed for a soldier but perhaps I just needed something worth it to fight for and someone to help me do it.

Garcel spoke little to me while we travelled and Nadia devoted her full attention to him when we rested. A few times though, Garcel asked me to leave him and let him die. I assumed it had something to do with Nadia's sweet presence and his present hideous state. Nadia did not mind helping Garcel, whatever his appearance may have been. It gave her something to occupy her thoughts and attention that wasn't the terrible place she had just escaped from.

Watching Nadia made me wonder more about Mercy. How she was. What she was doing. I hoped she wasn't worried about me for taking so long. Sixteen days away is six days more than I had promised. She probably had given me up for loss by now.

# RALIPH'S SURPRISE

**Mercy**

He'd been gone for sixteen days. I knew he wasn't coming back. It occurred to me, I could try to go after him but I have no understanding of the forest and Larcos would be sure to kill me if an Urfane didn't get me first. The boys needed me. Apart from that, my mother needed me and so did Adann. But more than anything, I just wanted to be with him.

I brushed my hair and put on some perfume. Tightly, I gripped my necklace in which I had hidden his note to my heart. I stared out the window intently. How I longed to see a light from the edge of the forest. Tears sprang into my eyes. Under my breath, I sang a song of lost love I'd heard my mother sing when I was young.

Sobs escaped my lips and wrecked my body. He wasn't coming back. Not now. Not ever. I stared longingly at the window. Nothing. No one. Wait!

A light at the edge of the forest. My heart skipped a beat. It waved up and down twice then sideways. Raliph!

In joy, I jumped off my window seat, threw my cloak over my shoulders and slipped down my window. The climb was hard but it brought me just beside the city gate. I didn't want to risk sneaking out tonight and miss him.

The gatekeeper stood quietly at the gate preoccupied with something or other. He turned around when my footsteps were too loud to be ignored as I approached.

"Princess Mercy?" he said, his eyes wide to see me at the gate so late at night.

"Open the gate for me, please."

"Your father's orders: No man..." He stopped when he saw some golden coins appear in my hand. We really needed to get a new gatekeeper. Sure, it's good I can bribe him but what about the other side?

"I'll return shortly with some others I believe," I said, dropping a few coins into his hand.

He raised a questioning eyebrow. I pulled a few more coins from my cloak and rolled my eyes at him. After taking them and eyeing them carefully, he opened the gate slightly so that I could slip through the bottom.

With that task done, I ran across the bridge and towards the forest as quickly as I could.

"Mercy, is that you?"

It was Raliph's voice!

"Raliph!" I called.

I fell into his arms and embraced him. He held me close in the shadow of the forest. I felt safe.

"I was so afraid you would never return..."

"I'm sorry," he said softly into my ear. "I was delayed."

"You are here." I closed my eyes and leant on his chest. "I care no more."

"Mercy, I need to show you something." He took my hands and led me deeper into the shadow of the trees.

In the dark, I could make out people. Raliph cast the light of the lantern over their faces.

"Meta," I whispered. "Nadia, Annae..." I embraced them. "Oh Raliph, thank you!"

"Mercy," he continued evenly. "There's someone else..."

I watched him as he knelt down at the foot of a tree. The

lantern light shed over the face of a man. A man who seemed vaguely familiar. A brutalized man. Tortured or possibly mauled.

"Mercy," the man whispered, meeting my eyes.

My heart skipped a beat. "Garcel!" I ran to his side. "Garcel, you're alive!" Tears sprang into my eyes from too many conflicting emotions. "What happened to you?"

"Larcos," said Raliph, deep resentment in his voice. "The pig wanted to kill him as slowly and painfully as he could."

"Like someone I knew tried to do to you, Raliph," said Garcel quietly.

Raliph ignored his comment. "We must get them safe and fed as soon as possible."

I nodded. "I'll bribe the gatekeeper to let us all in."

"You need a new gatekeeper," said Raliph.

I chuckled. "Tell me something I don't know."

Raliph hoisted my brother over his shoulder. I understood why he took so long to get back. We made our way back to Whitestone with a trail of women behind us.

Nadia caught up with me in the front. "You and Raliph are very much in love."

I smiled. "It's not exactly the best situation to be in."

"That is understandable," she agreed. She looked ahead at Raliph, carrying Garcel towards the city. "You cannot run away with him?"

"There are wrongs I must right, battles I must fight before my life is my own." I sighed. "But I wish I could be with him. With all my heart."

"I heard that!" said Raliph, in front of us.

My eyes met Nadia's and we giggled. It felt good to be caught.

The gatekeeper's eyes widened when he saw the huge party coming in at the dead of night. But I tossed him some more coins and he opened the gate for us.

I sent the girls to the orphanage except for Nadia who insisted on coming with me. We then went to the castle where I broke in through the cellar; me, Nadia, and Raliph with Garcel. I led them up to Garcel's room through the silent stone hallways and shadowy staircases.

"You must go now, Raliph," I told him as he laid my brother down on his bed. "Hide in the cellar and wait for me there."

He faced me. I was suddenly hit with the reality of his closeness. He seemed taller than I had remembered and broader as well. He smiled gently down at me. "I do not fear being caught."

"I fear for you so go."

He stepped away and bowed. "As your Highness so commands." Then he left.

I turned to Nadia. "Light another lamp and give it to me. I must alert the household."

Nadia found another lamp next to the bed and lit it with the fire of the other one in my hand. I left her with that light and ran up the stairs to find my mother.

I found her awake, sitting next to the window staring out into the starry night.

She turned to me and smiled. "Mercy, what is it?"

"Garcel…" I paused to catch my breath. "He's returned!"

"My son!" She threw her cloak over her shoulders and followed me down the stairs. "He's not himself though…" I began as we descended. "He…" I paused, not sure how to say what I needed to say. "He's been tortured."

She stopped midstep. Her eyes closed for a moment and she bit her lip. "Go to bed, Mercy, I will see him alone."

She opened the door. I stole a glance into the dimly lit room. Nadia was kneeling beside his bed holding his hand in hers. The muted yellow light of the lamp on the table reflected onto Garcel's torn face. Deep scars and burns covered his skin. He was whispering things quietly to Nadia. I caught a look in her eyes when she glanced down at his hand in hers. Nadia loved my brother!

The Queen opened the door wider. "He will speak to you when he is better."

I sighed. I needed to speak with him.

"You will see him tomorrow."

Sullenly, I disappeared into the shadows of the cavernous hall. I was not going to my room though. I had one more thing to do tonight. A smile crept onto my face for the excitement. Raliph.

I slipped down the stairs, through the kitchen, then down into the cellar.

"Raliph," I whispered, shining the light over the food lined shelves and dirt floor.

"Mercy," a voice said behind me.

I turned quickly, startled.

"It's me," he smiled, his eyes catching the glimmer of my lamp.

"Come." I led him up the hatch out onto the street.

"I must see my family," he said. "I will rest there tonight. Can you get us out of the city?"

I inspected my cloak for any spare coins but then remembered I'd given it to Meta to help Lillis.

"We'll have to slip under and swim the moat."

Raliph nodded. "That's alright. It's better than getting caught together here."

We made our way to Adann's secret passageway under the wall. He was significantly impressed at the ingenuity of my wimpy brother.

"I take it you and your brother do this sort of thing a lot."

I blushed. "The royal family has never been known for exceptionally good behavior."

I sent Raliph through first then I followed, making sure I didn't leave a trace of us behind me. He stood up unsteadily when he came up at the other side and turned to see if I was behind him. I laughed and pushed him into the moat and jumped in behind him. It was cold as always but I expected it.

We reached the other side and both stood on the bank dripping wet. I busied myself wringing my skirt out. Raliph poked me. I turned to him to see him grinning mischievously at me with a handful of mud in his hands. I screamed and ran, giggling all the while. He chased me laughing heartily behind me.

Under the starlight, we played. In the fields past Whitestone, we chased each other and laughed. Until we were both exhausted and paused to breathe.

Raliph took my hand; I looked up startled to meet his gaze. "I love you," he mouthed.

Joy overwhelmed my heart and I laughed with all my being.

I found my other hand in his and he drew me close. "I love you, Mercy," he whispered into my ear. I leant on his chest and heard his heart beat.

"I love you too, Raliph," I replied, my voice barely audible.

His arms went around me. I closed my eyes, making sure I would remember that moment forever.

# THE HEART OF SUNFARE

Raliph and I walked hand in hand to the house along the forest edge. The light was out in the house so Raliph walked in quietly, so as not to disturb anyone. He paused at the open door to embrace me.

"Tomorrow morning, I must leave back to the camp. I must be careful not to arouse any more attention or suspicion to myself. But when I can, I will do what I can to help more slaves out of the camp to Whitestone."

"I will be here to see you off tomorrow," I whispered.

Raliph smiled. "Thank you, Mercy. For all you've done for me."

"Raliph!" called a voice from inside the house.

I slipped into the shadows.

"Sunfare!"

The door shut.

"Oh Raliph, I was so afraid…" I saw the window light up from a newly lit candle or lamp.

I knew I should go home and leave Raliph to his family but I needed to know if Sunfare would keep her promise and speak to her brother about Adann.

"I'm sorry, Sunfare," said Raliph.

"It's alright. But stop giving me these scares."

"I will try."

They spoke on a series of uninteresting topics for a while. I was about to go back when I heard Sunfare's sweet voice venture.

"Raliph…" she paused. "I have been seeing someone."

"Why are you distraught? Has he mistreated you?"

"No." she said quickly. "He's alright I suppose. You see…"

"Just tell me, Sunfare."

She sighed. "Alright, he's the prince."

"Garcel?"

"No, Adann."

"Sunfare…" Raliph trailed off. I could tell by the sound of his voice that he was taken aback.

"I need to know what you think."

"Well, it's not really my thoughts that matter. You don't seem very happy with this. What do you think of him?"

There was silence for a while. Finally, she spoke. "He is young and foolish. Like a child who can't make up his mind. He does what his brother does though he cares little for violence. He pretends to be strong and wise but he can't because he's too afraid of his father and brother. He is hotheaded with a spoiled nature of an immature child."

"Sounds like my conclusion as well," said Raliph. "Why are you seeing him?"

"Mother is getting worse and Duelis and Natalia are growing thin. Adann brings money to buy me things; he doesn't know that it goes to the doctor to pay for medicine for Mother's failing health."

"It is not your job to support our family at the expense of your heart. I want you to have a chance at love. Not squander your heart on a rich fool."

"But Raliph, I have been cruel to him."

"He's the prince. A hardheaded idiot. Does it matter?"

"He's not just that…" Sunfare said, choking up. "He depends on me so much. I am his only friend now. I feel so awful."

"Why, Sunfare?"

"When I first knew him, he teased me and said I was coy because I never showed much emotion for him or anything else…" she heaved a shuddered sigh. "I thought he merely thought I was pretty and assumed that he was too shallow to have his heart broken. But he's not…" she sobbed quietly. "He's been asking me to depend on him. To talk to him and I can't keep up the facade anymore. But I cannot love him without telling him the truth. Even then, I don't know if duty will allow my heart to love him in these times of death and sickness."

"If I can, you can, Sunfare…"

I heard a noise behind me. Silently, I moved closer into the shadow of the house and listened. Oh no! Not now! I listened again. It was unmistakable, the slow unconfident gait of my brother Adann. "O Ellar."

Adann didn't bother to knock, he just opened the door like the house was his own. I peeked through the window to watch the dreaded scene.

"Sunfare, I have wonderful news! Garcel, he…" Adann stopped. "Raliph, what are you doing holding Sunfare…" The pieces came together. "Sunfare, you have a brother!"

They stood side by side. I realized again how alike they looked. Same hair, same eyes, both were tall and stood straight.

"And of all the men in Tarlen to have for a brother, it's Raliph!" He stepped back. "Sunfare, what has he told you of me?"

"Nothing," Raliph replied for her. "She knows nothing.

"What have you been hiding from me, Raliph," demanded Sunfare. "I have a right to know!"

"Just as I had a right to know you had a brother in the rebel army," said Adann, his eyes fixed on Sunfare and Raliph. His body was stiff and straight as it would be when he was angry or nervous.

"Sunfare didn't tell you because she was afraid of you," Raliph spoke for her. "And why should a spoiled young prince have any right to know the family secrets anyways?"

"Sunfare, I wanted you to trust me...not be afraid of me...why?"

"How could I?" Sunfare exclaimed. "I knew you hated him. I knew you had fought with him before. I knew there was a dark secret."

Adann hung his head in shame.

"I knew if I told you, you would be angered. I know better than to anger a prince."

Adann gripped the back of a chair to hold himself. His knuckles whitened. I did not want to imagine how white his face was.

Sunfare would demand to know the secret. Could she bear the truth? Or more importantly, could Adann bear the pain he'll see in her eyes when the truth is told.

"It is not you, Sunfare, who should be afraid," he said bitterly. "I cannot bear this!" He turned to Raliph. "Tell her, tell her why your presence is so terrible to me! Tell her all you know of the man that I am. Tell her the dark secret. Tell it all!"

Raliph took his sister's hands. Meeting her inquisitive eyes, he turned away. "I cannot your highness," he whispered hoarsely. "Why must you demand such a thing from me?"

"Tell her!" he shrieked. "You hate me, Raliph? Now's your

chance to exact your revenge on me!"

I shuddered hearing my brother's voice. He sounded half mad.

"Let her know the cruelty of my black heart and then perhaps the hate in her eyes toward me will be enough for even your satisfaction." He heaved a shuddered breath. "When the woman I love heart and soul hates me."

"Adann," Sunfare neared him and touched his shoulder. She longed to comfort him but feared to do so.

He slumped down onto the chair he'd been leaning on. Sunfare knelt down and took his hands. "Adann," she repeated.

"After Justice died, Garcel and I were grief-stricken," Adann began in a hoarse tone. "That same week, Garcel captured a common rebel. Instead of sending him to the mines like we usually would, Garcel pretended he had information we needed and we…" Sweat was beading on his face. His whole body began to shake. "Brought him to the dungeon and tortured him severely for two weeks."

Sunfare dropped his hands and fell back onto the floor. Tears filled her eyes. She said nothing, only shook with heart wrenching sobs. "Raliph, why do you hide so much from me?" she broke.

"I couldn't have you bear more of my troubles," said Raliph taking a step nearer to his sister.

She slid away from him, still weeping on the cold dirt floor. "I watched you be branded. I watched you kill a man and I watched you fall apart and grow cold afterwards!" Wiping her eyes, she slowly got up onto her feet. Standing tall, she faced her brother. "Want to know why I've been seeing that man?" She pointed to Adann whose face remained engulfed in his hands in desperate fear to look up at her.

"Because I wanted to get you out of there. If I saved enough, we would move into Whitestone where we'd be safe. Duelis could get a job, I thought, and you could escape to the mountains beyond the Dim Marshes. You could live, not be whipped, cheated, branded, tortured, beaten, or forced to do deeds you hate with all your soul!"

Adann straightened and slowly stood to his feet. "So, the only reason you said those words, smiled when you saw me, listened when I talked to you…was because you wanted my money?"

Sunfare's eyes met his, she mouthed, "Yes." Tears flooded her eyes and she looked down to the ground. She shook as sobs wracked her body.

Adann stood stock still. "The fool that I am…I thought somehow, in all my folly, I could be loved." He wiped his eyes of unwanted tears. "Yet, when I think of it, I wonder how I could have believed that." He bit his lip to disallow any more sobs to escape. "I want to be a great man just as Justice and Garcel. But I see now that I am nothing but a cruel, miserable coward." He turned to leave. "Goodbye, Sunfare. It was nice as long as the lie lasted."

He stepped out into the night. Hand on his sword hilt; he strode, with no hesitancy, towards the garden a bit beyond the house. I had once seen him go there with Sunfare before. When he reached the middle of the garden, he covered his face with his hands, fell to his knees, and wept.

"So, are you just going to let him leave?" Raliph demanded in the house.

"What else can I do?" said Sunfare trying to wipe away her ever replenishing supply of tears.

"Are you going to forgive the past and try again?"

Raliph took her cloak off the hook on the door.

"But I cheated him, broke his heart, used him…"

"If he loves you, he'll forgive you just as you'll forgive him for what he did to me…"

I turned back to see Adann. He had stopped weeping and was now walking purposely towards the forest. His dagger was drawn. Fear struck me when I saw where his blade was pointed. At his throat. I stood up to run and stop him when Sunfare rushed past me to Adann as he stood at the edge of the forest.

"No Adann, no!" she cried.

"Sunfare?" He dropped his blade onto the path.

"Adann…" she said in a softer tone when she neared him. "I'm so sorry."

"I'm not mad at you, Sunfare. How can I be? You love your family."

"And I love you." She began to cry again. "I'm sorry, Adann, so sorry."

"You know well it should be me apologizing."

"Adann, you know I forgive you. My brother has so I will…" she paused to wipe her eyes. "May we try again? This time in honesty and forgiveness?"

Adann drew her nearer and they wept upon each other. I smiled. For the first time in my life, I saw my brother, Adann, as a man.

"Touching isn't it, Mercy?" Raliph grinned down at me while I hid behind my bush. "You know I'm trained and drilled frequently on being able to detect spies."

I growled inwardly.

"There have been very few people who can sneak up on me."

"Raliph!" I whispered fiercely.

"Dawn is nearly upon us. You should return."

"I know."

"It is dangerous for you to be so near the forest."

"As if I didn't have enough people pretending to be my father," I said.

He laughed. I smiled a bit too. It probably was pretty funny to watch me huddled up behind a bush eavesdropping on my brother's romance.

His smiled dimmed. "I must leave and report to my commander else they may assume I deserted and persecute my family."

"Adann will do all he can to make sure your family is safe."

He nodded his face grim. "I will seek to discover Ellar's will for me, if there can be one in this cruel war." He looked at me and sighed. "I promise to return as soon as I can."

I nodded.

"Look for me at sunset every night at the edge of the forest."

"I will watch."

"Now go, Mercy. Before anyone realizes you left tonight."

Sadly, I stood and slipped past the house. The first morning light appeared as I ran along the path back to the city, the gate opened and I passed through and snuck into the palace. Only the servants were up and I knew they wouldn't tell on me.

# GARCEL'S COURAGE

"Your brother wishes to speak to you."

"He does!" I exclaimed. For days Garcel, had been carefully tended by my mother with only Nadia tending as the servant. I heard how he was faring through Nadia.

When I opened the door, the whole family was gathered around. Nadia stood in the shadows apart from the rest.

Father had been called home at the news of his son's return but didn't look too pleased to be there as he sat, scowling, in a decoratively cushioned chair a few feet from the bed.

Garcel looked to be himself despite the numerous scars and marks on him. He was propped up with many cushions on top of his intricately embroidered duvet. He smiled when he saw me enter.

"Your face is a welcome sight, fair sister!" he exclaimed.

I curtsied and sat down at the foot of his bed. "Garcel, it was so terrible when we thought you had died…I, knowing it was my fault…"

"No sister, do not speak so. Whatever happened was my choice and is all far into the past."

"All of you should stop taking so many risks or I'll be left with no heir to sit upon the throne of Tarlen and lead the troops into battle," growled the king.

"Perhaps, there will be no cause to go into battle by then, perhaps we will have peace," said the queen evenly.

The king's brows furrowed. "Don't you go preaching treason."

"Father, this war has gone on long enough. The time has come to make peace between our two armies," said Garcel.

"Garcel, you of all people should wish for revenge from Larcos! After all he's done to you, what he would have done to your sister."

"You do not care what happens to any of us, Father!" cried Garcel. "All you want is to capture more slaves to send to the mines so you may be richer and more powerful from their toil!"

Father stared, mouth open, shocked. "How dare you!"

"The people in your kingdom are ravaged by war, hunger, plague…"

"The rebels are bringing that upon us," the king protested.

"No! It is you! Stop lying to yourself, and us. And I want no part in it." Garcel fell back onto his pillows. "I will no longer send prisoners to the mines nor will I steal from the farmers to feed my army. I will not allow my soldiers to abuse the poor or harm their daughters. And I will do everything in my power to be just and fair to my enemy as I am to the citizens and soldiers of Tarlen."

My heart throbbed. My hands were clammy from cold sweat. I watched my father's face intently, wondering what he would say.

"You are a fool, Garcel!"

"If I am ever to be king, I desire to be a just one."

I glanced over at every face in the room. Mother smiled proudly, Adann stared in shock, and Father's eyes were ablaze. Nadia stood in the corner still, her eyes shining with affection for him.

Father was brooding in a storm at his son. "What has happened to my son?"

"Your son is tired of being cruel. Tired of hating himself. Tired of this devastated and corrupt version of a kingdom," said Garcel.

Father stood up and stormed out. Garcel watched, his face composed, but when his eyes met Nadia's they filled with tears. "I didn't plan to lose my composure to such an extent."

"What happened to you, Garcel?" said Adann huskily. In his darting nervous eyes, I saw fear was written on his face.

"I met some friends…unlikely friends."

"The rebel, the guards say, led you to the camp. The same rebel," Adann stopped.

Garcel nodded.

"The same rebel…?" Mother turned inquisitively to Adann.

Adann blushed and looked down.

"We have to tell her eventually. She needs to know." I said finding all the courage within me I possessed.

"You are prepared to tell her?" Garcel looked at me, surprised.

"If you are."

Adann stared at the floor.

"The prisoner we brought back for questioning a while ago…well, we didn't kill him…" Garcel began hesitant in his words.

"What did you do?" Mother asked, leaning in closer as Garcel spoke in a hushed tone. We could not risk our father hearing the secrets to be unfolded.

"We tortured him until he was unrecognizable…" he stopped.

"Then, I found him one night accidently and he begged mercy of me," I continued. "I took care of him and through that met both Morglin and Ellar." I placed my hand on the mark on my breast.

"They fell in love but I got wind of it and tried to kill the man."

"His name is Raliph," said Adann. His first words since Garcel began the story.

"By a miracle of Ellar, he survived and escaped but not before he had won our sister and accepted Ellar's brand."

"He escaped never to be heard from again until Garcel and I got into a fight and I ran away."

"She was angry with at me for what I did to Raliph."

"Then I was kidnapped and Raliph got wind of it."

"I was in rage but I had to trust Raliph to lead me to Mercy if I could hope to save her," said Garcel. "Along the way Raliph and I became unlikely friends. He told me of Ellar and I met him and was branded as you have seen, Mother."

"What is with this brand, anyways?" Adann demanded. "Isn't it illegal?"

"Justice wore it," I put in.

"He did?" said Garcel, slightly taken aback.

Mother nodded.

"Raliph and I got Mercy out of there but as I was the decoy, I dueled with Larcos so Mercy could escape," Garcel paused. "The fight was the bravest duel I've fought but the moment he had advantage, he called his men and they struck me down."

I tried to picture the battle my noble brother was depicting. I could only imagine his sword whizzing above his assailant's heads then striking down hard upon Larcos' blade. His dark hair flying as his powerful arms hewed a mighty sword over Larcos.

"You know the rest."

I stopped imagining Garcel's story.

"For some reason, Raliph found me and carried me to a camp where numerous women from the rebel army were hiding."

Nadia stepped out of the shadows. I motioned for her to sit next to me.

"Nadia being one of them," Mother assumed.

"Yes," Nadia smiled winningly.

I caught Garcel staring at her. She was still dressed in her torn clothes and her black eye was visible. But she was still lovely. Her face was sort of homely when I thought about it with mousy hair and thin lips but her tenderness was so endearing it was impossible for anyone to believe she was the most beautiful girl to walk the earth. Garcel sure thought so. He blushed when he saw my smirk.

"It was a terrifying journey back to Whitestone. We were almost caught and Raliph had to fight a few men to get us through but he led us all to safety with no great harm to us. My greatest fear was that Garcel would die on the way for he was very weak and the journey long," said Nadia.

"Besides the fact I was the most depressed man to ever have to talk to," Garcel put in.

"Wait," said Adann. "Raliph saved your life, saved Mercy's, and for some odd reason he was bringing people from the rebel camp to Whitestone…"

I sighed. "I am the Compassionate Angel unbeknownst to Father. I had met those women while I was being held at the camp. Raliph promised to bring them back so they could be safe from the horrors of the rebel camp. They help with my orphanage."

"Larcos will kill you all," Adann whispered. "As will Father."

"I know," I shrugged. "But he never knew anything I do, anyways."

"The mark is illegal," he reminded.

"Your father will be furious with you two if he knows of the mark. He suspects something," Mother warned.

"But he knows you have it," I said, careless.

"I am under a strict oath not to tell anyone of it or influence someone else to get it. Your father wanted the blessing of Ellar upon his home but he does not want his practices."

"What will happen if he discovers we have it?" I asked. Fear finally creeping into my heart.

"I will be killed."

# COURAGE OR FOLLY?

Thoughts of that day haunted me for many to come. What would happen if Father did find out? How much danger were Garcel, Nadia, and I in? Adann would not tell on us to anyone but Sunfare I knew but he had taken to stalking around the castle with a storm-cloud in his eyes.

Father left to make yet another overview of his generals and the posts in the main cities. He did this as often as he could for the next few months and when he was home, he would only speak to Adann. I hated to think what the king wanted from Adann. Adann wouldn't betray us but I couldn't know for sure.

The boys required less of my presence with Meta and the rest of the escapees there. They lightened the load on Lillis. She now taught them more of Ellar and peace so they could teach the boys. I was not needed so much anymore at the orphanage but I would often find my steps leading me there. The boys loved me and being there helped me understand why I was taking so many risks. I would tell them stories and sometimes sing quietly to them. It always scared me to go to see the boys because I knew the risks of getting caught.

Just in precautionary measures, I practiced my fencing and archery more than usual to prepare for the worst. If mother were ever put in danger through Garcel and I, we would be able to defend her. Fear loomed its ugly head at me. Something would happen soon. Either to me or someone close to me.

I did not see Raliph much anymore but every night I would watch for him. Two months passed. Nothing.

It was early as I crept up the stairs to my room after a night visit to Lillis and the boys.

"You know what you have been paid for?" I heard my father's voice whisper coarsely near my door. My heart skipped a beat. I slipped into the shadows, hoping desperately I wouldn't be caught. Unfortunately, I was in my disguise to roam the streets and visit the boys; if I were caught in it there would be many questions on why I was so dressed.

"You can count on me, Your Majesty." I recognized the voice to belong to Duelis, Sunfare's sister. I had hired her as my maid when I moved the family into Whitestone. What was father trying to get her to do?"

I hid in the shadow of the corner as they passed by. When I was sure they were gone, I went into my room and shut the door. Pulling off my disguise, I hid it in my old hideout. I climbed into bed and pretended I had been there all along. Nagging fears plagued me and it was near impossible to fall asleep. Whatever I did, I had to be much more careful in the future. I could not risk my mother or Garcel's life becoming endangered because of our convictions regarding Ellar. My identity of being the Compassionate Angel must remain under wraps. Our very lives hung in the balance of secrecy.

"Your Highness."

I rolled over and groaned.

"Your Highness, the prince Garcel wishes to speak to you."

I sat up and blinked. The sun had crept into my room and was now spreading its warm blanket over my bed.

I looked up to see Duelis smiling courteously at me as she delivered her message again.

"Fetch my robe; I shall meet him in his chambers."

I watched her hasten to her task. The girls in that family had a way of keeping secrets without causing the slightest suspicion. They had perfected the art of being fake.

When I reached my brother's chambers, I found him sitting on a chair looking out his window. We had all been pleased to hear he had been walking lately. I suspected he had walked from his bed to that chair then collapsed, exhausted.

Nadia had been waiting on him lately. She just brought in a steaming cup of tea or something as I was entering. When she saw me, she blushed and made her way to the door.

As I glanced around the room, I realized just how royal my brother's chambers were. Mounted on his wall was the shield of the royal family with the symbol of royal might and power. A bloodied Urfane falling under the power of a man with a crown on his head and a scarlet sword in his hand. Disgusting. His bed was ornamented with fine embroidery depicting battles Garcel had fought. Adann beside him every one. Some sort of art decorated his roof. His walls were bare except for broken swords hanging every foot or so. Each sword representing a mighty soldier he had defeated.

I blushed when I noticed Garcel had turned and was looking at me. "It's as if all my life, I've done nothing but kill."

Nadia curtsied and left.

"She's in love with you," I said when the door shut behind her.

"As I am with her."

"Will you make her an offer?"

"When I can walk a mile without support, yes."

"Pride?"

"What else?" He smiled and beckoned me to near him. "Larcos told you of what is the nature of your jewelry."

I nodded solemnly. "And the war in general."

"Do you want to see it?"

"What do you mean?" I whispered my eyes wide in apprehension.

"At the foot of the mountains Gandon, Forshant, and Caynas at the end of the marshes. Guarded by many soldiers. A deathtrap to any rebel who dares pass that way. Thousands of rebels toil in chains. They work either deep in the caves where the gases in the air slowly suffocate them and they die or with the purifying fires where the fire and sun scorch them until they die. All the while, they are whipped and abused by the bloodthirsty drivers and soldiers who are bored with their job. Some have survived four years but that is the record.

I stared at my bracelet. It was intricately ornamented with diamonds and red ruby. Red like the blood with which it cost to make it.

"I never used to care until I imagined Raliph as one of those men," he said quietly. "Something must be done. It's not enough merely to stop causing this evil. I must do something to stop it."

"We will. The day you can walk normally, we will begin."

"You know well we are already deep in trouble with both Larcos and our father. If we get caught there is no telling what will happen," he warned.

"Well, whatever happens, it can't be any more trouble than we'll already be in if we're caught. I'll be risking no more than I already have." I laughed but Garcel did not laugh.

"This is what has fueled the war for as long as it has been raging. There are men who are rich because of this. Including Father. By coming against this, we come against powerful men and their riches."

"We're powerful," I put in, still optimistic.

"No, only puppets of a powerful man,"

"Stop being so dark. We're both in hot water and will be for the rest of our lives. If we choose to bear Ellar's mark, we might as well have some fun with it!"

Garcel finally smiled. "Alright Mercy, I shall try. I've been like this since you were captured. Everything is changing for us so fast."

"I know," I said. Sighing, I looked at my brother carefully. His face was taut with worry and his eyebrows were furrowed as though he were bearing the weight of the world on his shoulders. "You have changed, Garcel," I whispered. "You no longer hold that same anger you once did. You no longer bear the air of a cruel man."

"I was humbled by Ellar, Raliph, and Nadia." He smiled slightly. "Now, I hate the man I was."

"Well, don't be too sorry company for poor Nadia."

Garcel blushed.

"You must be charming and dashing to win her affections."

He laughed. "I will try, Mercy."

Nadia entered and I stood up to leave. "The words I said…before I was captured…you know how sorry I am…"

He nodded. "I know. I have no anger at you for it."

"Will you forget them?"

He lowered his eyes. "In my heart, I will always bear the scar of what I have done, bared by those words you spoke to me that terrible day."

I sighed. "I wish we could go back…"

"But if we could, we would never have met Ellar."

# DOING SOMETHING

He told me to dress like a wealthy soldier. It must not be known I was the princess.

"You will be a greedy rebel captain offering to turn his soldiers in for a price but demand to see the treasures he will be granted for his act of crime."

It was an ingenious plan I thought when he told me. I had to remind myself that Garcel was a military strategist and had to remember everything down to the smallest detail. I felt proud to have such a clever brother.

Apparently, I had an obsession with fine jewels and was tired of Larcos getting them all.

"We will charge them all on an oath of secrecy so it does not get out back to father or Larcos' spies," he told me.

I nodded trying to remember everything. Tomorrow, we would put our plan into action.

Everyone was asleep as I perfected my disguise in the light of a small lamp. I remembered playing imaginary games as a child with Justice and we would dress up like this and think of stories. It was all fun and games then hiding in our little room by the light of a candle. Now this was real, this was no story. This was dangerous. Life and death. If I were caught, exile would be the best punishment I could get for this crime.

I hid my delicate hands in my long overhanging sleeves, put mail on myself and shoulder padding to hide my figure. After smearing dirt on my face, I pulled my hood over my eyes. I stepped into huge boots that went up past my knees to hide my shapely legs. When I looked into the mirror, it was difficult to suppress my laughter at the sight of myself. It was perfect. No one would recognize me as the beautiful princess, Mercy. I was a man now.

I strapped a jewel bedecked sword onto my side. Staring at myself in the mirror intently, I practiced my best mean expression. I used to practice my terrible faces on my brothers so I was pretty good at it.

I heard a knock on the door.

"Ready to go?" whispered Garcel when I opened the door.

I smiled enthusiastically. He glanced at my costume and smiling at my face, he chuckled. "You'll have to wipe that grin off your face when we get to the pit."

We couldn't afford to be caught at the gate so we had to slip under the wall and swim the moat. I didn't like the idea of having wet clothes for a long ride but it couldn't be helped. With the help of Garcel's most trusted servant, we had horses and supplies waiting for us. Dripping wet and cold, we mounted our horses and galloped past the city towards the Dim Marshes.

Through the marshlands was the most direct route to the mountains though it was hot, tiresome, smelly and the mud sometimes could swallow a horse whole. I trusted Garcel knew the best and safest way through as he had been through many times but I was still a little scared. I'd never been to the marshes before.

Garcel told the servants that if anyone asked where we had gone to tell them that Garcel had taken me to a trainer in Bellorn to help me improve my archery skills. He had noted I was practicing more and was pleased with my sudden interest in warlike activities. Little did he know the real reason I was training. Regardless, it was a good guise to slip through the radar undetected. Garcel had thought of everything and I was proud to call him my brother.

I glanced over at him astride his horse, sitting proudly like a great man of war. So noble and brave. I remembered the day he saved me from Larcos. Sword drawn and head back. His dark hair strewn over his face covering his intense forest eyes. I blinked to bring myself back to the land of the living. He was still ahead of me, sitting straight on his horse, leading me in the best pathway through the marshes. He cut a fine figure in the saddle with his broad shoulders back and his head held high in the wind. I felt safe with this brave and strong man as my brother. In that moment, I was proud to call him my brother. I loved him dearly. As if it was a first time realization, I stared at him for a while. Yes, I did love him. I loved him more than I would ever know.

"We ride tonight and tomorrow and the next day. We will reach the mountains at twilight the second day.

I swallowed hard trying not to imagine so little sleep and so much riding but if my brother so asked it of me; I would do it without question.

He led me through the marshes through the quickest path he knew until we reached the mountain pass. I was happy to be out of the marshes as soon as I could for they scared me. The Dim Marshes was the place of exile for all those who are banished from Tarlen. A vast land of many miles where misfits hid in grass and mud. I knew the bitter people would not attack us because we had the appearance of being two mighty men but I was still scared. No one dares attack the prince not merely because he is the prince but because he is the mightiest soldier in Tarlen. But there were many of them.

Sometimes, Garcel would point out what the people of the marshes would eat like a plant or animal or point to a rock or bush as a marking to show where they lived. "You look at that bush and only see a bush. But if you look closely you'll realize an entire family can live under that bush," he would tell me. "They dig a hole and then block up the incoming mud with roots, straw and clay. They live there for years. Convicted men, diseased families, and runaway children. It is in the Dim Marshes that they hide. There are some who are hearing every word we speak at this very moment. They never attack a Tarlen soldier but if we sleep and no one is on watch they will steal our belongings as silently as night can steal over sunrays at twilight."

"Doesn't anyone do anything about them?" I asked.

"They can hide so no one kills them. And they are outcasts so no one helps them. They are the people of the Dim Marshes. Those who live in mud."

In the corner of my eye, I caught a movement in the distance of the vast plains of water, plants and muck. Sorrow filled my heart. "What a terrible fate to be driven here."

Garcel smiled tenderly at me. "You cannot save the whole world, Mercy. You are a princess, not a god."

When we reached the mountains, Garcel led me up a steep path along the mountainside. The wind blew so hard on us it was hard to keep my seat in my saddle. I was so tired, I longed to fall asleep. The horses struggled to find footing in the rocky terrain. There were numerous loose stones that, more than once, caused our horses to lose their balance and almost fall.

Garcel suddenly stopped in front of me. "There." He pointed down. I looked where he was pointing. We were just above the slave camp providing us with a perfect view of what went on down there. I braced myself before I looked carefully but I could never be prepared for what I saw.

Below were men chained, working by purifying fires or carrying heavy loads out a cave mouth. Most stumbling with every step they took. Dirt char and blood marred their bodies as the sun burnt their skin and sucked the life out of them Slavers cried out harshly to them and whipped them brutally if they slowed at all with their tasks. I watched horrified as one man collapsed into a fire. The slavers laughed and the man was pushed completely in the fire as though he were merely firewood.

Garcel looked at me, concerned. "Are you alright?"

I bit my lip and nodded.

"We don't have to do this. We can go back and you can pretend you never even heard of this place."

I shook my head. "We're doing this. I don't care."

He smiled. "As you like."

He dismounted and led his horse down a steep hill to a flat place just above The Pit. It was growing dark as I saw tents with lights inside. As we drew nearer, we saw the shapes of men in the tents. I heard voices. Laughter, cruel laughter. Something or someone was causing this uproar. I hated to think about it.

I glanced down at The Pit where dying men labored in hopelessness. Fire, blood, and slaves, all for the price of jewels like the ones which bedecked my rich ornaments. The Pit was a hole cut into the mountain shaped much like a cylinder. Beside it was a cave that opened its yawning mouth and devoured the stumbling dehumanized creatures I saw below.

Jagged rock kept them enclosed and chains held them fast to their tasks and from destroying their own lives in their dungeon. There was a ladder up out of The Pit situated opposite from the yawning mouth of the cave.

The sounds of clanking and pounding and agonized cries resounded in my ears making it difficult to focus and evaluate on the scene and our plan to change it.

The sun's light was fading but no one seemed to notice. They kept on. The clanking, the pounding, the shrieks and the blood. I watched another man die.

Garcel remained unfazed. Boldly, he marched into the well-lit tent where all the laughing was. When I entered, I saw clearly what they were laughing at. A man, chained to the ground by his ankle was getting tossed around and made fun of. One man pulled his clothes off in front of our very eyes then hit him in the stomach. He laid sprawled on the floor moaning and crying until another man picked him up to have his fun with the unfortunate slave.

When they realized Prince Garcel had entered, the laughter died quickly. They stood to their feet and bowed to him. I counted five of them.

Garcel smiled sardonically as I remembered he used to do so well. It scared me to see him transform himself into that fearful man once again so quickly. "Partying are you? Having fun while the king is paying you to get the lousy Cansten asses moving!" He kicked at a chair and it fell broken on the ground.

The five men, slave drivers or Tarlen soldiers, stood still and silent. They knew better than to talk back to the prince.

"Wasting good slaves on sick games?!" He kicked at the man chained on the floor. He groaned and crawled pitifully in the dirt away from Garcel.

Garcel hit the face of one of the men as he stood stock still. He didn't flinch at the hit but I saw blood trickle down his nose in a few seconds after his hand made contact with the poor man's nose.

"Now, all of you! Get these worthless beasts fed and gather today's work for our honored guest to see." He motioned to me as I stepped more into the light.

"Yes, Sir," one young man replied. "May I ask why, Sir?"

"No you may not!" Garcel bellowed and struck him. "I will tell you brutish creatures all later. Make a good impression on our guest and do as I tell you. All of you!"

The five men, shaking and bowing repeatedly, unchained the slave and proceeded to leave the tent and go down to the work pit.

Garcel motioned for me to near him. I tried not to think about the blood on the floor.

"Now, after you see the jewels, I will put on a celebration in order to impress you so you'll agree to our proposition."

I nodded, knowing the whole plan already.

"The wine in my saddle is drugged and will make the beasts pass out and remain so for the night until noon unheeding even the loudest sounds. In order not to arouse any suspicions, I will drink some of the wine as well so as to make it seem that you, the rebel captain, planned this alone. After I pass out, you are on your own." He looked at me squarely. "You sure you can go through with this?"

"Yes," I said, hoping I didn't sound as scared as I was.

"You're doing great. You look very convincing."

"I feel very uncomfortable."

He chuckled. "The other drink is in your saddlebag. The key for the chains are on the belts of every slaver. Set as many free as you can but there are hundreds so if you cannot save them all, know you saved some. Escape on your horse. The brutes won't be able to stop you until at the earliest noon tomorrow."

I nodded.

"I will meet you behind the mountain we have specified. I will be weak but we have food for them and us there already. Remember where we hid it." He put his hand on my shoulder. "Don't be scared, Mercy. Ellar will protect us."

I was taken down into The Pit of Treasures; they called it, to behold the jewels that were apparently to be mine. I pretended to be a greedy man as I gazed at the many precious stones and metals in which I had once worn on my neck and arms in the past. I felt hot anger rise in me at the cost of blood these stones had.

Garcel laughed innately and filled a sack with the jewels. In the sight of the slavers, he cried to me, "This all will be yours if you betray your charge to us here!"

I took the sack eagerly and weighed it in my hands. The precious stones felt like worthless rocks in a sack.

A slave passed by and spat in Garcel's face. "Morglin curse you!" he spat.

A slaver took his whip and prepared to beat the audacious slave.

Garcel wiped his face. "No!" he bellowed. "Bring him to the tent. Tonight, we will have a party in honor of our guest who is soon to provide more of these maggots to us, with him," he struck the angry man. "As our entertainment!"

The men laughed and unchained their newest victim. He had his head bowed to the ground now and he stared with thunderstorms in his eyes at the dirt in shame.

I wanted to faint. The stench of blood and death was too great in that place. I pretended to laugh but inside my stomach was lurching from the terrible sights I saw and the foul stench of cruelty I could smell from a mile away.

The slaves were pulled out of the cave and fed some disgusting grime and if they didn't eat it, they were whipped. Sometimes, when the slavers pulled the men out of the cave they pulled them out dead. After they were fed, the slavers checked their chains and then led us back up the ladder.

"His name is Sander. He is a rebel captain. The king has offered to pay him an ample share to betray his regiment. I brought him here to see a token of our generosity." Garcel announced once all inside the tent. The men laughed.

Cautiously, I glanced around the tent again at the grimy cruel faces. The slave who had spat on Garcel stood silent, chained to the ground and staring at the dirt.

"Sander! Bring the wine! We shall give you a Tarlen welcome!" Garcel cried and hit the slave, knocking him to the ground. He laughed innately. I ran out of there to the saddlebags to get the wine.

Cruel laughter filled the tent. I entered with the wine and Garcel, still laughing hard and cold, poured it. The men guzzled it down then began to kick and taunt the slave. I held the cup in my hand but drunk none. Silently, I watched my brother as he reeled around like a drunkard. Hitting any man he saw and laughing hollow at everything he saw. Watching him made me wonder if he had always been like that before he had met Ellar. Drunk with power and cruelty. The slavers followed him like dogs with their tongues out mimicking everything he did. They taunted the poor slave. Telling him horror stories of things they would do to him then tripping him, hitting him or kicking him when he lay helpless on the ground.

Within an hour before things escalated further, the drunks began to fall. I watched as one by one, they each dropped off. The slave in the tent watched in surprise. After the last man fell asleep, Garcel smiled and nodded at me. Then he collapsed and he was out.

I stood up and took some keys from the belts of the snoring drunks. Then, wordlessly I unchained the bloody slave on the floor. He stared at me in silence.

"Get up," I ordered him in a deep voice.

He slowly ventured to his feet. "Who are you?"

"Ask no questions, do as I say and you will get out of here alive," I told him.

"Follow me."

He staggered after me. I took the brew out of my saddlebag.

"Drink this."

"What is it?" He eyed me suspiciously.

"It is a drug which will give you unnatural energy. Flee to the mountain before the marshes." I pointed beyond the ridge. "Wait there for me."

He drank a sip of the brew then ran out of sight. The drug made it impossible for him to sit still though the poor man was in excruciating pain.

With the keys from each slaver in my hand, I climbed down the ladder into the pit. The slaves lay in the dirt, most sleeping, some staring up at me, too weak to move. I knelt down and unchained the nearest one to me.

"Go straight to the mountain just before the Dim Marshes to await my orders," I told him still using my deep man voice. I forced some liquid down his throat. He jumped up immediately.

"Here," I passed him some keys. "Help me first with these."

Obediently, he ran to the next man and unchained him quickly. The process was repeated until I grew so exhausted I longed to drink some of the drug I was carrying.

Garcel got it because he had access to all things for the war. The drug was sometimes used to give soldiers energy to fight if they had been walking for days. The drug was hard to conjure usually so it was rarely used but Garcel could get it whenever he wished.

I shook one man but he didn't stir. "Get up! You're leaving!" I shook him furiously.

"He died over the night, Sir." A voice said behind me. "He'll be burnt tomorrow."

I stepped back. "That's horrible." Tears filled my eyes. He only had to live through one more night and he could have been free. Sorrowfully, I went to the next man.

"Who are you?" the voice asked.

"One who is saving you."

"You aren't a rebel leader," he persisted.

I did not speak but began unchaining a half starved man who looked to have been in The Pit for a while.

"Who are you?" the man asked again.

I turned to face him. "Do as I say and you'll escape danger! Persist in your questions and I cannot help you." I pointed to the ladder out of the pit. "Go!"

He turned sullenly away. I continued work. That man had obviously not been in the pit for long to be willing to stay there because he was curious.

As the morning light appeared, I unchained the last man and poured nearly the last drop out of the skin. I was exhausted. Slowly climbing up the ladder, I yawned. "I did it." Joy filled my being. I had just done the bravest thing in my life. "Father will kill me if he finds out," I whispered. "Kill Garcel." I sighed. Whatever, I wouldn't let anything spoil my moment of glory.

I hid my face in my cloak. If ever the slaves found out who I was, they could tell Father. I had to keep my identity hidden. I growled. "Oh the horrors of being a princess."

I mounted my horse and left that dark place. I hoped someday the stench of my father's greed would eventually leave my nostrils and the sight of it, erase from my memory but I could not forget. I would always remember the feeling of a dead man on my hand… The expressionless face… Death.

Some called it the Pit of Treasures but I knew what it was. It was the Pit of Death. Where bodies are burned like firewood. Where the ground is crimson from the blood of slavers' whips. Where chains restrain men from killing themselves. Hate, cruelty, hopelessness, fear. Slowly, they die and more are brought. Life cannot be so cheaply bought as Father thinks. One day, he will pay. No one can get away with such cruelty. Not even the king.

When I reached the mountain, I saw them waiting. The drug was wearing off and many of them were collapsed on the ground. I dismounted and tied my reins to a tree branch. All eyes were on me.

"Each of you find one man to leave with!" I commanded loudly. "Leave with your partner in different directions so their search parties will be stretched too thin to find all of you."

"We have no strength to do so. No supplies," one man protested.

I removed a rock from the side of the mountain to reveal a small cave filled with small bags of food and a skin of water enough to last two men through a three day journey. "I was prepared for that," I said proudly thinking again of my brother's genius. "Each party, take a bag then leave. You must be out of here as soon as possible."

I stepped back as each group took their supplies then left. There must have been at least two hundred of them. Did we bring enough supplies for them?

"Should we report to Larcos?" one man asked as he and his partner were leaving.

"Escape the king! That is my order. However you choose to do it, I don't care!"

They obeyed. I watched as men with bloody ankles in torn tatters passed by me with their bag of food and water. I sure hoped they would make it. Most of them should at least.

The sun beat down on me as the crowd thinned and chaos died down. My head felt dizzy from lack of sleep and the heat. I leant against the mountainside.

"Who are you?"

I turned to see the final man. He was sitting alone against the mountainside, clearly unwell. I recognized him as the man who had spat on Garcel the day before.

I neared him. He was bashed up and bruised terribly from both his work and from being the 'entertainment' in the night.

I poured some water onto a rag and washed his face. Then I rinsed it and cooled his chain scarred ankles. They were hot and red and bloody marred with grime and scarlet stained.

"You must escape."

He breathed hard. His eyes were glazing over as I had seen Raliph's do when he was dying. I poured water down his throat.

We were running out of time. The slavers would have begun to track us down now. I went to my saddle and pulled out some good meat, my own supply. Then I even dug deep for a piece of fruit to give to him. Perhaps they would give him strength.

"Who are you to care if one man dies?" he croaked, his voice raspy losing breath. "You…are no rebel captain."

I sighed. "No, I am not a rebel." I felt his forehead. It was hot like a sunbaked stone, lifeless.

"Who are you…?" he protested.

"The Compassionate Angel."

His eyes caught light. His lips parted into a smile. "Someone in Tarlen cares about people."

I met his eyes. "More than just one."

"You are a girl!" He forced himself to sit up, curiosity giving him strength.

"You must leave!" I told him.

"I could tear off your disguise and know who the Compassionate Angel is…" he heaved a breath. "Only man in Tarlen to know." He collapsed back.

"If you had the strength to stand to your feet," I said, mocking him. "The less you know the less danger you and I and others are in. I save lives who keep silent." I held my head high. "Those slavers will be here looking for us. We're both in danger if you don't get a move on."

I found a last drop of the drug in the wineskin and squeezed it into a small skin of water. "This will give you strength to flee." I threw it to him. "Now…" I stopped. The sound of a horse's gait reached my ears. "Hide!" I hissed and shoved him behind a tree.

I drew my sword and waited.

"Mercy?"

Garcel, oh no!

He entered the valley and reined his horse to a halt. Slipping out of his saddle, he ran to me. "Mercy! Mercy we did it!" He took me in his arms and swung me around laughing for joy. "You were so brave!"

"Garcel," I said. "They're not all gone!"

He dropped me. "Oh no." He sighed. "Alright, where did you hide him?"

I went to the tree and yanked him out before my brother.

Trembling, he fell on his face before Garcel. "Please your Highness, don't make me go back there. Don't torture me. Kill me now if you must, just don't make me go back…" He began to weep.

Garcel knelt down and touched the shaking man's shoulder. "You are in no danger from me, Mantar."

"You know him?" I said.

"Every name of every man I threw in that pit has haunted me for years."

Mantar looked up at us both. "You two were together in this. You planned the wine, her disguise. You wanted us to escape!"

I blushed. "Garcel planned it."

"You had to do the dirty work," said Garcel.

Mantar's jaw dropped. "Why?"

Garcel sighed. "Why must you know everything?"

"The prince captures me, drags me through the swampland all the while hurling abuses at me and my fellows. Then throws me into a pit where I am beaten and worked to death. Almost die. Hate you. You come back. Pretend to be the man you were. Beat me up, treat me like scum, then later I find out the whole while you're planning a mass escape for the very slaves you captured and threw into that Pit of Toil!" Mantar slowly looked up to meet Garcel's eyes. "With all due respect, I should be excused for my curiosity."

"He does have a point," I said.

Garcel picked Mantar up onto his feet. "I was a cruel man but not as hard as you think. Guilt plagued me as it does anyone else and I hated myself for what I did."

"The blood of hundreds of men is on your hands!" Mantar cried.

Garcel stepped back like he'd been struck.

"Of the ten you dragged out there with me two years ago, there are three left of us. I watched them die and be burnt. My comrades! Nothing you can do can make up for those lives you destroyed.

Nothing. Not even this elaborate scheme!"

"Thousands, actually," Garcel said quietly. "The blood of thousands if you include battles as well." He reached for his dagger and tossed it to him. "Kill me if you want, Mantar. You have every right to do so."

Mantar picked up the knife and looked at Garcel.

"Mercy, don't watch," Garcel warned.

I stood still as a statue. Why was Garcel letting this man act so? What was he doing?

"Why should you two royalties care about us?" Mantar demanded his hands shaking. "Why should you," he pointed the dagger at Garcel, "come back like this to save us after you've destroyed so many? Have you come to mock us?"

Garcel stood silent.

"Why?" he cried. "Why?"

"I met someone who changed me," said Garcel quietly.

Mantar's strength gave way and he collapsed. Garcel caught him before he landed hard on the ground. He stared up at Garcel's strong face. "What is with you royalties?"

Garcel smiled.

"What is that on your chest?"

I let out a small scream.

Garcel quickly covered up his golden mark of which his shirt had failed to do so at the impact of Mantar's body on Garcel. "Nothing of importance."

"What is it?"

"Listen, Mantar." I said kneeling down to him. "My brother and I are stuck between Larcos and our father, both of which have ample reason to kill us if they find out all what we've been doing.

We're traitors to all causes because we have chosen to follow the way of mercy and justice. We don't want you to get entangled into the mess we are in. Please, ask no more questions. Hit my brother in the face and be on your way."

Garcel chuckled at my solution.

Mantar shook his head and slowly stood up. "For you, the Compassionate Angel I will do anything. There is a rare kindness about you that demands my instant servitude."

Garcel held him up to his feet and passed him his water skin. "You cover up your guilt in good deeds but I know the truth," he whispered to Garcel.

Garcel did not reply. He only opened the water skin and brought it to Mantar's lips.

"I hate you."

"I know."

Mantar accepted the drink and revived quickly because of the drug in it. He sighed. "I don't understand you royalties. I hate you but yet I owe my life to you. And to the princess…" he turned to bow to me. "Whatever you ask of me, I will do."

"Keep our secret and my identity as the princess. The one who freed you was a rebel captain if anyone asks questions."

He nodded. "Yes, your Highnesses."

We watched him leave.

"We did it." I said happily.

He did not respond.

I turned to see his face in his hands weeping. "Garcel!"

"I hate myself, Mercy," he whispered. "I hate myself so bad."

# NADIA'S CHOICE

"What if he doesn't like me in this?" Nadia's sweet face was flushed in her long purple gown. The gown she had picked for her wedding.

"He thinks you're pretty in anything,. Besides, after the ceremony, it won't matter," I said.

She blushed. "Oh Mercy, do you mind?"

"No," I touched her blushing cheek. "I couldn't ask for a sweeter sister."

"I'm so scared." She gazed out the window at the forest beyond the fields. "I'm so young, weak. He's a strong man of war."

"Who needs a strong young woman to encourage and help him." I took out a necklace from a small wooden box and put it on her neck. "You saved his life, Nadia. He would not have lived if you had not cared for him."

Nadia did not reply only stared out the window.

"When I was a child, I used to dream of marriage, a family, a young girl's dream..." she finally spoke. "Then I was taken...all the terrible things that happened to me in the rebel camp..." She turned to meet my gaze, her eyes overflowed with tears. "Now my dream is coming true and I am terrified."

"Why?" I gave her a handkerchief to wipe her eyes.

"In my heart, I know terrible pain awaits me with this man," she whispered. "But I cannot go back...I will not!" A soft sob escaped her lips. "Black fate has followed me all my life and I know it can follow me even into the chambers of the Prince of Tarlen."

She turned and stood at the window sill. Her long gown gracing her gentle form, her once short shorn hair nearly reaching her chin, her small white hands clenched at her sides.

"But there is love and joy too." My words felt empty. I knew she was right. Something terrible would happen to Garcel and I and Nadia, by her choice to marry Garcel will be deeply affected.

"I love him, Mercy," she whispered. "Of all the fates that await me…I choose him!" Her soft voice grew stronger. "The fool that I am! I will bind myself to the brave and troubled heir to the throne. For despite the warnings in my heart, I cannot deny my love for him."

# RALIPH'S DESPAIR

**Ralph**

The forest seemed twice a dim as I entered it. I sighed thinking how much I did not want to leave you and my family. When I was with you, I always felt like I knew what Ellar wanted me to do, but now, in the forest, everything seemed so much dimmer.

"Ellar," I whispered. "What do you want me to do? Who do you want me to be?"

I wondered why I expected an answer. It was unlikely he'd hear me at all. But I felt lonely and needed to talk to someone, why not the one who caused my whole troubling dilemma in the first place?

I remembered your songs. Your laugh. I wondered how I would bear it now. I broke off running. Angry, sad, and determined all at once and I was tired of trying to understand my feelings. I longed for a good fight or a chase. It was easier that way. Easier than dealing with unpleasant and uncertain emotions. I could sooner defeat an army of a thousand men than comprehend the emotions I felt when I passed from the sunlight into the darkness of the forest.

I ran over my plan in my head. When I got back to the camp, I would report to my commander with a good story that is only partially true on my absence, if anyone even noticed I was gone in the first place. I had the scars to excuse my absence without getting into trouble with my commanders.

I took the quickest route to the camp as I had no reason to hide from the rebels and could easily hear a Tarlen soldier if he passed by. Tarlen soldiers were notorious for being loud and thrashing through the forest leaving intolerably obvious trails.

The rhythm of my feet as I padded through the forest helped me not to think too much but your face, Mercy, haunted me however fast I ran. With all my heart, I wished to be with you again but the risk was too great for us to be seen together. I was already in danger from Larcos if he discovered I saved Garcel and those slaves. I didn't need King Twallor discovering I was the secret lover of his only daughter. It was like walking on a tightrope, one wrong move in either direction and I plummet to my death below. But after all I'd been through now, death didn't seem too bad to me.

The sun was setting when I reached the camp the fourth day. Before I went to report, I stood on a hill to look down at the camp. I could hear the pounding of metal and the cries of slaves working the fires. Beyond that, new recruits were being trained to fight. When they slacked off, they were whipped. Tents of wealthy captains dotted all about and Larcos' was at the end. The soldiers who were returning from battle began to fight over their spoils and drinking. Larcos would let them brawl and enjoy their spoils when they came back from an assignment as long as they didn't kill each other. It was his method of making us fight harder and be tougher but it was a deplorable sight to behold. Two hundred men getting drunk, fighting over fine clothes, weapons and women. Larcos came out to meet them and took a sword and a girl. No man dared oppose him.

"Once again, you have been victorious! Eat, drink, and enjoy your spoils today and tomorrow. You and the seventh division will launch an attack on the city of Bellorn. We will take that city once and for all!"

Cheers arose and they resumed their drinking. Larcos dragged a poor screaming girl to his tent while those watching laughed. I wondered why I had never seen the horrific acts that were committed by these savages.

I spotted one man in a corner of the camp. They were tying him up and throwing him around amongst themselves. I remembered being that man. They beat him up and laughed at him, taking his clothes and weapons. He was probably about eighteen years old. This same thing happened to a few more young and weaker soldiers.

I watched as the whole place became a mob. The last thing I wanted in the world was to go down to the camp. But I had to. Sighing, I made my way down into the abyssal hole of drunkenness, bullies, and victims. I avoided the mob and went directly to my captain's tent. When I entered his tent, Caraph, my captain, was strapping his sword to his side, preparing to go out and join the brawl. His eyes opened wide in surprise to see me.

"Raliph!"

I bowed respectfully.

"So you report at last. You had better have a good explanation on your absence or I will have to make an example of you."

"I was taken when I was spying but I escaped before we reached The Pit."

"Have you any proofs?"

I showed him some of the scars from the urfane attack. They were so deep and still slightly infected they looked new enough to prove my false argument.

Caraph inspected them and nodded. "Alright, I doubt you could escape anything, Raliph, but these wounds would prove otherwise." He took my arm firmly in his steely grip. "Come, prove yourself around the fire."

I sighed. That was the last place in the world I wanted to go.

Caraph threw a drink at me. I drank it readily as I was growing very thirsty from my journey. A staggering man approached me.

"Your sword is nice." He grabbed my drink from my hands. "Give it!" Another man, slightly less intoxicated eyed my dagger. I rolled my eyes at the foolish brawlers.

"Not tonight. I'm not in the mood to fight."

Caraph stared at me in surprise.

"Ooh, is that so!" The first man drew his dagger. Shouts went out that another fight was coming. Men stumbled over to see it. I had no choice now but to fight with the low creatures.

When my first adversary charged me, I didn't even bother to draw my weapon; I just ducked his dagger and hit him down with my fist in the stomach. He fell back and I slipped into the crowd. I didn't want to fight tonight.

A girl's screams pierced my ears. I glanced around to see a young girl in a torn blue dress. It had once been a nice dress; she had once had a sweet innocent face too I imagine. Drunk men were passing her between them. I knew how well things would escalate for the poor girl. She was already getting beaten up. The firelight reflected her terrified eyes. They met mine but quickly lowered in shame and fear. Unthinking, I stepped into the circle and caught her. She didn't bother to fight me. Holding her with one arm, I drew my sword with the other to oppose the reeling beasts.

"I'm taking this one tonight. Any who wishes to fight me for her, step up. I fight two at once." They want a fight. I'd give them one. The girl deserved a night of peace.

Two sour faced men drew their swords in response to the challenge. They were drunk and unkempt as they growled at me. I knew it would be little competition to beat them because I was sober and they were far from it. Passing the girl to Caraph, I drew my blades. I had two swords carefully sharpened, somewhat difficult to wield but effective enough to ward off drunks.

With a few strong blows, I sent them both sprawling. Cheers arose when the first man lost his blade. I pushed him down with my shoulder then hit the blade out of my other opponent's hand, disarming him.

Two more men charged me and another staggered after them. Apparently, I hadn't given them all enough of a show yet.

I crossed my blades behind me and brought them around. Then, I turned and struck a man behind me. They were surrounding me on all sides. Closing in.

I ducked a sword and let it whizz over my head. Then, I stabbed my attacker's foot. I rolled out of the circle and struck the farthest one on the shin with my sword. Blood spilt and he faded into the crowd. There wasn't a second's delay for three men to wield their blades above me. I stood still for a moment, drawing them in. Then, I sidestepped their attack. The blades thudded on the ground. I tripped the man nearest and stepped on his sword. To thoroughly rid myself of him, I kicked him in the face with my other foot. He howled and disappeared. Well, apparently it was too easy again so two more joined. I got a slice on my arm but that was not a wound worth stopping for. I twirled my swords together yanking at the hilt of the weapon of the one then dodged that of another.

"Alright, that's enough!" Caraph hollered. He didn't want good soldiers killed for a small squabble. "He's earned his woman!" He shoved the girl at me. "Take my tent and take your blade elsewhere."

Obediently, I sheathed my swords and took the girl's wrist. Dragging her to my commander's tent, I heard cheers arise for me. I had given a good show.

I let the girl go when I entered the tent. The girl fell onto the ground and the tent flap closed behind us.

"How may I please a noble soldier as yourself, who fought so bravely?" she said in a low soft voice. Her hair was strewn over her face and her head was down. She would not look up at me or meet my eyes. Her body was shaking. She looked thin and tired. I judged her to be around seventeen. I wondered what your reaction, Mercy, would be if you were to behold her in that moment. "Your servant, my lord."

"Do not flatter me, child," I replied. "You only hope I will favor you and give you something good to eat and a warm place to sleep tonight."

She did not reply, merely stared at the ground.

I slung my sack off my back and took out some meat I had killed. Kneeling down to her, I put it in her hand. "Here, child."

Taking it, she held it protectively and began to devour it. I unpinned my cloak and put it over her shoulders.

"Thank you, my lord," she said quietly.

"What is your name?" I asked, taking care not to make any sudden movements that may scare her.

"Terti."

"Look at me, Terti."

She slowly raised her eyes. As she raised her face for me to see her, I noticed scars and bruises. I was sure I could not live one more day in this terrible land with so much cruelty to the innocent. In that one moment, I saw the cruelty of Tarlen, all embodied in a young girl curled up in a corner terrified to look up and covered in scars and bruises. My eyes no more beheld Terti but they beheld every tear of every mother who lost those dearest to her to war, the terrified face of every girl dragged by her hair to the rebel camp, the sad, hopeless eyes of every soldier forced into this war by fear and duty, forced to a place filled with shame and regret, all the while the fears of those so tired of guilt and instead have grown coldhearted. It was all wrong.

Terti didn't deserve this. She once had a family. A hope. A future. Happiness. Now she is reduced to flattering drunken senseless louts into granting her simple necessities while they use her, beat her, and destroy her heart.

I could not bear it. Tears filled my eyes. "Why?" I whispered hoarsely.

Her sad, dulled eyes, met mine. She did not say a word. Anything I could do would never be enough to heal even the tiniest piece of her heart.

"You do not need to fear me, Terti. I only wish I could make up for some of the cruelty inflicted on you by my fellow men."

Terti stared at me in surprise. "Who are you? You cannot be a rebel."

"I am a man who caught a glimpse of justice and mercy and now that I see it can never be the same." I bowed respectfully. "You will be safe here. I will watch outside the door. Caraph will pass out drunk before he gets to this tent."

She watched me, silent as I left. I closed the tent flap behind me. I sat down at the door and covered my face with my hands. There, I wept.

"Ellar, why did you put me here?" I watched the campfire and reveling fools, drunk and senseless. "What would you have me do in all this darkness? How can I, a mere shell of a man, change this place? All this despair... I...can't."

My body shook violently as I wept at the entrance of my commander's tent. Tears flowed until I wondered if I could have any left.

# RALIPH'S VALOR

Caraph and his command were preparing to attack Bellorn. According to Larcos, the city was holding out too long. It was loyal to the king of Tarlen. The city was rich and powerful and situated twenty miles above Whitestone and fifty miles away from Fardstone. If Larcos could launch a successful attack and take it in the night then he would have ten times more advantage to take the remaining fortresses the king still held. The king held three strongholds all within fifty miles away from each other at the most. They formed a triangle of power that the king used to control the land and fend off the rebels. If Larcos could take Bellorn, the smallest of the three cities, then Larcos would put the king at a serious disadvantage. Bellorn and Fardstone stood about ten miles away from the marshes. From these positions, the three cities controlled the main farmland of Tarlen and forced the rebels to the forest to only ravage out-skirting villages and small cities. Larcos looked on Bellorn with greedy eyes, anxious to have the upper hand. Though we were ordered to obey our leader without question, some of our commanders wondered if Larcos' restlessness was causing him to be blinded to our odds. The Tarlen army was richer and more powerful than Larcos knew and no amount of small attacks on villages and small cities will cause that to diminish the organized Tarlen army. Larcos was an excellent strategist but his impatience could prove fatal to our cause. Not that I cared. If we lost, I'd die or become a slave. If we won, I would be stuck hiding my convictions from men who would use it against me in a world too dark to see goodness. Death seemed like the best option in my present situation, but then, there was you, Mercy. I was to seek Ellar's will for me but it was impossible to see how I could do what was right in a place so distorted and corrupt as the rebel camp. Then again, perhaps that was the case for all of Tarlen.

We travelled at night through the forest, attacking any traveler or hunter who was unprotected and a man of Tarlen.

We hid during the day so no Tarlen spies wouldn't catch us and warn the great cities of an attack. One of the first things a Cansten soldier learns is how to be invisible, even in large numbers. A few times, I had to admire my trainers who, though they whipped me a lot, taught me to be excellent at hiding and slipping past unseen.

The sun was setting on the third day of our journey and I prepared to find a hideout for the day. A large fallen tree with its roots exposed looked good as there was a large hole formed in the dirt from its uprooting.

"It's my hideout." I turned to look behind me. Marat. He hadn't realized it was me.

"Marat." I nodded.

Marat's eyes widened. His fear for me had gone up since I'd almost killed him and I defeated four men singlehandedly around the campfire for Terti. I doubted he'd betray me but it could still happen. It would be easiest and smartest to kill him quickly so my secret would die with him. He read my thoughts and stepped back hand on his hilt. My hand went to my dagger as though to threaten him that if he did one wrong move, I would throw my knife at his heart. I needed this man to fear me.

"I haven't betrayed you, Raliph," he whispered.

"Give me the hideout."

I smirked as he backed away then turned and ran. It was odd having men afraid of me. But I knew Marat as I knew every other rebel. There was no code of honor except the code of strength. If Marat did not fear my blade, he would willingly turn me in despite his oaths. It meant money and favor. But then, Caraph would likely disbelieve Marat's account as I already had a convincing lie complete with scars to prove it. Still, Marat was a great threat. I needed to lay low for a while. I curled up in my hideout. It occurred to me, I should've let Marat have the spot but I shrugged it off and went to sleep.

We took the long route to Bellorn along the out-skirting farms and villages to avoid being detected by Tarlen troops. There were a few soldiers watching for small attacks so Caraph sent us in groups disguised as farmers and merchants through different villages and fields in the surrounding area. Our meeting place was Bellorn at dark, in three days. We were drilled on our tasks as it was a stealth attack. I was in Caraph's group in charge of swimming the moat and jumping the wall. There were ten of us. After we climbed over the wall, we were to open the gate to let the rest of the troops in. There were twelve other groups like ours. Each in divisions of ten. After we stormed the city, we'd kill all the men of the city. Soldiers or otherwise. Then take the boys and brand them and take the women and girls for slaves. It was the biggest attack we'd done since our defeat by the prince Justice. The same battle that ended his life.

Larcos sent a smaller scale attack to a city called Tantarse nearby Fardstone. Hopefully, the attack would draw the extra Tarlen troops to Tantarse so they wouldn't reach Bellorn until we had our victory secured. It was a battle I had hoped desperately to avoid. Not only for the mere danger of it but also for the brutality of the attack. How could I claim I was against taking slaves and branding boys if I helped do those deplorable acts? Truthfully, I was hoping to get into a fight and be somehow disabled before the day of the attack. I imagined what you would say if I were with you, Mercy. You would probably tell me that I was coming at it all wrong and should use my present position to do right not only avoid doing wrong. But I was not brave nor was I mighty. I was scared and a pathetic fighter.

We were getting closer to Bellorn every day and I began to despair. How could I ever be anything but a coward?

---

Caraph motioned for us to be silent. His powerful form stood silhouetted by the city beyond. The moon lit the night in a sorrowful gleam. Perhaps, it was merely my own morbid heart which caused me to see it that way. The walls of Bellorn stood high in the shadows, a fortress to block any attackers. Caraph had chosen the most nimble to climb it. I did not know why he had chosen me. In the past, the likeliness of myself being chosen for any important task was slim to none.

I closed my eyes for a moment to envision the scene I had seen before but this time I saw it in a different light. The scene of the bloody mess of men, stabbed in their sleep, unable to cry out even a warning to the others. The flames of burning homes as those who once lived in them run out in a panic only to be caught by brutal soldiers. I saw the many corpses on the stone streets. I heard the cries of the women and the screams of their children as they are torn from their mothers' arms. In that moment, I almost turned and ran.

Silently, Caraph slid himself into the moat. We followed, trying our best to copy his methods. To avoid detection from the watch on the wall, we held our breaths and swam underwater across the moat and came up on the other side under the shadow of the wall. Each of us had been carefully drilled on what to do from here. Without a word, one man stood still along the wall while another climbed up onto the powerful man's shoulders. The rest of us used them as a human ladder and climbed up and over the wall. We jumped down, careful to land quietly and waited in the shadows until Caraph followed the last of us and appeared on the other side of the wall with us.

He motioned for us to follow him and we did so in silence. We passed along the wall, hiding in the darkness. Other divisions, at other points of the wall, followed the same process.

We reached the gate. The gatekeeper was sitting down on the ground beside the gate, snoring. The watch stood on the wall; waiting for their shift to end so they could crawl into their warm beds and sleep until daylight. We passed several barracks but no one stirred inside for we heard no sound but snoring from the barracks.

Caraph stabbed the gatekeeper in his sleep. Two others took care of the lazy guards. With that done, Caraph put us on the large wheel which was used to pull up and let down the gate. The wheel was five feet around and took at least three men to turn it. Slowly, the gate creaked and moved upwards but before we were even half way, I heard shouts from behind the houses in the city. I flattened myself against the wall when I saw hundreds of fully armed Tarlen soldiers appear out of the silent city. They had been watching us all along, waiting until they knew just how many there were of us.

I drew my sword and prepared to fight as the rest of my comrades did as well.

"Do not fight, fools! Escape while you can!" bellowed our powerful commander as he pulled out his battle-axe from its place on his back and hacked at the advancing soldiers. After buying a bit of time with his powerful attacks, he singlehandedly turned the massive wheel to open the gate so there was just enough room for us to get through. In the confusion of the battle, I could only hear screams and moans as the men desperately pushed themselves through the small opening. Stomping on each other in their haste, they forsook the dying and fled the city for their lives. Many fell. Their cries echoed into the silent cold stars. Dead bodies of both Tarlen and rebel soldiers alike lay on top of each other in that terrible bloodbath at the gate. Caraph now held the gate with one arm and swung his battle-axe with the other. Finding courage in the chaos for once, I let out a shout jumping over the dying and twisted my blade around and onto his attackers. My comrades were now either dead or escaped. It was only Caraph and I still fighting in the bloodbath at the gate. I looked over at Caraph, he was badly wounded.

"Fly, Raliph!" he shrieked over the noise.

My eyes fell on a dead man at my feet. A bar was underneath the wheel to stop the gate if a strong board was placed between a prong of the wheel and against the bar. I struck another man down. Something scratched my arm. Blood gushed out. We would quickly run out of time. They were closing in on us. I bent down and hoisted the dead man up and put his body between the wheel prongs and against the bar. Pulling my axe out, I wielded it above my head at any who approached. We needed to make it three meters to the gate. If I could keep the gate behind us and the soldiers before us we might make it. But our attackers were more than I could count. A hundred at least trying to keep two from reaching their escape.

I slung Caraph over my shoulder and swung my axe with all the power in me to keep them from getting behind me. In this way, I backed my way to the gate. I pushed Caraph through then followed. He was unconscious at this time now. My foot barely made it out when the gate came slamming down. I felt more blood spilling in my body but I did not have time to merit attention to that, it was a sword wound at my side while I was making my final efforts to flee the gate. We were in danger of archers. I dove into the moat under the bridge still bearing Caraph in my arms. I remained underwater until I felt faint. I surfaced at the bank near the city. I knew we would hide best in the shadow of the wall rather than risk trying to run out of the archers' range in the fields beyond the moat in the moonlight.

I heaved a breath and turned my attention to my commander. He was soaked with water and blood. His clothes were torn revealing every spot a blade had pierced him. He opened up his eyes and looked at me, confused.

"Raliph?" he whispered.

"My lord, we must be quiet."

Caraph fell back on the wall and sighed. "We failed."

"But you saved so many of us."

"I am a commander. It is my duty to put my life at risk for my men," he explained in a hushed tone. "It is not your duty to do the same for me."

"What would we do without such a noble captain?"

"I would be replaced with another mighty man."

"But not one so noble."

"Ba, there's no such thing as nobility in Larcos' command. No honor among thieves."

"Then, why did you save us?"

Caraff lowered his eyes. "When I saw the terror, the pure terror on the faces of my men who I had led, I could not let them all die like animals in a cage without a fight." He coughed quietly. "If I am to die for something in this coldblooded army, I'll die for my men."

I listened in silence.

"The fear in my eyes in my first battle…" he slowed. I realized he was about to pass out. "Fear…" He collapsed.

I checked his breathing. He was alive. The archers on the wall probably assumed that I had drowned by now so I bore him up and swam the moat with him in one arm. Exhaustion was overtaking me. When I reached the bank, I threw him over my shoulder and escaped quickly out of sight of the city. There was a safe house in a nearby village so I set my coarse there. If I could make it that very night, Caraph's chances would be much higher. I glanced over my own bleeding body and quickened my pace. I too needed help quick.

# RALIPH'S CONVICTIONS

"Raliph the mighty warrior! One against a thousand, he swung his axe with all the strength of his arm..." The storyteller swung his arms around holding an imaginary axe. The firelight from the center of the camp reflected off his expressive features. His eyebrows went up and down. I always thought he would be a better comedian than storyteller of great battles. "Few have seen such a feat before..." and on he went. The men cheered. At least, they were enjoying it. And they lifted me up on their shoulders. "With no fear in his eyes or tremble in his hand, he brought the mightiest of them down. The greatest of them all challenged him," the storyteller paused to add affect, "Roaring like an Urfane devoid of its prey, he stood between the gate and the noble hero. Did he flinch? Did he cower? Did he run? No! He struck him down like he was a child. And with the very body of his challenger, he blocked the gate from closing in time to escape with his wounded captain."

I rolled my eyes at the exaggeration. Caraph approached the circle and more cheers arose. He met my eyes and smirked. He motioned for me to come to him.

Obediently, I jumped down from my exalted height and left the circle towards Caraph's tent, eager to disappear again.

He welcomed me into his tent and closed the flap so that we were alone. Meeting my eyes again, he chuckled at the foolery of the firelight stories. "You're a mighty man now, Raliph. Never thought I'd say that to you."

I shrugged.

"You don't care?" he asked.

"Sir, if I were to request anything for my supposed bravery it would be peace. This recognition is both undeserved and unasked for."

Caraph smirked. "You are a strange one, Raliph. Ever since you returned from your 'escape' as you call it."

"You doubt me?"

"No, but I know there is more to your story."

I chuckled.

"Because you didn't tell me, I will not press it for my curiosity's sake as I am presently in debt to you. But," he smiled. "I demand an opportunity to repay you somehow. I owe you my life and I demand such a chance."

I thought for a moment. "If you demand it and there is no way that you will merely accept it as a soldier's duty then I will make one small request."

"Anything I can give you."

"More training."

He looked at me with an odd light in his eye. "None of my money? No slaves? No weapons?"

"No."

He laughed and shook his head. He had clear amusement in me. Taking his blade out of its sheath, he said, "If that is all you ask for let us go out to the forest where it is quieter."

"Much obliged."

He paused and scrutinized me. "No chance you are trying to take my place?"

"No sir."

"Then why?"

"As a soldier in your command may I be permitted to keep that to myself?"

He smirked and shook his head at me. "Whatever you say, Raliph. Like I said, I owe you my life." He faced me and put his hand on my shoulder. "Are you in danger?"

Without looking up, I replied in a low voice, "Every man, woman, and child are in danger in Tarlen in these times and I am not exempt."

---

Since that day, Caraph made me his assistant. He trained me to be stronger, faster, and smarter.

No man dared get into a fight with me. However, I was discontented because I did no good in the camp as I was too busy maintaining my mighty soldier façade and training under Caraph. As I was almost always with him, he and I became friends. Though he often stated that he would trust me with his life, I could tell he still wanted to know my dark secret.

Every night, I would sneak away to pray to Ellar to give me strength and courage to stand for him. Every day, I hid my mark and my convictions with it. Fear.

One day, Caraph was wanted for a private meeting with Larcos. As usual under such circumstances as Caraph's assistant, I stood outside the door waiting for my commander to come back out. However, Larcos' tent was almost directly next to the training grounds for new recruits. There were ten of them and two commanders. One of them was yelling at a young boy, crying in a ball in the dirt.

"Get up, useless ratbag! You wanna get whipped?" he said and kicked the boy further into the dirt.

Unthinking, I left my post at the door and neared the scene. I had become known now as a man never to challenge. With all the training Caraph had given me over the past few months, I was known as a man to be feared.

The two men were some of the few older rebels who managed to reach their fifties without getting killed. They backed away as I entered the scene. Only the young boy in a ball in the dirt didn't see my approach.

I knelt down onto the ground and touched him on the shoulder. He looked up, startled. When he saw me his eyes widened in fear. Guilt seared my heart like Morglin's hand once did my flesh. I had known of these cruelties and did nothing. Too worried about saving my own skin and being the man I thought Ellar wished me to be under the claim I had to prepare more. What rubbish. I had turned my back on innocent children such as this boy, that could never be who Ellar wished me to be.

I drew the boy into my arms and let him cry into my shoulder.

"It's not fair," he sobbed. "I hate this place…"

I listened quietly.

"I don't want to become…like them."

"Don't," I whispered into his ear.

"I…have to."

"No," I touched the boy's chest at his heart. "They can do anything to you. Hurt you, steal from you, make you do things you'd never in your worst nightmare see yourself doing. But your heart is your own. They can't get to it unless you let them."

He slowed his blubbering.

"Be strong."

I stood up, everyone staring at me. I didn't care. For once, I felt I'd done something good and if I was killed for it, at least my life would no longer be in vain.

Caraph approached me. He'd witnessed part of the scene. I bowed respectfully to him, left the boy's side and neared the cruel man who had threatened to whip the boy. I wrenched the whip out of his hand and broke it.

"Make these boys soldiers not animals."

Caraph stared at me like I had just hit him hard on the head with a club.

I turned away. Caraph followed me.

"Who are you?" he demanded.

I neared my tent and stepped in. Caraph entered and the flap closed.

"Raliph," I answered. "The man you've commanded for years."

Caraph shook his head. "No, you are a mighty man who cares nothing for fame. A man of wisdom but does not wish to be known for it. A man of mercy who hides it so as to avoid detection. And a man of many secrets."

"I am not half as intriguing as that," I replied, turning my face to the wall away from his probing eyes. "I am a man of convictions. Convictions which are never vocalized in this camp. I am what they call a mighty man because I fear I will someday soon have to defend these convictions. A man of wisdom I am not, merely caution and cowardice. And as far as secrets, I cannot deny that I hold many dark secrets. Some of which could kill me, but I am Raliph. Still a coward, still a weakling, I only show my weaknesses differently.

"You underestimate yourself! Why you've caught even Larcos' attention!"

I turned, terror written in my eyes. "No, he must never think anything of me...he..."

"He wants to make you his assistant. He heard you are loyal, courageous, strong, brave..."

"No!"

"Any offences you have committed could easily be defended by your blade in a few little fights..."

"No! You don't understand," I paused and drew a shuddered sigh. "This is no petty offence."

"You have a compassionate heart which is rare in this camp; I'll warrant you that and I'm sure it will cause many fights. Larcos cares little for such a quality but you have others to make up for it."

I tore my shirt to reveal my mark. Caraph's eyes widened. "That mark, I've seen it before..."

"I serve Ellar," I said, my voice hoarse. Caraph's eyes remained fixated on my mark. "My convictions are from him. I have already committed two crimes in which Larcos would pay a huge sum to know to hang me from the highest tree." I sighed and sat down against the tent, hanging my head in my hands. "This mark is only part of the story, the beginning of a man who can't go back."

"That mark is on the prince Garcel, same place. What...?"

"It is illegal in Tarlen. Don't know how Larcos would feel about it. It..." I stopped. How much could I tell him and remain alive. "In many ways, it causes me to see injustice and cruelty as a result..."

"You do things which Larcos and the Cansten regime object to."

"That's the truth of it."

"What did you do?"

I shook my head.

Caraph knelt down on the ground in front of me and touched me on the shoulder. "Why would I betray you?"

"Money," I replied meeting his eyes. "Or duty perhaps."

"You have my loyalty and my respect, Raliph."

I smiled halfheartedly. "Thank you, Caraph."

Caraph stood and offered his hand to me. I stood to my feet. "If you are standing against a thousand men alone, I would stand with you," he whispered.

I bowed my head. "What if it was Larcos?"

"Then I would fight Larcos."

I smiled. "Perhaps, for this moment, I'll believe you."

# THE DARKEST STREET IN WHITESTONE

**Mercy**

She said she wanted me to see something but I had to dress like a peasant. Over the past while, I had a nice collection of rags to pull out whenever I played the part of the Compassionate Angel.

Nadia told me she would lead me there but that I had to take it in alone. She had been exploring the vast city of Whitestone as of late and knew it better than I did. It was dark, I was ready, and I heard a knock on the door.

"Mercy, are you ready?"

I nodded solemnly. Garcel was gone to protect Bellorn for a while as it feared attack.

Nadia would spend the days Garcel was gone to explore Whitestone. This time she was taking me with her.

We snuck out through the cellar and she led me onto the broad street. The light of the moon shone on the stone streets. The normally gray stones shone back white as the city was so named, lighting our path. These stones were known as star stones, for on a starlit night the stones shine white. Over this light, Nadia led me through the streets. It all felt surreal though I had walked the streets at night before.

We passed by many streets I had never seen. Slowly, I began to notice a change. The star stone was barely reflecting white for the light was barely reaching it. The shadows grew too deep.

She stopped before an ominous street. I peered on. The starlight had not reached it. Only the light in the windows of the buildings lining it gave light and even them, not much.

"Listen for the sounds, watch the people, smell their stench, and feel the grime," Nadia whispered. Then she disappeared.

Cautiously, I braved the first step…

"So tell me, Mercy. What did you find?" she asked when I reached the end.

Tears were in my eyes. I closed them and imagined it again.

"I pass by the darkest street in Whitestone

An old man lies dying at my feet

Three dirty children pass by in a hurry

And harlots cry in the street.

I hear the drunken calls from the tavern

I smell their puke and I see

A young child begging in raggedy clothes

In Whitestone in the darkest street.

In a house by the corner a woman's shrieking

A child cries from her wrath

My eyes are adjusted, now to the dim light

As I continue to pick out my path.

Dust rises with every step I take

Dust covering the beggar I see

It all isn't right, I wonder how I can live my life

When I know of this place and this street."

It all isn't right, I wonder how I can live my life

When I know of this place and this street."

# TO BEAR THE MARK OF ELLAR

I watched at my window again. Every night since he left. Three months had passed and I had not seen him. I wondered if he had died. Often questioned if I really loved him at all but I still waited every night to see if he'd appear. He did. I saw his lantern wave up and down twice as we had agreed would be our code. I jumped up in nervous expectation.

He was waiting for me at the edge of the forest. I ran into his embrace and he swung me around. We laughed.

"So much has happened, Mercy. I have so much to tell."

"How long can you stay?"

"I have two days until I must return to my new post," his face grew somber, "As Larcos' assistant."

I covered my mouth to keep from screaming. "Oh no! Oh Raliph, what happened?"

"It's a long story." He set me down on a log and sat down beside me. Taking my hand, he began to tell me his adventures since I had seen him last.

He had to leave. I feared this would be the last time we would see each other. He wiped the tears from my eyes.

"Will we ever get to be together?" I whispered. I could hear his heart beating next to my ear while he held me close.

"Someday, Ellar knows."

I sighed. "I hate Tarlen. Why can't people who love each other be together? I hate Tarlen, I hate this place."

"Somehow…" he dropped off. "It'll be okay."

I didn't believe him. I just cried. We both knew with him as Larcos' assistant and with myself already in hot water with the King. This would be our last meeting. Here as we were.

---

**Nadia**

Garcel, the King, and I were in the dinner hall. I had come later with Garcel. We didn't mean to be so late and we certainly didn't mean to eat with your father. The meal was had in silence. Garcel tried a few times to start a conversation but to no avail. In the wide hall covered in tapestries of noble deeds done long ago, the King sat, as head of the long table of dark wood, staring anxiously at the door. He was clearly waiting for something. He would glance at Garcel with clouded eyes then at the door again.

A guard entered and nodded at the king. He smiled and stood to his feet. Two guards entered after the first one carrying a struggling prisoner.

I glanced at Garcel, a look of sheer horror came over his face which he quickly covered up.

The prisoner was dragged to the middle of the room, crying and begging for mercy. Garcel stood as still as a statue beside me. His hand reached down to his sword-hilt.

The king smirked. "Well?" He turned to the prisoner.

The prisoner met Garcel's noble eyes then dropped to the royally carpeted floor.

The king nodded to one of the guards who took out a knife. Kneeling down to the ground where the prisoner was groveling, he placed the knife behind the ear of the poor man. They were going to cut his ear off! Blood spilt as the knife cut at the root of the ear.

"Ahh! Your Majesty!" he cried.

The king indicated the guard to stop.

"It was the Prince! He drugged our slave drivers…" he began to sob.

"And?" The king nodded to the guard.

"He masterminded the plan," he said when the knife was placed at his bleeding ear again.

"And?"

"The Compassionate Angel was disguised as a rebel captain."

The king stepped closer. An imposing figure above the whimpering slave. "And who is the Compassionate Angel?"

Garcel's eyes widened in fear.

The prisoner begged and wept piteously at the feet of the king. The king kicked him in the face. He sobbed more.

"Tell me!"

"The…" he stopped, "Princess Mercy."

The prisoner looked up to meet Garcel's eyes. "I'm sorry, Your Highness. They were going to torture me," he wept.

Take him away to the dungeons!" The king smiled wickedly.

"Let the poor wretch go, Father! Your quarrel is with me!" said Garcel, standing tall. He was taller than his father.

The king glanced over at his son. His eyes clouded with rage. "You! My own son!" He pointed at Garcel. "Betrayed me! Betrayed Tarlen! Betrayed the royal family! You are not worthy to ever be the king!"

My eyes widened in fear as the king in rage yanked a spear off the decorated wall. "Let the poor devil go free…" He kicked at the prisoner. His eyes wild with fury as he stared at his son. The warrior. The prince. My noble husband who I was soon to have a child for. He stood tall. A tear escaped his eye. He met his father's gaze bravely. Love and fear for my husband overcame me.

"Let the saving of that wretched worm you're so fond of be your last wish!" With that the king threw the spear into his own son's stomach.

"You don't love me, Garcel. You are not my son."

Blood spilt as the son of the king fell to the ground. His shirt had torn by the spear in his gut and the gold in his mark caught the king's eye. He approached.

"Nadia!" Garcel heaved. "Go find…Mercy!" His blood gushing out of his gut. "Get out of here!"

My husband's final wish. I ran past the guards before they had a chance to stop me. For a pregnant woman, I was fast.

"Stop her!"

I heard the clattering of the guards behind me. I ran down the halls and up the winding stairs. The image of my husband being speared by his own father running through my mind as I ran. Fear gave me strength.

I barged into Mercy's chambers. "The guards are chasing me! The king is after us!"

---

**Mercy**

When Nadia came in with that cry, my first thought was Justice and my hiding place. I grabbed her hand and dragged her into it. When I shut the doors, I heard voices in my room.

"They must've escaped through the window."

"A woman that big?"

"Well, they aren't in here."

Nadia whimpered. I covered her mouth. We sat still in the black room inside the palace walls. It was cold and I was already shaking in fear. I could only but imagine how Nadia was feeling.

The voices faded and the footsteps became faint. I removed my hand from Nadia's mouth and let her cry.

"He killed Garcel," she whispered.

"What?"

"Now he wants to kill us too…" she sobbed some more. "He saw the mark."

Oh no! I had to go warn Mother. "Nadia, stay here. If I don't return at midnight escape alone to the marshlands."

She grabbed my hand. "Where are you going?"

"Mother."

I strapped my sword to my waist with my dagger on the other side. My only thought was to warn my mother and protect her if it came to that. I slipped through my door and up the stairs towards my mother's secluded tower room. On my way upstairs, I met a guard. His eyes opened wide to see me. I punched him in the jaw and knocked him out with the butt end of my dagger.

When I finally reached her room, I noticed the door was ajar.

"Mother?!" I called.

Silence.

I looked around the room. Her favorite chair by the window had been knocked down and her needlepoint was on the ground.

"Mercy," a soft voice called.

I followed the sound to her bedroom.

I found her, on the floor, in a pool of blood.

"Mother," I fell to my knees beside her and took her hands.

"He did this, didn't he?"

"Mercy, listen to your mother," she said, her voice soft and hoarse. "My work in Tarlen is finished now."

"No, Mother!"

"I am so proud to call you my…my daughter…" she paused to catch her breath. "You have become a braver and stronger servant of Ellar than I…" she coughed. "Could ever be."

"Father will pay for this!" I said swearing under my breath.

"He has in his heart and that is enough."

My tears fell down onto her scarlet body. I hated him. I hated everything. I hated myself for my part in causing her death.

She looked up at me and met my eyes. "Mercy, don't regret my death…" she whispered. "I knew it would happen. It was my choice…"

I wanted to scream. I wanted to cry. I wanted to kill that scum of a being I called my father. I hated him. I hated Tarlen. I even hated Ellar.

"Don't forsake Ellar," she said softly, her eyes fading as they stared into mine. "I love you…my child."

Her eyes dropped. Her body went limp. Her face grew cold. She was gone.

"No, no, no," was all I could say. All I could whisper as I wept over my mother's dead body. Ooh, how I hated that cruel selfish man. Looking at her lifeless face everything felt so pointless now. I looked around the silent room. Sanity slowly returned to me and I realized I had to return to Nadia. We had to escape. I didn't want to. I would rather die with my mother and brother but Nadia couldn't escape alone.

# MERCY'S DOUBTS

I returned to Nadia in tears. She had waited silently for me in the room. Despite my grief, I couldn't help but be amazed she had not gone insane while I was away reliving her husband's death. She remained calm as she gently and fondly spoke of the courage of her husband when he faced the king in his death.

We waited in the dark until the whole palace was silent. When we were sure it was safe, we slipped out of the hiding place and down to the fated hall in which my beloved brother was speared. Nadia found him on the ground and knelt down beside him gently stroking his still face.

The hall was silent and the dark shadows remained still reflecting off the tapestries and furniture around us. On the opposite wall, I saw an arrangement of weapons. Two swords crossed and a place below which had once held a spear. I shivered in the eerie room. Not a sound. Only the sound of a young woman on her knees, weeping over her husband's silent body. His torn shirt was stained with blood. I could hardly bear to look at the huge gaping wound in his stomach. Beside him lay the spear which the king had dropped beside the body of his once beloved son.

I knelt down beside Nadia. Gently, I touched the face of my brother. My heart leapt. It was warm. "Nadia," I whispered. "Check his heart."

She put her ear to his breast. "He's still alive."

Nadia instantly began to bandage the wound from material from her skirt.

"Get two horses ready in the stable. Be quiet. I'll carry him," I ordered. Nadia obeyed.

I gathered all the strength I had, I picked up the powerful bloodstained form of my brother and threw him over my shoulder. I blessed the day I chose to train in the war and weaponry arts. It did good things for the muscles in my arms.

I prayed to Ellar that no one would awaken and stop me as I made my escape. Slowly, I made my way to the stables. The stone walls and floor echoed my every breath back to me. I struggled under the weight of my brother. With every step I took, I realized more that I was an outcast leaving my home forever. My comfortable life. My family. My orphanage. My happy dreams for the future. Soon to be mine no longer. I did wish to die but I knew Nadia needed me to be strong.

I descended a narrow passageway down the stairs towards the palace stables. Cautiously, I picked my every step so as not to trip and fall onto my face and crack my dying brother's head. I heard footsteps from around the corner. A shadow. I prepared to put Garcel down and draw my sword.

"Mercy, I know it's you," said a pretty voice.

It was Duelis. She had seen me. Should I kill her? Knock her out. Make her swear everything to secrecy.

She faced me, her eyes red and puffy as if she had been crying. "I found your disguises and told the king."

I stared at her unsure how to react.

"I didn't know he'd try to kill you…" New tears filled her eyes. "I'm so sorry. I was just trying to help my family…"

I bit my lip. My arm burned from the weight and I longed to cry myself from sheer exhaustion.

"Duelis," I began. "Steal my jewels from my room and everything of value I have in my room. Take it to Sunfare. I want her to be the Compassionate Angel."

"Duelis nodded.

"Don't tell anyone you met me tonight or what I said and you are forgiven."

Duelis wiped her eyes. "Yes, your highness."

I knew Duelis wasn't exactly the best person to trust with riches as her family was notorious for being thieves and traitors but I needed the task to be done and Duelis was the only person I was in a position to ask. Sunfare would become the next queen and in that position my orphanage need never fear for lack of financial help.

I stumbled to the stables exhausted. Nadia had two horses prepared. "How are we going to get through the gate?"

I sighed. Bribery would not be enough for convicted criminals to escape through the gate alive. We could go to the darkest street in Whitestone. No one would look for us there. But anyone could turn us in if we remained in Whitestone. We needed to get out of the city and get to the Marshlands.

"We will have to get of the gatekeeper and bring it up ourselves."

"How?"

I shrugged. "Pray to Ellar."

We strapped the unconscious body of Garcel onto the horse and led the horses out of the stable and into the street. Together, Nadia and I slipped through the shadows each holding the reins of a horse. I feared for poor Nadia. She was pregnant and had already had a terrible scare.

We edged along the shadow of the city's high wall. The streets were silent and the only light on the streets was the star stone under our feet. I stopped suddenly.

"What is it?"

"Shh. Don't you hear it?"

Nadia paused. "I hear weeping."

I gave the reins to Nadia and placed my hand on my hilt, ready in case of danger. Turning the corner, I saw a man on his knees weeping in the shadows holding a knife in his hand. Remembering the sight of Adann when he had been rejected by Sunfare, the pieces quickly came together and I cried out.

The man dropped the knife and it clattered in the shadowed star stone. He caught sight of me and bowed down to me when he recognized my face. Weeping, he groveled at my feet. "Your highness, please kill me. It is because of me your brother and mother were murdered."

I knelt down and lifted him up to face me. "It was our own choices which caused these misfortunes for us. Choices I would not change even if I had the chance to. We did what we knew we should and now we are paying for it dearly."

He continued to sob. I reached down and touched him gently with my hand.

"My brother is not dead. He is dying and we must get help for him but he is not dead."

Hope entered his eyes. "Let me be of service to you."

"I forgive you freely as my brother did."

"Please, let me do something or I shall destroy myself in guilt."

I sighed and thought for a moment. "Open the gate for us and escape the city of Whitestone." I pulled him up to his feet. "When you escape, find Ellar." Tears filled my eyes at the mention of Ellar. Thankfully, he did not see my tears. He disappeared into the shadows.

I wiped my eyes and returned to Nadia. How can I be benevolent and loving after witnessing the cold-blooded murder of my mother? Because of Ellar, the whole mess happened in the first place. Under my breath, I cursed the day I met Raliph and the day Ellar first touched me.

Mantar opened the gate for us. I did not know how but I did not care. We galloped out of Whitestone without looking back. Shouts sounded behind us from the watch on the wall. I hoped desperately the hard riding would not kill Garcel. It was a long ride and dangerous enough because we were now hunted not to mention Garcel was at death's door. I did not wish to pray.

# MERCY'S STRENGTH

We rode hard for a night a day and a night until we reached the outskirts of the marshlands. The sun's rays were barely reaching the dismal place as it hid behind the huge mountains beyond in the early morning. Vast stretches of mud, water, and overgrown weeds went on for miles. It was silent, except for the insects which whizzed about and sometimes hit my face. What a fool I was to think we'd find a safe haven in the Marshlands. We'd be safer with the rebels or in the villages.

Nadia turned to me. "How do we find them?"

I gulped. "People of the Marshlands!" I called. "We are weary wretches chased from our homes."

I noticed a movement in the distance.

"We ask for help and shelter in exchange for these horses and our services!"

Ten figures approached. They were covered in mud and had their hair matted in the straw of the plentiful weeds of the Marshes. Their clothes looked like straw interwoven in fish skin. And their eyes were sad, all sad.

Suddenly, I felt sick to my stomach. I might become like these people.

There were four men, one grey haired. Three women and three children. All dressed alike, all sad. I noticed one man did not have an arm. Another had a scar in the place of an ear. One of the women was bald. I swallowed hard. They took the reins of our horses and wordlessly led us through the marshes. We stopped at a small hole. A grey haired old man appeared out of it. He scrutinized us. "Take them all down to me. Take their horses."

A tall lank man bore Garcel off the horse and took him down into the hole. Another man pushed us down the hole after him.

I climbed down a rope ladder in a small tunnel-like decline. Nadia followed me. I wondered how she was doing with that child in her stomach.

We reached the bottom and I looked around. It was a small cave-like room. Stones lined the walls and the walls melded into the roof. The room was dimly lit by a strange glowing lamp which held no flame only a pale green light. The floor was lined in stones and fish skin. I wondered how they kept it from rotting or shriveling up. Seats from large stones were arranged in a semicircle covered in animal fur. The old man motioned for us to sit down.

Garcel was laid on the floor in the center of the room. I looked up to see the old man seated in an elevated chair. I assumed he was the governor of the Marshlanders. I glanced down at Garcel. He was still unconscious and barely breathing.

I heaved a deep breath and began to speak. "We have been banished from Tarlen and fled for fear of our lives. The man who lies here is this young woman's husband and my brother and…"

"You hope that I will heal this dying man and give you shelter from your enemies?" the grey haired man interrupted me.

"That was our hope," I said bowing respectfully.

He scowled. "We are a harsh people who live a harsh life. If I heal your brother, I demand payment."

"We give you our horses and all our jewels. Our weapons…"

"You must work!" He pointed at me. "You must provide food for yourself and that woman," he motioned at Nadia. "And you will pay me for my services."

I gulped. By no means was I too proud to work even though I came from a palace but I could not fathom how anyone could work hard enough to satisfy all he demanded. "Sir, I mean no disrespect but how can I as I do not know the ways of survival in these cold plains."

"Enstar!" he hollered. A young girl appeared dressed like the rest of them but she had soft eyes. She looked up at me curiously. "You will teach this genteel lady how to work for her keep!" He spat at the mention of me. I wanted to cry.

"You!" He pointed to Nadia. "Will aid me with your husband."

"Yes sir," Nadia replied showing no signs of intimidation. I wondered how she could remain so unfazed. Then I remembered how she was used to being yelled at by hard men from the rebel camp. This stern old man would seem like nothing compared to what she had been through.

I glanced around the room to notice strange symbols carved in stone in the walls. I shivered. This place felt evil.

Enstar motioned for me to follow her. She went up the ladder out the hole into the night. She led me to another hole hidden by a bush and pointed for me to get into it. It was a smaller version of the stern old man's hole. The same lighting fixtures, the same symbols. A boy probably a few years older than Enstar was sitting on the ground working on something that looked like a slingshot out of bone and skin. He glanced up at me as a slight light of interest caught his eye, then he lowered them back to his work. He was dressed like the rest of them.

Enstar led me to another room and removed a stone from the wall. It appeared to be a sort of cupboard from which she pulled out a dress identical to hers except bigger. She motioned for me to put it on. I did so.

I wondered why she never spoke to me. If she was afraid, forbidden or perhaps a mute? Maybe her tongue had been cut out like Meta's.

After I had been fully clad in the clothes of a Marshlander, Enstar took my previous clothing, gathered them up and put them in a corner and spread them out like a bed. Contented with that, she indicated me to follow her out of the hole again. My feet dragged for I had not slept in two days.

When we reached the top, I saw the sun had fully risen now. I smiled but Enstar did not pay attention. She gathered a big handful of mud and began to plaster it all over my nice skin then all in my hair! She messed up my hair then put grasses into it. I was so cold and tired, I just wanted to cry. Enstar did not speak and did not smile. I tried talking to her but she would only look at me then continue her work. What a dismal place these silent plains were.

Enstar dug her fingers into some mud and pulled out a worm. I followed her example. I found a big one. She nodded and motioned for me to continue. After gathering many slimy creatures, Enstar pulled out a slingshot made out of bone and skin that she kept in her belt. Slinking through the marshes and weeds, she made her way to a flat plain that was somewhat dry. She spotted a movement and hit it with a stone from her slingshot. It was a small furry marsh animal. It fell and laid stunned in the grasses. When we got closer to it, I realized it was a pandar. A marsh creature under a foot long that slinked through the marshlands with its long body and caught large insects. Though it was skinny and only about the length of my wrist to my elbow, it had a lovely pelt. Enstar drew her knife and cut its head off. Then she gave it to me. Together, we gathered up all the worms and carried the pandar back to her hole. She left the worms there but indicated for me to keep the pandar.

We left her hole and went back to the old man's. I found him over Garcel's body applying herbs to the wound and Nadia was watching above him. Beads of sweat were gathered on her forehead. I guessed she had been working long and hard.

"Only a pandar!" he exclaimed angrily. "That's all you can bring me after I've been slaving away for these many hours!"

I bit my lip. Enstar did not speak. I now understood why Enstar gave me the pandar. To appease the old man.

"If you don't bring better things than this by evening, I'll kill this man myself!" He pointed to Enstar. "Don't help her, Enstar. You're nearly Shatam' next victim. We might as well just give you up just to rid ourselves of your useless hide."

Enstar motioned for me to follow her out. I did. I did not wish to stay and listen to the old man rage. Out of the corner of my eye, I noticed the mud on Enstar's face was streaked in a line down her cheek. She was crying. As well she might. What sort of man would threaten a child because he suspected her of being kind?

I sighed. There was so much despair here. And who was Shatam?

"Listen Enstar, thank you for helping me today." I knelt down to her height. "I am so scared and so tired and your help has been the only kindness I have been shown since I ran away." I wiped a tear off her cheek. "If there's any way I can help you tell me."

She turned away from me. Her shoulders shook in silent sobs.

"If you are in danger, I can defend you. I am a warrior. If you need love, I can give it," I ventured further. I touched her shoulder. She grabbed my hand and dragged me further into the marshes.

We reached a muddy pond. Enstar knelt down on the ground next to it and began to teach me to fish with my bare hands. By the evening, I had two fish for the stern old man. Maybe he would spare my brother.

# MERCY'S BITTERNESS

Enstar gave me some roots to eat then sent me alone to see the old man. His eyes lighted to see what I had brought him. "Enstar too scared to come down and face her grandfather?" he sneered.

"She's your granddaughter!" I exclaimed shocked to think what an awful man would treat his granddaughter so.

"She needs to toughen up or she'll never make it. I'm hard on her for her own good," he said seeing my horror. "Her mother died from the sword of a Tarlen soldier. If she doesn't toughen up, she'll get killed." He met my eyes. "There are no free passes in the marshlands."

"There are other ways to help people become stronger…" I ventured.

"Not here. Not in the Marshlands."

I sighed. Nadia had fallen asleep and Garcel was still unconscious. I knelt down to him as he lay on a skin on the ground.

"How is he?"

"He has a good chance. Who is he?"

I bit my lip. If he learns that my brother is the prince of Tarlen, he'll hate us all. And if there is a reward on us why wouldn't he hesitate to turn us all in?

"He's a mighty warrior isn't he?" he pressed.

I shrugged. Not willing to meet his gaze.

"You're in the Marshlands now. No one cares who you were, what you did…"

"We're in a lot of danger from many people. I do not wish to risk anymore lives on our account or make any more enemies. At least not until my brother is well."

I noticed Garcel stirred on the floor. I took his hand. He opened his eyes. The old man instantly took a cup of something and forced it down his throat. He coughed.

"Ow," he said weakly.

I smiled. "You had us so scared."

"I'm not dead?"

"No, Tarlen probably thinks you are though."

"Nadia."

"She's safe, resting."

He relaxed. "What happened?"

"We escaped with you on horses to the Marshes."

"What are you wearing?"

I laughed. "I'm wearing what the Marshlanders wear to blend in. So people passing by won't see us."

"To get to the Pits and back…" A deep pain passed over his eyes.

"Yes."

He paused a moment thinking, a cloud passed over his face. "Mother?"

I bit my lip. "Killed by the king."

"The monster," he swore under his breath.

Tears welled up in my eyes. I looked around nervously remembering that we were not alone but the old man had left leaving us a moment of privacy which I was grateful for.

"Ellar be thanked you two are safe."

"Ellar," I whispered more to myself than anyone else. Tears filled my eyes. "If it hadn't been for Ellar, we wouldn't be stuck here in this deplorable hole."

A strange light entered Garcel's eye but I did not care. "I hate Father. I hate this place. I hate Ellar," I said.

Garcel was silent for a while. Finally he spoke. "He loves you, Mercy. You'll understand someday."

My eyes filled with tears. I turned away and left his side. I saw Enstar waiting for me at the top of the hole. Wiping my eyes, I went up to her. I noticed her looking at me oddly when I wiped my eyes from leftover tears. Biting my lip, I set my face forward.

The old man appeared suddenly and pulled me aside. "Your brother bears a strange golden mark on his breast. What does it mean?"

"Ask him," I said coldly.

He sneered at me. Even with an old decrepit face, I couldn't believe how anyone could make themselves look as ugly as he was. Poor Enstar for having such an awful ugly grandfather. "Get to work with the little brat," he pointed at Enstar.

"No wonder she doesn't speak," I whispered. He heard me.

"She doesn't want to be found by Shatam and his servants. She's nearly his."

I wondered what he meant but I had a terrible feeling. His voice sent chills down my spine. He disappeared. I turned back to Enstar. Once again, tears.

She led me away and we worked together for hours. Enstar taught me many things. She also taught me how to eat everything disgusting without making it look gross.

She slurped a worm and swallowed it then motioned for me to do the same. I grimaced but did it. She smiled. I was entranced.

Enstar was a rare child indeed. Her soft eyes sometimes dulled and I wondered if they were weak.

She gathered many roots and a strange red berry which grew on a scarcely found bush. Sometimes, she would bring many of her findings to the boy in her hole. We saw other Marshlanders. All sad and most silent. I myself began to feel their damp hopelessness settle in on me.

It was getting dark again and I was growing tired. Enstar was beginning to stumble and her normally alert manner began to wane. We neared a plain covered in bushes. Enstar tripped over something in front of me.

"Enstar!" I exclaimed when I realized what she had tripped over. A sleeping Tarlen soldier. I ran and hid behind a bush but Enstar was grabbed before she could follow.

"Marsh scum!" The angry soldier growled holding her by both her thin wrists in one hand. Then, he drew his knife. There were five of them. Two soldiers, the rest I suspected were judging by their chains were rebel prisoners. They all awoke.

"What is it Jasor?"

"A little Marsh worm," Jasor replied.

"Kill it and go back to sleep."

"No!" I stepped out from my hiding place. The other soldier got up and drew his sword. I drew my stone knife.

He smirked and approached me in confidence. I blocked his first blow then pushed my dagger's handle over to his and twisted it so he lost grip of his sword. It landed on the ground and I kicked him in the stomach. He joined his sword on the ground. I pushed my knife onto the back of my opponent's neck. "Let the girl go or I will kill your friend."

Jasor let go of Enstar.

"Run, Enstar!" I commanded. She obeyed.

Jasor grabbed me from behind and pushed me to the ground. He held his blade at my heart.

"Jasor, wait! Look at her!"

Jasor's eyes widened. "Princess Mercy!"

He backed away and dropped his sword. I looked toward the bushes. Enstar had disappeared. The three prisoners watched in silence. I didn't take a lot of time to observe them though. I sat up.

"She's hiding from her father," Phintas said quietly. Jasor just stared at me.

"There's a reward for her isn't there, Phintas?"

I clutched my dagger ready to defend myself.

"Give her a break! Her father killed her brother for doing one of the few decent things done in Tarlen history by men. Then in his rage, the king killed her mother for who knows what. And instead of wallowing in her grief she, singlehandedly, spirited her pregnant sister-in-law and herself to the Marshes. The whole while fleeing her angry father for helping her brother and trying to make Tarlen less of a perilous place for children," said Phintas pushing Jasor away and offering me his hand to help me up.

I stared at him in shock.

"I'm sorry about all the grief your father has caused you," he said gently, helping me to my feet.

Hot angry tears welled up in my eyes from anger at my father. I bit my lip.

Phintas met my eyes. "If there were more people like you, Tarlen wouldn't be such an awful place of oppression, greed and bloodshed."

I could not speak. Unsure how to react to the sudden kindness from a soldier, a soldier who had not given a thought to the life of Enstar. Why should my presence cause such gentleness from a trained killer? I tried to think of some benevolent speech as I often would use in such instances but my heart was too full of bitterness. It would be awful for him to see how far I had fallen from such a noble savior to a bitter slave. Inwardly, I cursed the day I chose to help a soul. "You…" I paused to draw a shuddered breath," could change it."

"No," said Jasor. "No one can and no one will, so what's the point? Just get what you can out of this damned place."

I stepped back. "And why can't you change it?"

Jasor smirked at me like I was some sort of joke. "Because we're all too scared for our own skins, Princess," he pointed at me. "Look what happened to royalty for doing something good. We're common people trying to survive and keep our families alive."

"You're scared," I whispered.

"Yes," said Phintas.

A million thoughts went through my mind at once.

"What you did, all the good will be forgotten and nothing will change," said Jasor. Phintas glared at him.

Tears flowed down freely from my pent up emotions. "No." I stifled a sob. "No! I refuse to believe that. My life has not been pointless."

"Everyone's is!" said Jasor. His brows furrowed, angry. I searched his eyes and saw hopelessness. "You're no better than the rest of us, Princess! You and your fool brother!"

"Jasor!" Phintas rebuked. "Shame!"

Jasor shrunk back. Phintas could be an intimidating man when he wanted to be, glowering down at Jasor who was shorter than him. Jasor bowed his head. Phintas looked up and met my eyes.

"You could. If I am to die, let my legacy live. Do something to stop the oppression. Love somehow."

He bit his lip and shook his head. "No, Princess. I am afraid."

# MERCY'S DARKEST HOUR

I stepped away. I disappeared behind the bushes. I didn't know where I was going nor did I care. I ran. Reaching a desolate plain, I knelt down and wept. The soft breeze blew my dark tangled hair. I touched my skin feeling the cold mud and grime covering my body. The mud and grime made me feel like the scum I was kneeling on. Tears overflowed my eyes. "Ellar," I whispered. "Please."

No one came. I felt nothing. I saw no one.

"Ellar," I said more frantically. I began to feel frightened. Howls like that of Urfanes reached my ears. Fog settled down on me. I stood to my feet. Fear fully upon me.

"Ellar!" I screamed. "If you care at all! Help me!" I fell to my knees again numb. "I don't want to fade into this nothingness of fear…" I sobbed into my hands.

I heard no one. I felt nothing. I saw no one. I cried more.

Dark shadows passed through the fog. The howls grew closer. The fog grew thicker. An icy hand of terror gripped my very being.

I closed my eyes and remembered his warm hand on my shoulder. I had to believe he was still good. I had nothing to hold onto but that. Putting my hand on my shoulder, I dreamt of the first time I had ever felt his hand. Something, even just a memory of hope. A memory of goodness and love in this desolate place. I hated him but in that moment, in my fear, hopelessness and hurt, he was the only one I could hold onto. If he even still cared.

I opened my eyes to see the fog had thinned and the dark

shadows were moving away. My mind was clear now. What were those shadows, I wondered. I did not know.

"Perhaps, there is more darkness in this place than I imagined," I whispered to myself.

I clutched my heart in fear, did Ellar care about me anymore in the Marshes as I couldn't save Tarlen? Would he still save me?

I bravely passed away from the fog and dark shadows. There was another task I had to do.

# WHAT MERCY CANNOT CHANGE

Trembling, I made my way back to the camp where the two Tarlen soldiers were sleeping. However much I wanted to pretend I didn't care, I did. Ellar had forgotten me or perhaps the evil in the Marshlands was too strong for him. Either way I heard no one, saw no one and felt nothing. All I could do was remember. But did I even want to? Why should I? But there remained that burning power within me making me care.

In the silent way I knew so well, I neared Phintas' sleeping body. At his belt, the key to the prisoners' chains hung. I unfastened it. Stealthfully, I unchained the sleeping prisoners. That accomplished, I shook them each awake. All of them had been beaten and appeared weak. They stared at me in shock.

"Princess Mercy?"

"Go now, before they wake up."

Two of them ran glad for the chance to escape the Pit. The other stood before me without budging an inch.

"My name is Taran but I am known as a Blackheart," he said softly. "Don't know if you recognize me, I was your guard."

My eyes widened.

"But as I watched you even I could not hate you. I'm sorry."

"For what?"

"For never seeing anyone but myself. Phintas was right, Tarlen would be a decent place if there were more people like you and your late brothers."

I noticed Jasor stir.

"Go," I whispered fiercely.

"Forgive me," he pleaded.

I nodded. "Of course, now go."

He obeyed and disappeared behind the bushes. I drew my knife and cut the dirt where the prisoners had been sleeping.

"*Bring Adann here to meet me*," I wrote, "*Princess Mercy.*"

---

When Enstar saw me, she embraced me. Since that day, she did not leave my side. We told no one what happened that night.

---

I worked hard for weeks with Enstar in order to pay the old man. His name was Cranteng, suited him, he was a crank. Garcel, Nadia and myself did not reveal who we were to him for fear of betrayal.

Poor Nadia got bigger and bigger as she stood by Garcel for many long days and nights. Garcel slowly improved and Enstar and I worked hard to appease her grandfather so he would continue on that path.

I didn't have time to think anymore. The remembrance of Ellar and Raliph faded and I began to forget about everything but hard work and sad eyes. I was becoming one of them. Nadia and Garcel weren't. But they hadn't seen what I had or done what I did.

Ellar didn't care anymore, so why should I?

# MERCY AND SHATAM

"He's here!" His wide eyes darted about. "Where's Enstar?"

"She went to bring her brother some worms," I replied.

Cranteng's eyes fell.

"I'll go find her."

"No! You must hide! Shatam is greedy!" The poor man shuddered and stumbled around half mad in fear.

I didn't care. If Enstar was in danger, I sure wasn't about to sit around and let it happen.

"Get my brother and Nadia, I'm going out."

I crawled out of Cranteng's hole unsure who, or what, I was going to face.

It was twilight as I stepped out. I saw dim blue lights in a distance with moving cloaked figures. The Marshlanders watched me approach the lights in fear. The more I neared the lights the more I felt a heavy evil settle on me. Terror began to grip me and I longed to run back.

"Ellar, if you can. Help me now," I whispered.

I looked back to see Garcel and Nadia watching me. "Pray to Ellar for me," I mouthed. Garcel nodded.

Swallowing hard, I approached. The cloaked figures matched the descriptions of Morglin's servants I had read in that history book. The shadows of Urfanes flitted past me and I heard their howls. I could not make out what all was happening but I could hear Enstar's screams. As I neared, I realized the cold blue lights were lanterns being held by Morglin's servants. They stood, solemnly, motionless, ominous. My hair stood up on the back of my neck when I caught sight of them. I forced my feet to go forward.

"Ellar, I'm sorry," I whispered tears filling my eyes. "Help me now."

The silent figures saw me and parted. Now, I could see what the creatures were surrounding. Enstar was lying on her back on a stone crying. Beside her stood the creature I knew so well. Morglin. I saw the black and red marks on her skin. Her clothes were torn and written on her face, bitter agony.

My anger gave me courage. "By Ellar," I called. "I demand you, Morglin to leave that girl alone!"

Morglin looked up at me, startled. In that moment, I remembered how terrible his eyes were when they met my own. His blackened form backed away a bit from Enstar. I continued to approach him, my hair still sticking up at the back of my neck. The cloaked figures did not dare near me. An Urfane snarled at me but did not attack.

"Ellar, Ellar, Ellar," I whispered over and over again.

"I bear the mark of your victor, Morglin!" I called and, trembling, bared my heart to show the golden letters. The light from the golden word shone up at my face and nearly blinded me. The blue lights went out immediately and the cloaked figures turned into black shadows and disappeared. The Urfanes yelled and ran. Morglin flashed his smoldering eyes at me. I kept walking towards him.

"You think you're so strong, you faithless outcast!" he hissed at me. "You turned your back on him so why should he help you now? Why should he care about you now? You're no use to him."

I thought on his words. The hope in my heart dimmed as did the light from my mark though it did not disappear. Tears welled up in my eyes. I stopped. Morglin slunk towards me his claw-like hand reaching towards me ready to take hold of me. "You're worthless now. Look at you. He despises you. You're nothing but a coward. You can't compete with me. Stop fooling yourself. You're not a princess, you're my slave!" He grabbed my wrist. It burned. He grabbed me with his cruel eyes tearing me up inside. His words seared through my being. I screamed. My knees buckled. I felt my body grow cold. My strength left me. I could not tear my eyes from his as they burned a hole inside me. His words repeated over and over in my head, *"Worthless, despised, coward, outcast, slave."*

With the last bit of strength I had, I cried, "Ellar!"

Morglin let go. He backed away and ran away like an animal. Behind me, a hand gently touched my shoulder. The touch I remembered but had not felt in so long. "Mercy, I was always with you," he said.

Then, he approached poor Enstar who was weeping where she had been left. He gathered her in his arms and held her. Ellar.

The Marshlanders began to appear. They neared us cautiously.

I went to my brother, still trembling from my brush with death, and he embraced me. He was still very weak but I felt safe in his arms nonetheless. I cried.

Cranteng neared his granddaughter in the lordly figure's arms. He knelt down in fear to he who had saved the child. Enstar's brother limped to the scene. I soon found myself in a crowd of many Marshlanders making no effort to hide themselves.

I glanced back to Ellar, Enstar, and Cranteng. The people watched but would not near Ellar any more than ten feet.

"Can you protect Enstar?" he begged. "Take her wherever you want just protect her from this evil." The desperate man began to weep at Ellar's feet. I felt sorry for him suddenly. Perhaps, he did love Enstar. Ellar raised him to his feet and gently passed Enstar into his arms. I noticed gold underneath Enstar's dress. He touched Cranteng's shoulder and said something I did not hear.

He turned to me again. I ran to him and fell in his arms. "I'm so sorry, Ellar," I sobbed.

He stroked my hair softly. "I never left you. I will never leave you. Whatever happens. However you feel, I will not forget you."

Garcel neared us. Ellar turned to him. Garcel bowed nobly before him. "My Lord."

They walked away from the crowd. I wondered what they were discussing. The crowd of people around me distracted me from watching the two as they ventured off. Enstar took my hand. She smiled broadly. She showed me her mark.

"We match!" she laughed aloud. "I'm not scared anymore."

Cranteng glanced at her nervously. Enstar wasn't about to be quiet. She ran over to her brother and hugged him. "I'm not scared! I'm not scared!"

He brother broke a smile.

"I have Ellar so I'm not scared."

She danced and laughed. For once, she finally looked like a careless happy eight year old. I laughed and danced with her.

Ellar and Garcel returned and all the children crowded around him. He knelt down and touched them all. More and more people appeared. The adults looked worried to see their children around such a powerful being but the children wouldn't be stopped. Soon the entire ground which had been crowded Urfanes and Morglin's servants was covered in laughing children. I smiled but the reality of what I had just faced hit me. I breathed hard. Garcel caught me as I fell back.

He drew me away from the crowd. "Tired?"

"Yes," I replied. "Shaken up."

"Not your daily routine."

I smiled. "No."

His eyes darted over to Ellar. His face was troubled.

"What did Ellar say to you?"

"He asked me if I wanted to go through with it," he whispered hoarsely.

"With what?"

"Following him."

"What did you say?"

Garcel met my eyes unwavering. He bit his lip and drew a shuddered breath. "I said yes."

# RALIPH'S SECRETS

**Raliph**

I cannot lie and tell you Mercy that I refused the position. I had to take it or I would be sure to be questioned. But how could I defend a man I wanted dead? A man I resented with the very core of my being.

"I'll go in with you to speak to him. Perhaps, he'll change his mind," said Caraph.

I strapped my weapons onto my person.

"But perhaps he'll train you beyond what I ever could."

"Train me so I am strong enough to fight him himself? Some man I am."

"Larcos is not loveable but he's scared. He knows if he doesn't become king before he grows old, he'll be killed and preceded. He chose you because he's heard you're loyal to your commanding officer."

"He thinks that I will respect and defend him as I do you, though he has done nothing to deserve such?"

Caraph sighed. "Raliph, you are a fine man. You don't have qualities I myself envy to great extent. Do whatever your convictions grant as right. May the power in you preserve you."

I bowed.

I stepped to the door of Larcos' tent. Caraph gripped my shoulder. "Whatever happens, Raliph, your fool convictions. I will defend you, even to Larcos."

I put my hand on his and met his eyes. "Thank you."

I stepped inside. Larcos sat on a decorated chair. The room held many beautiful tapestries of red, purple, blue, gold, and silver. On the ground, rich carpets were laid out to cushion where the detestable creature walked. A few extensively adorned wooden chairs were dotted around the tent. Larcos himself was no more modest than his tent. His jewelry, of which he was notorious for wearing in excess, studded in precious stones, weighed his neck and adorned his person. Apparently, he considered himself a king already in regards to his extravagance. The band of gold and sparkling precious stones circling round his head added to the allusion. Behind him stood his guard.

"Raliph," he greeted me with a smile. "I have heard many things of you; I wanted to discover the truth of them for myself." He stood and walked around me, inspecting every inch of me like I was a prized horse. "You are strong enough," he said. "Kill him." He pointed to his guard behind his chair.

The guard drew his sword. With wild imploring eyes, he begged me to spare his life. I looked back at him, evenly evaluating him. His hand trembled as it gripped his blade. I looked down at my hand to discover it was shaking too.

"No," I said.

The guard's eyes widened in surprise. He lowered his sword slowly but remained still on guard.

"Why not?" Larcos demanded.

"Why?" I said back at him. I knew he had a temper that few should reckon with but I knew I would have to die eventually and I hope to cause the fewest to die as possible in the process.

"Because I, your commander, demand it."

I bowed my head to the furious man. "In no way do I belittle your authority but I will not kill a man for no real reason."

"He's a terrible guard."

"Perhaps, I could request the opportunity to train him?"

Larcos tightened his grip on his sword hilt in anger, then seeming to change his mind, loosened it. "Caraph was right," he said quieter now, his tone even. "You allow none to terrify you."

He motioned to the guard. "Leave us!"

The guard bowed to me then left.

Larcos sat down on his elaborate chair. I stood erect before him.

"Caraph informed me that you are brave, loyal, skilled, and valiant," he began. "The only thing you aren't is obedient."

I remained silent. My eyes fixed ahead, my fists clenched behind my back as an outlet for my anger towards the man standing before me.

"I see you are strong and intelligent…"

His voice went on but I was not listening. Instead, I observed him. Considered the man who had tortured Garcel, threatened Mercy, and killed thousands. I studied him carefully and noticed a troubled light in his eyes. Yes, Caraph was right. Larcos was scared. Possibly scared of me, for though I knew I was little short of a coward, I was a better man than Larcos. Within me, my heart became weary suddenly when I thought of all the bloodshed and cruelty I observed in this camp from the Cansten Army. I desired to die, change it, or die trying. I was trapped. If Larcos wished me to be his shield bearer, I would be forced to hide all goodness from Ellar in order to obey the cruel monster. What could I do? Could I refuse the position without question? No. What could I do? How could I avoid this position which would be sure to be my person or my morality's end?

"You are a man of few words, Raliph," said Larcos, bringing me out of my thoughts.

My face burned. His smug expression showed he clearly

believed I was afraid of him. Maybe I was but still I hated him. Those cold hungry eyes darting around the room like an animal looking for a meal, his haughty smirk, triumphant and sure to get whatever he wanted, augh! It took all my willpower not to draw my sword and murder the man in that moment.

"The king is drawing some of his fortifications away from Nalstrom. I intend to lead the battle," he said.

Nalstrom lay three days away by horse. It was one of the few fortified cities in the center of the farmland. It was mainly used for the king's purposes to collect tax from the farmers in the villages surrounding it. It was only a day away from Bellorn which made it difficult to keep because Bellorn was a strong Tarlen fortification and would not hesitate to save the city of Nalstrom. The city had once been taken by the rebels about fifty years ago but the king took it back and fortified it to be even stronger. The city would have to be taken in stealth and burned to the ground if we were victorious so it could not be rebuilt again.

"May I ask why Nalstrom?"

"Prisoners and supplies. If it falls under our power, we do not have to fear it when we attack Bellorn. There are many who we could recruit in that city and we can collect some crops from the villagers around who are not in allegiance with us."

A thousand images passed through my mind. Scenes from battles past that I knew all too well. No, how could I go to war against a city that never did me wrong and cause such horrific devastation that should only happen in a nightmare? I did not want to attack Nalstrom. I did not want to attack anyone.

"You will be my shield bearer for that attack and if you do well, you will have the position permanently. What do you say?"

I bowed stiffly. "My lord."

"Good! We leave tomorrow. Inform Caraph that I will need

him and his command for this job."

I step out of the lavish tent hating my very name. "Ellar, why? What am I to do?"

My mind raced trying to rationalize my morality with my situation but whatever way I looked at it, I was still trapped. I could not take prisoners to be branded, enslaved, tortured and raped. The thought of it made my stomach lurch. I wanted to die. Anything to avoid fighting alongside Larcos and helping him in his devises.

I walked over to the smithing tents where young boys were trained and adjoining that where those who refused to join the rebel army were tortured and killed. It was a scare tactic Larcos used to turn the boys into fighting machines. I hated it that he forced the poor boys to train nearby the horrific torture instruments. It was beyond cruel in my mind. I hated that man. And I was not better as I did not oppose him.

My young friend saw me and ran up and embraced me. Other young recruits shyly ventured near. They each were clumsily holding swords in their hands and were cut up from training and doing a bad job of it. I motioned for them to come closer, drew my sword and showed them each how to hold their swords.

"Now imagine I'm going to kill you with my sword, what would you do with it?" I slowly held out my sword at the boy nearest to me.

"I'd push it away," he said and used his sword to push mine down to the ground.

"That's right. What if I were coming down on your head? How would you react?" I positioned my sword above his head and brought it slowly down towards the boy.

"I'd step away," he said as he did so.

"Now what if you wanted to bring me down while I was in this position?"

He hit my legs lightly with his sword. I went down dramatically, much to their amusement. "Now, you could try to disarm me or stab me quickly," I finished and stood up again.

I continued to teach them basic defense and attack strategies. The boys' previous trainers did not dare interrupt me. No one but Larcos or a cocky commander would ever try to challenge me. That was how it was and I was okay with that.

Night began to show its signs of appearing. I sent the boys all to bed to get a good sleep for their training tomorrow which I unfortunately wouldn't be a part of. Looking at their faces, nearly peaceful and happy, I felt accomplished.

I set my pace towards my own tent. I had to check my weapons and supplies for a four day journey.

"My lord, Raliph." A shape approached me as I was about to enter my tent.

I put my hand on my sword hilt.

"It is I, Larcos' guard, who you spared."

"What do you want?" I said impatiently, not wishing to have a long conversation.

He faced me forcing me to pay attention to him. "Thank you, for sparing my life back there," he bowed. "I expected him to kill you."

I shrugged. "I suppose he'd prefer to procrastinate that event."

"I owe you a debt beyond what I could ever repay."

I sigh inwardly. "What is your name?"

"Anwell," he replied.

"Anwell, no man should thank another for doing him the service of not murdering him in cold blood. If anything, I should apologize for even considering it." With that, I went into my tent.

Staring at the roof of my simple tent, I lay on my back on a pallet. Right and wrong melded together in my heart causing my blood to boil up in the fury. They do not mix. They cannot. Rage fills my heart so I could barely control myself as I stared into the darkness around me. No place should be so terrible. No war so brutally unjust. And no man should have to choose between torturous death and being a coldhearted beast.

---

The stone walls loomed above us. Larcos smiled when he saw it, his eyes hungry for battle. "Caraph, take half your men to the third watchtower. Leave the rest with me," he ordered.

Caraph motioned for half his men to follow him and disappeared toward the third watchtower.

I looked up at the stone walls in the stillness of the night. The city was not large but it was well fortified. The only way to defeat this city would be to do it quickly. If the alarm were to be raised, we would have half the Tarlen army on us from Bellorn. Larcos and the rest of us were hiding behind farmhouses or any shadow which would sufficiently conceal us. I stood beside Larcos as we waited for a signal from Caraph to move in.

"Prepare to approach," he said. I set my eye on the next shadow I would run to.

"Go."

I darted to the shadow and prepared my arrow on the string. Took my target and let it fly. Arrows whizzed up above me and took down the watchmen in the watchtowers before they could make a sound.

We slunk from shadow to shadow to the moat in silence but in haste. We knew the drill. We had done this many times. I swam the moat and pressed my body against the wall. Larcos copied me. A man climbed onto my shoulders, and another man hoisted himself up the human ladder. I stood my ground and set my teeth for the uncomfortable procedure. Not a word was said nor sound heard from among us.

After several men reached the top, they pulled us up with rope. We slunk along the wall to hide in the watchtowers. Caraph and his men had dismantled the alarm bell in one watchtower, the rest of us dismantled the rest in the second and third. The city remained silent in its slumber.

Caraph and his men went to the barracks where the Tarlen soldiers slept and set it in flames. Cries of fear erupted from the building and many men ran from the flaming houses shirtless with no weapons to defend themselves.

The rebels laughed at them, beat them up, and roped them together. Larcos liked Tarlen soldiers as slave soldiers to take all the missions that it would be unlikely to escape from alive. He would brand them and once branded it would be impossible for them to return to Tarlen society. I did not linger my gaze upon the poor soldiers, burned out of their slumber at night by their enemies to be beaten and taken away forever.

Larcos and I jumped down off the wall and raised the gate. Hundreds of Cansten soldiers ran into the city with flaming torches bellowing war cries. They ran from house to house pillaging and murdering whoever stood in their path. Taking whatever they wanted prisoners, money, wine, and weapons. Screams of terror arose in the city and echoed in my burning heart. The city had been taken. We tore down the walls and burned every house.

I watched in horror as a beautiful homes burned in red furious flames of the wrath of the rebel soldiers. A man in his nightdress, an older woman, and a young girl with a child in her arms fled from what was once their home. They killed the man and the woman and tore the screaming baby from the girl's arms and tied her up. The child cried alone in the street, abandoned. My conscience seared me like the hot flames burning every building I could see. How could I be part of such evil?

"Hey you!" I pointed to the man who was dragging the girl towards the gate. "Give her to me!"

"But sir…" he protested.

I drew my sword. "Give her to me!"

He let go of her and dodged into the ally. I looked around. Flaming houses, dying men, and screaming women and children. I stepped over the girl's dead father. Making sure no one was watching me; I picked up the crying child. I drew my knife and cut the ropes on the wrists of the girl. "Stay close to me and you will keep your child," I said. Her eyes were wide in terror but nevertheless she obeyed.

We had taken the city. Now in the quickest way possible, we had to loot it and burn it to the ground. With my axe, I tore down a part of the wall. At least doing that job, I would not be watching all the terrible things going on in the city.

"Someday Raliph," I whispered to myself. "You'll be brave and do the right thing."

The sun was beginning to rise. Larcos ordered us to take our newly attained possessions and fly. We would meet at camp. I took a horse and one for Larcos from a burning stable, tied our personal prisoners to other steeds and on them, we fled back to camp.

The city had been demolished. The dead and dying were strewn all over the streets. The whole city was in flames. I had helped do that. I was part of it. I looked back one more time as we galloped away. Living flames and smoke devoured the once beautiful city. The cries of the dying faded only to the cries of the child in the young woman's arms sitting in front of me on my horse.

Larcos smirked as he looked back at the city. More jewelry than normal was hanging on his neck and arms. Rage seethed me at the sight of the greedy man. I tried not to look at him. But he would not allow that as he reined his horse nearer to mine.

"You did well, Raliph," he said. "Kill the child." He nodded to my prisoner and her baby.

"I'd rather not."

"I don't like soft men."

"You know I don't kill pointlessly."

He glared at me. "Alright, do what you want but don't go spreading your ideas around, could become vastly inconvenient."

I bit my lip. I had every intention of spreading my ideas around. So far I was doing a bad job of it but I would, eventually. Someday, I would get the courage to be more than just a 'soft' man, but I would be a fearless man who would fight for right causes.

The girl trembled as she sat in front of me, her child, bound to her, wept feeling her fear. I could only imagine how terrified they both must be. The girl wept softly. I hated myself. Why was I such a coward? I could have saved her family. I might have been killed but then at least my life would have been worth something. The only way I could be a servant of Ellar would be outright rebellion. Wait! I had a plan.

# RALIPH'S PLAN

Larcos agreed to allow me to return home before I officially began as his shield bearer. I planned to see Mercy and talk to her about all that was happening before I made any decisions.

It was a dark night when I reached the edge of the forest. I waved my lantern to her window, up and down then side to side twice. Then I waited. No one came. I waved again and approached the castle.

"Raliph!" someone said to me.

I turned quickly. "Sunfare!?" I was alarmed. "Where is Mercy?"

She breathed hard. "Raliph." she embraced me. "Garcel was murdered by the king. Mercy fled with Nadia to the Marshlands."

I stepped back. "Oh no." I felt like I had been struck.

"Raliph, are you okay?" She took my hand.

"The woman I love is in exile and a dear friend of mine is dead." I slumped down onto the ground. "What of her orphanage?"

"I'm taking care of it."

I covered my face in my hands. "Will she forget me?"

Sunfare sighed. "I don't know."

I wept.

---

I returned to the rebel camp in full resolve to count my life as nothing. On my return journey, I left small strips of purple material on stones. No one would notice unless they were looking for them.

When I returned, I pretended to be happy with my position. My tent was placed beside Larcos' and I was also in charge of checking his weapons before each battle.

Larcos was basking in his victory and sending out small raid parties. He had the soldiers we took branded then put some in irons to sharpen his and his army's weapons, others he enlisted in the army for dangerous missions, and the higher ranking ones he tortured for information on the fortification and defense strategies of the other mighty cities. It made me sick.

I went to my tent and collapsed on my bed. I sighed angrily.

"You seem disturbed, my lord."

I looked up. I had forgotten I had told her to stay in my tent and she would not be harmed. She was sitting in the corner rocking her child quietly.

"Very disturbed."

"What is wrong, my lord?"

I growled. "I hate this place! This entire place. I hate Tarlen!"

"Why, my lord?"

"Just call me Raliph. I'm not a lord."

"You saved me, my child. To me you are a lord."

"Well, not to me."

"Why do you hate Tarlen?"

"What good is there in Tarlen that is not destroyed by the greedy and the bitter?"

"You are not like the rest here?"

"That child had a father, grandparents, possibly cousins," I pointed to the baby in her arms. "…Could've been raised, healthy and happy. Everything being provided…now…" I ran my fingers through my hair; bit my lip to keep myself from exclaiming out vocally in my anger.

"There is more to this, isn't there?"

I nodded my face down. "The girl I love has been banished to the marshlands and her brother murdered in cold blood."

A soft hand touched my shoulder. I turned to see her face. It was tearstained, dark circles were under her eyes. "I got to get you out of here." I stood to my feet.

"How?"

"I'll tell you tonight. Stay here."

She watched me go, puzzled. I walked towards the fire. As usual, men were drinking. They had a Tarlen soldier stripped and were doing their best to humiliate him as much as possible. There were only about a hundred of them, a small raid party just returned from their small mission. Larcos was in his tent having an important meeting with the commanders.

When the drunks saw me approach, they stopped and stared at me, it was uncommon for me to approach the center of the camp where the brawls occurred. The soldier laid face flat on the ground. A few women were also there but they weren't the main entertainment.

"I want a girl!" I yelled.

Obediently a young girl, probably around sixteen was pushed at me. I grabbed her wrist then approached the Tarlen soldier. He moaned as he lay there naked, near the fire.

I stooped down and picked him up by the hair. "And a slave to prepare my weapons for the morning!"

I yanked the poor man up and held the girl by the wrist. No one dared move a muscle to protest my actions. I dragged the two to my tent.

The soldier groaned when I shoved him inside and pushed him

on the ground. "Here!" I threw a robe on him. He writhed and moaned underneath it. I studied him for a moment to notice that he had burn marks on him as well as blood. That oh so familiar anger came rising up inside me again.

I knelt down to him and touched his bare shoulder. I covered it with the robe.

"What is your name?"

"Ultan."

I lifted him up and set him down on my bed. The two girls watched intrigued. He kept his eyes lowered. I could only imagine the pain and shame he was experiencing. Pouring a cup of wine, I gave it to him. Then I turned to the girls.

"What is your name?"

"Timma," she replied shyly

"Nice to meet you, Timma," I said. "My name is Raliph."

Her eyes were wide staring at me.

"Listen Timma, I know a safe way out of the forest. I have the path marked in red. I need you to take it, with her," I pointed to the girl in the corner holding her child. "But before you escape you must tell another slave. The path begins at the boulder past the smithing tents."

Timma stared at me wide eyed. She reminded me of a ten year old child the way she stared at me.

"Tell no one that I am behind this."

Timma nodded. "Yes sir."

I neared Ultan and placed my hand on his shoulder. "I need you to protect this young woman and her child with your life as she escapes, understand?"

Ultan looked up and nodded.

"Are you a Tarlen spy?" Timma asked.

I shook my head. "No."

"Who are you then?"

I shrugged. "A warrior." I took some bread and meat and packed it up with some blankets. "Tell no one I am behind this," I repeated as I dug around in a chest in the corner until I produced three cloaks. "You leave tonight when everyone is asleep or passed out." I put a brown cloak in Timma's hands. "But you must tell another slave of the escape route before you leave."

She nodded, adventure shone in her big brown eyes. I was glad she had the beautiful purity of joy still in her. The rebel camp had not completely ruined her heart yet. Looking at her golden smile made me miss Mercy. I remember the time she had taken my hand and we ran through the fields. I stopped myself before I thought more of her. This was no time to break down.

"You are in a lot of danger," said Ultan quietly.

I shrugged. "I'm in the Cansten army. Of course I'm in danger."

# RALIPH'S FACADE

We were attacking Bellorn. Larcos had spent a week trying to figure out the perfect time and strategy.

"The only way to take it is from the inside," he explained to me as we were discussing strategies late one night. I was taking on a highly successful double life.

"There's a shipment from the mines coming to Bellorn in two weeks. It is manned by some Tarlen soldiers. We leave tomorrow to interrupt them."

My heart leapt at the thought of going to the Marshlands. My mind raced to Mercy's beautiful face and my heart pounded in excitement.

He continued on about his elaborate scheme. My mind wandered to a world of joy again when I thought of seeing the wonderful girl I was in love with.

"Raliph!"

I blinked and shook out of it. "Sorry, my lord. I am tired," I lied.

"As I was saying, we'll infiltrate the city in the Tarlen uniforms and overpower the gatekeeper and open the gate."

I nodded not really paying attention. The possibility of seeing my stunning princess was all I could think of. I left for my tent when Larcos was finished explaining his strategies to me.

"I tell you! It was the princess!" I heard one man say.

I slipped into a shadow.

"I was fast asleep when she shook me awake," the man went on. "She released us all then sent us away. Ask Terran."

"The princess would have to be crazy to save your life!" another man said.

"I know! I'm a nobody! A guard who failed his task while guarding the princess."

"You claim the princess saved you from the mines when you were one of her guards when she was being held here?"

"She's crazy I know, but why would I make up a story like that?"

"Why was she banished?" the second man asked in a quieter tone.

"I heard one of my Tarlen guards claim she and Garcel saved two hundred slaves from one of The Pits and that she was the Compassionate Angel," the first man replied also in a hushed tone.

"What is happening to Tarlen's royalty?"

"What happened to the prince? He was always cruel but then out of nowhere his own father murders him for saving slaves and refusing to take us to the Pits anymore."

"I don't know what to make of it."

The two strode past me. I followed in the shadows.

"One of our captors told the princess her life was useless..." said the first man. "She cried and ran away...I heard a scream, Ellar. It echoed all through the Marshlands. It was a dark night that night. The very air felt evil."

"You mean Ellar the god? The mark on the prince that would not disappear whatever we did to him?"

"Yes."

"What do you make of this?"

"I have no idea."

"Listen, you know how I am under Caraph?"

"Yes."

"The day Lord Raliph saved Caraff his shirt ripped and I saw some gold on his breast."

I held my breath.

"You don't think he has something to do with Garcel do you?"

"I don't know. They are all crazy. Have you seen Raliph when Larcos is not around?"

"No."

"He trains the new young recruits without the whip. I once…" he lowered his voice. "Saw him comforting one."

"You think Ellar has something to do with this?"

"I don't know."

They separated and slipped away. I had heard all I would hear now.

I retired into my tent and thought. Mercy was in trouble. I was being talked about. My façade was not as successful as I had hoped. Slaves were disappearing every day and never coming back. No one knew I was behind it but some were catching on that I wasn't cruel. My mark had been seen. If Larcos found out, he'd be sure to put two and two together soon.

---

Dressed as peasants, we travelled in small parties through the out skirting villages of Tarlen. Some of us would go on to the Marshlands, others would stay near Bellorn for the gate to open. Larcos wanted to be one to enter the city first so him and I were part of the group of soldiers to go to the Marshlands.

Though I hated the thought of destroying Bellorn, the hope of going through the Marshlands to see Mercy redeemed the dread of such war. I had no idea how I would find her. I hoped she would find me but as I neared the vast plains of seemingly deserted swamplands, I began to doubt.

We reached the edge of them and I glanced over those never-ending marshes. Only the mountains in the distance dictated an end to the plains. I sighed. How could I ever find Mercy without scanning every inch of it? I prayed a silent prayer to Ellar.

# A FORBIDDEN DEVOTION

**Mercy**

I gasped when I saw his face. He was glancing around, anxious as he followed his cohort. I wondered what he was looking for.

I became suddenly nervous of my appearance. My clothes were like the marshes. My hair had been knotted with twigs and muck to blend into its surroundings. I touched my face. It was covered in grimy mud. Sighing, I continued to observe him as I remained hidden.

He was with other rebels. Larcos was one of them. But I did not pay much attention to those around him. My eyes were glued to the face and form of my lover. I feared he had forgotten me. He looked different than my memory of him. More powerful and imposing. His blond hair curled long, down to his shoulders, his eyes held a deep seriousness I had never seen before. I gulped when I observed his muscles. Never had I seen such a warrior in my life. I blushed at my own silliness and hid behind the bushes as they passed. When they were gone, I ran to Nadia's hole.

Nadia, who was feeding her son Armon, stared at me in surprise when I entered in such haste. I attacked an old chest and finally produced a soft white dress. I washed my face, hands, and started on my hair. "Garcel!" I called.

Garcel emerged. He had been building he, Nadia and Armon's hole. I still stayed with Enstar. He was covered with dirt from digging. When he saw what I was doing, he looked at me in surprise. "What is it, Mercy?"

"Wash your hands and help me get the dirt out of my hair. Hurry!"

"Why?"

"Garcel!"

Obediently, he washed his hands and helped me rinse my long tangled hair. "What is this about, Mercy?"

"Raliph's here."

"Impossible!"

"No! He and some other rebels are marching through the Marshlands as we speak. I was waiting, hoping to see Adann. Instead, I saw him and about thirty other rebels."

"I wonder what they want," Nadia mused.

"Mercy, if you reveal yourself to them, it will be the worst for both him and you," Garcel warned.

"And wearing that white dress you'll easily be spotted," Nadia added softly in the corner.

"I haven't seen him for a year!" I exclaimed throwing my head back. Garcel sputtered when the dirty water from my hair splattered on him. "I haven't seen the man I love for a year. At this point, I don't care what happens to me."

Garcel sighed. "Wait until late when all are asleep. Then meet him. I suppose in that dress if you are seen in the dead of night, they'll mistake you for a spirit. It's that sort of place and everyone is superstitious when they are in the Marshlands."

I nodded obediently. I had learned from hard experience to listen to my brother.

The last man was snoring. Every man but the one on watch and he was not facing me. I stepped silently over the sleeping figures until I saw the troubled face of the man I loved. I paused for a moment. Hesitant. My dress blew softly in the night breeze. I sighed remembering the day we had slipped under the wall and ran through the fields before Whitestone. So much had changed since then. I was no longer as careless and free as I had been a year ago. My face was long and dark circles were around my eyes. My hair was course and my dress was simple and plain. I could not find any perfume so I smelt like a marsh. How could I be beautiful? What if he forgot? Didn't matter, I'd make him remember! But if he did not remember, how much would that break my heart? What if he didn't love me anymore? I stopped before I lost all my nerve.

Kneeling down, I swept a curl of his hair from his eyes. "In his memory, can he see an Angel of Mercy?" I whispered in his ear.

His eyes flew open. I covered his mouth. His eyes met mine. Recognition. I breathed a sigh of relief and removed my hand. Standing, I beckoned him to follow me through the sleeping camp and beyond. He did.

When we drew out of sight of the camp, he embraced me. "You saw me!" He held me out at arms' length to get a full look at me. "Mercy! Mercy! You're so beautiful! A sight for sore eyes." He spun me around and laughed. "How I hoped you would find me!"

We laughed together. He touched my face gently with his hand. "How are you? Are you alright?"

I nodded.

"Oh, Mercy!" He embraced me again.

I sighed a happy sigh. It had been so long. So long. I smiled and laughed again. I felt like I was in a world apart from any other. Like I was a child again. The terrible things I had seen had disappeared in his embrace. Everything of darkness and sorrow faded away. I was happy.

He held me for a while, then he released me.

"What is it, Raliph?"

He looked down into my eyes and sighed. "Mercy, how long have we been doing this?"

"What…what do you mean?"

"I'm a fugitive, you are a fugitive. We hide our love waiting for a moment that we can uncover it."

"We can't tell."

"No…but when will we?"

"What are you saying?"

"Let's marry tonight!"

"What?" I stepped back. "How?"

"There must be someone here who could marry us."

"We yes, but Raliph, our families."

"We're both outcasts, Mercy. We'll never marry at this rate," he complained.

I smiled a little at his impatience. But the thought. Imagining marrying him. It seemed so tempting. I looked at his face. It had changed in strength and age but was still recognizable. So much had happened since we had last spoken. Who was he now? Did I really still know him?

"Tell me about what has happened since I last saw you," I sat down on a rock.

He smiled. "You want to know what kind of stranger you're talking to?"

I blushed.

"I understand. I've been gone for a long time. You have changed too. I would like to hear your story as well, dear one." He sat down beside the rock on the dirt and began.

I listened as he told me daring tales of an inner struggle to serve Ellar. "You see, I have been needing to talk to you for so long, Mercy. I've been so scared of Larcos and of being found out, I am going mad in fear!"

"Meanwhile, you can't sit by and watch all these horrors happen?"

"Yes."

I thought for a moment. "You remember the night Garcel stabbed you and we were so sure you would die? Or the day the poison of the Urfane was penetrating your heart? Ellar came through. He's kept you alive for a reason."

Raliph sighed. "I know, Mercy. It's just…"

"What?"

He shrugged and blushed. "I'm scared."

"What is the worst fate? You die a hero or you cow in the corner and slowly die inside."

"But I do not want your brother's fate."

"Garcel?"

"Yes. Killed by his own father."

I glanced at the sky. It was getting lighter. Smiling, I took his hand. "I'll find you again tomorrow night."

He nodded. "I've gone with less sleep before."

I smiled then disappeared. He glanced around confused. "Mercy?"

Clearly, he hadn't realized that I was a Marsh-girl. That I had been trained to disappear any moment I wanted to.

He sighed, stood up, and trudged back to his camp. He passed out on the ground on the edge of the camp. I hurried back to Garcel and Nadia's hole.

"How did it go?" Nadia asked when I appeared. "Did he remember you?"

I laughed. "He had been waiting for me."

"Of course he had." Nadia smiled. "Who could forget you?"

"Where's Garcel?"

"Digging. I told him I am quite satisfied with this place. I've lived in worse holes before. But he refuses to stop trying to make this place better for us."

I chuckled in amusement at Nadia. She sure did love Garcel and Garcel certainly loved her back.

I found Garcel covered in mud putting grimy stones along the walls. "Garcel."

He turned around. "Mercy, how did it go?" He wiped his forehead with his muddy hand.

"He thinks you're dead."

A shadow passed over his face. "I guess that's what everyone thinks."

"We never discussed what we should do. We can't stay here forever," I said.

Garcel sighed. "I know. Something will come up. We will return to Whitestone someday. You will see your orphanage and no longer be ashamed to show your face," he bit his lip and turned away. "You should rest."

I left him in his mood and went to my hole five minutes away from his. Enstar smiled broadly to see me when I entered our hole. Her eyes shone mischievously. "I saw you with a man. You were holding hands. Who is he?"

I blushed. "Were you spying?"

"Of course I was," she giggled. "A strange man is having a rendezvous with my sole responsibility. Who knows who he was? I had to make sure you weren't in danger."

I roll my eyes. "Enstar, I can survive on my own."

She shook her head. "No, you can't."

I chuckled. "He and I have been seeing each other before I ever came here. I was only seventeen when I first fell in love with him. It has been a long time."

Enstar dumped a sizzling concoction into a stone bowl. "Breakfast?"

"I can go find my own."

She shook her head. "I got extra on purpose."

I took the bowl. Even if it was bitter roots and unwan worms, Enstar could make it taste good. She amazed me every day with her impressive skills in hunting and cooking. It seemed like her sole goal in her life was to make everyone else's lives easier. Sometimes, I even catch her trying to help her sour old grandfather. After meeting Ellar, she would do it without fear.

After breakfast, I went to my little bed on the ground. Enstar's brother saw me come in. He smiled. "Hello, Mercy."

"Hello, Shantan," I replied prepared to have a conversation.

"You should sleep now, Mercy," said Enstar at my elbow.

I chuckled again. "Very well, Enstar."

"Garcel?"

Merely the sight of his face made me laugh aloud.

"You're alive?"

Garcel chuckled. "Since last time I checked."

"Everyone thinks you're dead."

In the moonlight, I glanced over the faces of Raliph and Garcel. Garcel was grinning at him but Raliph just stood still, shocked, like he was seeing a ghost.

Garcel laughed. "Are you glad to see me?"

Raliph touched his shoulder. "The moment I realize you aren't a spirit, I will be."

I giggled. "Cranteng healed him."

"Cranteng? What kind of name is that?" Raliph asked.

We all laughed.

"Don't insult him, he's the chief," I said.

"Sorry."

Garcel shrugged. "He wouldn't dare to pick a fight with us now."

"Why?" Raliph asked.

"Ellar," Garcel and I said together.

"You two must tell me your story."

"It's long and depressing," I said.

"So was mine," said Raliph.

"Nadia might need me," Garcel protested.

"Nadia is well?" Raliph asked.

"She has a baby now," I said.

Raliph shook his head. "It's been too long."

I sat him down and told him about the slaves, about the Marshlanders, about my own folly, about Morglin, and about Ellar. Garcel only stayed for part of it because he was worried about Nadia so he went back to his hole.

Hand in hand, we walked the Dim Marshes. I looked up at this man I had loved for years now. When he looked down at me, his mouth broke into a fond smile.

"I've decided to do as you say," he told me when I finished my story.

"In what?"

"I'm going to cast aside my fear of Larcos and serve Ellar."

I paused for a moment to think of what my rash advice of courage would cost me. Though I did not wish to believe it, I knew that it would cost me the very life of the man who I loved. Perhaps, I could sound brave and instill courage in others but my trust in Ellar to keep Raliph safe was minimal. I feared for him. A thousand thoughts ran through my head. I tried to appear unaffected and proud and brave but my courage gave way and I fell into his arms unwilling to let him go. I loved him. I wanted to marry him. I really did. But how far and unlikely that dream was. I could not marry him now and be ashamed to admit my love for a rebel. If only it were different! If only I could proudly, in no shame or fear, both show my face and proclaim that I loved a rebel. I sighed. But what if that day never came? What if he died?

The sun was rising and I had to let him go. I walked with him as far as it was safe. We embraced and he kissed my hand. I wished he would have really kissed me but he didn't. Probably for the better but I was beyond caring what was wise.

"I love you, Mercy," he said then turned away.

"I love you too," I whispered hoarsely. He looked back at me and smiled. I disappeared into the Marshes before I broke down crying. Oh to be with him forever! No! I cannot, I must be brave. I must be strong. I must let him go to do what he is meant to do. But how can I go on without him? When will I be so safe as when I am in his arms? When will I be as happy as when I am with him? But it is not about me. There are too many starving people for me to concern myself over my own happiness. But still. I would give my right hand to be with him even if it wasn't forever. Even if it was only a year, a month, a week. No. I cannot. Perfect dreams of happiness and love do not belong in Tarlen. At least not dreams that include a rebel and an outcast princess living happily ever after.

I walked alone over the silent marshes. Praying for him and dreaming of him. It was foolish. I knew not to linger so long in a dream world but every time I would see him, I could not help but love him more. Now, my mind is filled with his smiles, his eyes, his gentle words, and by Ellar, his muscular embrace. I did not wish to face Nadia, Garcel, or Enstar yet. The only one I could face was Ellar, if he was listening. Perhaps, he was listening to my pleas for his life, perhaps he was not, but at least I felt like I could talk to someone about him. I hate love.

The next day, there was an ambush on some Tarlen soldiers and some jewels were stolen. I knew it was the rebel party but I did not see Raliph after that night.

# RALIPH'S STORY

**Raliph**

I left her, again, heart heavy but strengthened in the knowledge that she loved me and her prayers to Ellar were always for me. When we parted, her pale face was clearly imprinted in my memory.

I slinked into camp and went to my place on the ground. Before I could lie down, several men stood up around me. My hand went to my sword hilt.

Larcos approached me dragging a bound and beaten Marat. "Tell him what you saw him do!" said Larcos pressing the knife against Marat's throat.

"I saw him…sneak away with the princess Mercy…" he coughed and trembled but Larcos would not let him go. "…and I saw…him kill Garcel's guards…" his voice quivered as he spoke and he looked at me fearfully. "…and take him away."

I drew my sword from my belt.

Larcos smirked. "One against thirty, the traitor tries to save his skin!"

He threw Marat to the ground. He groaned. I felt sorry for him. Kneeling to the ground, I offered him my hand but he recoiled from me.

"Fool!" Larcos cut his bonds and spat on Marat. "And you!" He drew his sword. I gripped mine ready for an attack.

"Raliph the mighty man? No! Raliph the soft, the weak. Raliph the traitor!" he shrieked. "Bring him back to camp!"

Three men ventured near me, swords drawn. With a few quick

movements, I wounded one in the arm, he dropped his sword. I stabbed one in the foot, he hopped about in pain. And I knocked the other one down with my foot.

"Cowards!" Larcos shrieked and stabbed one of my attackers in the heart. He turned to Marat. "You do it!"

Marat met my eyes. I drew my second sword and clutched it tightly. He cowed and slunk away.

"I'll do it myself!" cried Larcos as he jumped into the circle, swords poised ready to strike. I waited for him to make the first attack. He charged me with a cry and brought his blade down for my head. I blocked it and swung my sword at his legs. He sidestepped my attack and jabbed at my stomach. I pivoted out of the way and made a jab at his foot. He blocked my sword by putting his in the ground then aimed his other sword in a wide swing towards my chest. I was stepped back too far for his sword to do any real damage on me but my blood spilt across my chest from the corner of his blade. I cried out. In anger, I charged him, both blades in the air. Something hard hit the back of my head and I fell. Light began to fade in my eyes.

"Good Marat, maybe I won't kill you after all."

He rolled me over and spat in my face. Semiconscious, I was unable to fight back. He kicked me hard in the stomach and laughed when I groaned. Almost out, I could still feel pain. Blurred faces of others surrounding me beat down on me. Course laughter filled the air. Their faces faded into a dream of pain. My head!

Faintly do I remember ropes around my body. My head ached. My body burned in pain. It was impossible to name everything that hurt. I was being dragged but I did not open my eyes to see where. I wanted to die.

I opened my eyes and looked around. I was tied to a chair in a tent. Everything on my body ached. I struggled in the ropes but to no avail.

"Where am I?" I whispered.

"In your tent."

I looked around for the speaker. In a dark corner, I saw the figure of a man hidden in the shadow almost as though he were trying to blend into the wall. "Marat?"

"Yes," he said quietly.

"What happened?" Everything was in a haze all muddled together from Mercy's painful farewell to this.

"You were caught in the act of treachery and sent to the rebel camp to await Larcos' disposal." His voice was cold and detached.

My head throbbed. "You hit me with something from behind so I'd go down?"

Marat recoiled deeper into the corner. "I had no choice. My death was secured with Larcos unless I did something!"

"What did you do?" I asked. "How did you find out?"

He sighed still hiding in his corner. "I had been spying on you the night before. I heard you call the dark haired angel Mercy then a little marsh girl appeared, drew her knife, and told me to leave."

"You didn't harm the girl did you?"

Marat shrugged. "No, I was scared you would hear me and I had enough blackmail already so I left."

I breathed out a sigh of relief; the girl was probably Enstar, protecting Mercy as she had been known to do.

"When I returned, Larcos met me. He asked me where I was and I couldn't think of a good lie…"

"So he…ah…forced you to tell about Mercy."

"And the incident with Garcel. I don't know how he did it."

I sighed.

"After I hit you, we all beat you up then Larcos sent me and two others back here to await him. If you escape, we die," he added almost as though he were pleading with me.

I closed my eyes and thought of everything I was losing. My love, my strength, my family… "I knew this would happen I just…" I paused. "I wanted to do more before."

Marat left the shadows. I saw his form clearly. Slunk down, he hung his head ashamed but at the same time almost afraid of me, terrified of something about me, and it wasn't merely my strength.

"You bear the same mark the prince does," he ventured carefully.

I nodded. "True enough. Ellar's mark."

"I learned about it after I saw it on Garcel," he said. "Many mighty men in the past had it before it was outlawed." He glanced at me curious. "Why would a prince wear it knowing the danger?"

"The benefit outweighs the cost," I replied simply.

Marat's eyes grew greedy. "What is the benefit?"

I thought for a moment looking at the greedy yet fearful eyes of a Cansten rebel. Perhaps, this could be the final difference my life would make. There would be no point to be scared anymore to speak of Ellar or my strong morals because I would surely die anyway. "It's not what you think, Marat. There is no gold or great might to be gained from this mark," I said. "The mark, when it is branded on a person by the hand of Ellar, protects them from the power and damage of Morglin."

At the mention of Morglin, Marat's eyes widened in fright. He had a good reason to be afraid. Morglin's power was rampant in the rebel camp. Mighty men would mysteriously disappear sometimes in the night and bystanders would report a dark creature dragging his victims away as they screamed in fear. I remember being such a victim.

"I had been taken by Morglin; one night I was being held at the palace where I had been tortured," I began. "In the torture chambers, I was branded Worthless Scum and when Morglin took me, he marked my skin with black words and curses upon me."

Marat stepped closer to listen.

"Princess Mercy called upon Ellar to save me when she saw my ghastly form and heard my terrible shrieks."

"Princess Mercy?"

I nodded. "Ellar did come and Morglin fled. I was in agony. No amount of pain could match what I felt while in the hands of Morglin. He ruined me. His hand burned and he grasped my heart and mind in his clutch…" I shivered. "It was as if I was chained but not merely my body but every part of me. Ellar found me like that…" I paused in remembrance. "He took me in his arms and healed me." The wonder of that moment so long ago hit me again like it never had. I smiled almost as though I were in a trance. "It was then I took his mark."

"You have no other brand on you," he whispered hoarsely.

"He took them away."

"Strange story," he said softly, in deep thought.

"Ellar desired me not to be ashamed of his mark but I feared the discovery of my treachery in saving Prince Garcel so I hid it. I regret that now."

Marat neared me, his face pale as he immerged from the shadows. His eyes darted around. His hands shook and glistened in cold sweat. "Tell me more…about Ellar."

# FAREWELL TO THE DIM MARSHES

**Mercy**

"Adann is here!" said Nadia down the entrance to the hole I shared with Enstar and her brother.

"Adann!" I cried and sped up the ladder out of our hole. Before I lost myself in excitement, I took the time to quickly cover the entrance with a rock and some grasses.

Nadia and Garcel led me to the edge of the Marshlands. Adann stood alone, wringing his hands. He looked at us blankly for a second then his eyes widened in surprise.

"Garcel!" he exclaimed. The brothers embraced. "I thought you were dead."

"So everyone thinks," smiled Garcel. "No, Mercy and Nadia spirited me away here. The Marshlanders healed my wound."

Nadia showed him Armon and we all wept together. I had never been so glad to see Adann in all my life.

"Come and eat," said Garcel.

"I will eat but I cannot rest for long."

We went to Cranteng's hole because it was closest to the edge of the Marshlands where we met Adann. Enstar met us there and made Adann and the rest of us some food. Adann received it with little hesitation though it was a far cry from the food of royalty that he was used to. He was nervous and restless though. I could tell by the way he would not sit still and his eyes would dart around the hole. He wrung his hands and tried to steady them. I noticed his hands were covered in scars. A huge bruise marred the side of his face.

"Bellorn is taken," he said after he could hide his anxiety no longer.

"Bellorn! That's not good," said Garcel.

"They infiltrated the city in the guise of Tarlen soldiers bringing a shipment from the mines," Adann began. "That night they opened the gate and let the rest sneak in. The call was sounded and father and I led our troops to save the city but they had an ambush waiting for us. They wiped out half of our troops. The rest they sent in panic. The king…" he stopped. His hands shook again and he quickly hid them at his sides. Swallowing hard he tried to continue. "He…"

"What is it, Adann?" demanded Garcel standing to his feet.

"The king is…mortally wounded."

Nadia's breath caught. I bit my lip. Garcel looked like he'd been struck.

"Larcos stabbed him and I saw him go down. That was when our troops fled," Adann now poured out the story freely. "I heard that you two girls," he nodded at me and Nadia, "had fled to the Dim Marshes."

"The king has discovered us?" I asked, afraid.

"The king is dying, Mercy. The only family he has left is I," said Adann.

"And whose fault is that?!" I exclaimed, angry. What had my father ever done for me that I should risk my life to visit him at his deathbed?

"Mercy!" said Garcel sternly immerging from the shadow of the wall he had been standing in. "We must return, if not for the king, than for Adann."

I sighed, tears filling my eyes. "He tried to kill us."

"We can't hide in the Dim Marshes forever," said Garcel.

"I have horses and some men to escort us home at the edge of the marshes," said Adann.

"You must remember, we are criminals," warned Nadia.

"Garcel strapped his sword to his side. "Get your quiver and your sword, Mercy. We are going home."

# A MARKING IN BLACK

**Ralph**

"Larcos is back!" The call went out. I sighed. I had hoped he would be killed at Bellorn. Marat came in, tightened the ropes that bound me, then left without meeting my eyes.

Battle cries and victory hollers were heard all throughout the camp. That and the screams of the prisoners. I knew that Larcos would currently be sending the young boys and captured soldiers to the training and smithing tents to be branded and put in irons if they protested. Sometimes, I wondered how Larcos hadn't been assassinated yet by some bold traitor who grew so angry at the brute that he snapped.

"Bring out the wine! Divide the slaves! You've earned it tonight!"

I listened to the screams and the cruel bellowing laughter from my tent where I was hopelessly bound. My blood boiled in rage. I hated this place more than I could put into words no matter what vulgarity I could procure. What a dark and cruel land I lived in.

I waited until the night was almost spent. The reveling had died down and I only heard the moaning of those in irons or being tortured. The sun began to rise and the slaves were hurrying to make breakfast.

Larcos entered his tent. His huge powerful form blocked the door. His arm dangled over a young woman who he threw out when he stepped into the door. I hated that man. He stumbled and paused for a moment to gain his bearings. Of course, he was drunk.

"So, you! The man I trusted with my life…traitor…" he said, his speech slurred. "I should have known you were no good the day you first opposed me." He drew his dagger and put it to my throat. "You led Prince Garcel here, didn't you?"

"Yes, I did," I said quietly.

"If it hadn't been for you, I would be king by now!" He cried and punched me in the nose. Blood dribbled down my nose and into my mouth.

"How long have you been seeing the princess?"

I shrugged pretending to be unaffected. "Before you captured her."

"Have you no fear of me?" he demanded.

"I see no purpose of fearing you as it won't save my skin."

Larcos sneered at me and pulled a sharp wooden hatchet from his belt. "Your skin will be the first to go."

I shuddered. Swallowing hard I bowed my head. "Oh Ellar," I whispered. "I knew it would come to this but please…"

He brought the hatchet down onto my back and tore at my skin. I cried out in pain.

"Do you fear me now?!" he bellowed laughing drunkenly.

Furious anger stirred inside of me. This is what Larcos did. He brought strong men down and humiliated them to grovel at his feet. This man lived off of power, being the strongest and mightiest man of all, but there were powers of higher authority than he. He hit me again on the shoulder. I cried out. He laughed almost in delight. He grabbed my neck with his huge hand and punched me in the face. I noticed on his wrist strange black letters when his arm band slipped down. "Weak," I whispered.

"Perhaps, you can overpower me, Larcos," I said. "But your master is stronger and him I do not fear."

He stopped and stepped back. "What?"

"You try to prove your strength to me, make me tremble before you. But you are under a power that you cannot wrench free from," I said my voice finding its strength. "And you tremble before him in fear and weakness. Just as that mark on your wrist dictates."

Larcos drew his sword and put it shakily at my heart.

"I bear the mark of Ellar. Your master's enemy," I looked up steadily to meet his wavering eyes.

"I have no master," he hissed.

"You think that if you become king, he will have no more control of you. You think you can prove you are strong to him but you can't!"

His hands trembled so much he had to lower his sword. Fear and fire blazed his eyes.

"I know the burn of his claws when they touch you," I whispered. "I've felt it myself. But I had not the strength to oppose him and I fell into his hands."

Larcos' lips trembled. Sweat beaded on his forehead. He looked like a madman.

"Ellar saved me, Larcos! He can save you as well!"

With a cry of fury, he gripped his sword and prepared to drive it into my heart but he stopped suddenly. He fell down as though someone had struck him down with their hand. Infuriated, he picked up his sword again.

I studied his eyes for a moment to realize that he had lost himself. They were wild and possessed. I stared in horror as a black marking etched its way on his forehead. Larcos was not my greatest enemy in that room.

"Ellar!" I cried. "Take Morglin out of this tent!" I shrieked. That old terror I had once experienced in the darkness of Mercy's hideout was taking hold of me. I breathed a sigh of relief when Larcos' eyes centered back and he began to move normally again.

But the beginnings of a brand remained on his forehead. Only an F and an E.

He glared at me with intense hatred and fear. "I need no one." He stood to his feet. "I will defeat Whitestone. And you will serve me in chains while I sit upon the throne of Tarlen."

"Your fate is decided by you," I sighed. "You have chosen Morglin."

Larcos ran out of the tent. "Secure the prisoners. All able soldiers, we leave for battle tomorrow!"

"Your pride is bringing this dark fate upon you, Larcos," I whispered. Blood trickled down my face and my back as it burned in pain but I cared little of that now.

"There is only one stronger than Morglin and he is not Larcos."

# A MIGHTY PRINCE'S GREATEST BATTLE

**Mercy**

"Why do you have to leave?" asked Enstar as she packed my food for the journey.

"Because Garcel wants me to," I sighed.

"It's so dangerous."

"I can defend myself, Enstar. Besides, we'll have protection from Adann's guards."

I could tell by her expression she didn't believe me.

"Take me with you, Mercy! Shantan and I!"

"What about your grandfather?"

"Grandfather could do without me to worry about," she said frowning.

I knelt down to her. "Enstar, you need to tell your people about the hope in Ellar."

She sighed. "Alright Mercy. Just don't get hurt."

We embraced and then I turned to finish packing up my things. I dressed as a warrior princess again and strapped my sword and dagger to my waist.

Garcel, Adann, and Nadia with Armon in her arms were waiting for me just outside my hole. Together, we fled the Dim Marshes and met Adann's guards with some horses at the edge.

I closed my eyes as I urged my horse forward. The joy of

riding again tingled in my fingers as I gently touched the reins of my mount. I had forgotten how much I had missed being a warrior princess. My black hair blew in the wind and often got into my mouth. I didn't care. Beside me, Garcel rode straight and tall. His eyes held the same excitement as mine did. Nadia did not get the same thrill from riding as we did. She stared at the mane as she sat in front of Garcel, clutching Armon tightly though he was already bound to her body. Garcel controlled the reins behind her but did not bother to go slower for her. The wonder of being on a horse again was too much for even his generous nature to cause him to slow down.

It was a three day ride to reach Whitestone from the edge of the Dim Marshes so we had to stop during the first night along a small outlaying wood. Adann sent the guards several paces away from us.

"Father has been trying to make me king material since you first returned from the rebel camp," said Adann when swallowing a bite of bread. He leant against a log and watched the sparks of our campfire leap up in the air. "It is like trying to make water stone."

"The king has different views of what makes a good king in Tarlen than what is accurate," said Garcel.

"I know," said Adann. "And I know that everything you are, Garcel, is what makes a good king."

A shadow passed over Garcel's eyes. He stared at the ground.

"Outlawed or not, when the king dies you are heir to the throne. Please take this burden from me!"

"Adann, I do not want the throne any more than you do!" cried Garcel.

"But you can do it though, I can't," he whispered. "All I want to do is marry Sunfare and have a family. I am a weak man, Garcel. I can't even command a regiment properly when you are not around." He played around with a twig on the ground, staring at it intently. "You could make changes in Tarlen. Good ones. You have courage. I have none."

"I have courage only through Ellar, Adann,"

Adann threw his twig into the fire. "And what has Ellar done for you?"

"A lot more than you think," replied Garcel.

"Garcel, why do you protest this so much?" I asked.

Nadia looked up at her husband's face, intent to hear what he would say.

Garcel shrugged as if it didn't matter to him. "I am an exile. It would be more in the king's wishes for Adann to take the throne."

"I know you, Garcel. That's not the answer," I pressed him.

Garcel sighed. "You don't need to know everything, Mercy. It is of no consequence anyways." He stood and left the campfire into the dark woods.

Nadia's eyes filled with tears. I ran to her side. "Nadia, what's wrong?"

She shook her head and continued sobbing.

"Nadia, we're going home, everything is going to be okay."

"No," she whispered. "I know him…" she continued to cry. Armon began to weep too. I took him and tried to quiet him while Nadia buried her face in her hands.

Adann watched silently. He bit his lip but remained silent. Deep lines creased his forehead. He looked away.

I sighed. What would become of us? What would become of all of us?

Adann disguised us as his guards to get through the gate and we snuck into the palace through the cellar.

The walls were dark and my footsteps echoed in the dim hall as they always had but I had forgotten. The light was low and I could barely see the daring battles painted brilliantly on the roof. The place was dark and sad, just as I had left it. I pulled the cowl off my hair and glanced around the place I had once called my home.

Adann led us through the winding halls and up the stairs until we reached the dimly lit bedchamber of the king. Adann sent everyone out and pulled Garcel and I into the room. Nadia did not go in with me though I wished she had because I longed for her strength and support.

My whole body trembled as I approached my father's bedside. Garcel put his arm over my shoulder. Adann lit another lamp to brighten the room. I looked at my father. Pale and thin. His eyes were closed and his face deeply troubled as he lay on the lavish bed of costly silk duvets.

My whole body trembled as I approached my father's bedside. Garcel put his arm over my shoulder. We approached him together.

"My lord the king. My father." Garcel spoke softly but with strength.

The king stirred.

"Father," said Adann. "I brought Mercy and Garcel home."

"Garcel?"

"Yes father. It is I," said Garcel. He knelt down to the king's bedside.

The king, my father, covered in sweat and bandages, heaved an unwilling breath. He looked at his son. His eyes scanning the broad powerful figure kneeling at his bedside.

"The king…is going to…die," he croaked.

Garcel remained silent.

Tears welled up in the king's eyes. "I thought I wanted the

stones...of the mines..." he paused to try to shift amongst his myriads of pillows. "I thought I wanted the heads and the strong slaves of the rebels..." he broke off.

I bit my lip. Not sure if I could let go of my anger to cry with my father.

"I was a fool."

"Father, I bear you no ill will," said Garcel.

His body shook from silent sobs. "No son...should have to flee from his father!" His eyes rested on me. "No daughter should have to save her family...from her father."

A tear unwillingly spilled down my cheek. "I bear you no ill will, Father," I repeated.

The king took Garcel's hand with his sweaty and blotchy one. "Promise me, you'll be a better king than I was. Promise me..."

Garcel closed his eyes and nodded. "I promise."

"Treat Nadia better than I did Laria...be a good father..."

He nodded faintly.

"It is Ellar...isn't it?"

"Yes Father, because of Ellar I did what I did and am who I am."

"I'm sorry," he whispered. "I wish..."

"No Father, wishing makes no difference. Don't wish. It is too late to change the past. But not to change your life."

He nodded and closed his eyes.

Garcel motioned for us to leave. He followed and shut the door behind him. Sighing, he turned to the stone wall and drew deep shuddered breaths. "Ellar, give me strength. Give me strength..." he whispered.

Tears sprang into my eyes when I watched him. Wisely, Nadia held back. She left down the hall to feed her fussing child. I followed her but slowed as the hall began to curve. Pausing, I glanced back at Garcel again. His body wrenched with desperate sobs. I could barely even watch him. Dare to feel the turmoil that he was feeling.

The father, who almost murdered him, asks for forgiveness which he grants then immediately, followed by his father's death.

"Ellar," he whispered hoarsely. "Take my strength, take my sword, and take my heart. Take my life." He sank to the ground. "Whatever you wish of me I will do."

A light appeared beside him. I slipped around the corner out of sight then up to my room for fear of getting caught by Ellar.

# A DIFFERENT SORT OF LEGACY

I went up to my room and shut the door. Everything was just as it had been. I walked to my window and saw the edge of the great forest. Plopping down on my bed which had remained in the middle of the room with numerous pillows and frills adorning it, I stared at the roof. The brilliant colors overwhelmed my eyes. So much blood. So much hatred. So much war. I hated war now. Closing my eyes, I remembered the time I longed to be painted on that roof or on those walls. Now the very thought repulsed me. The only thing that changed in my room while I was away was me.

I sat up and got off my bed. Digging around in my closet, I pulled out my paints. I go to my solid wooden door and begin to paint with brilliant colors a mighty warrior. This warrior wore gold embroidery. In his hand, he held a glittering sword, not tainted with blood, but holding back from taking a life. His eyes, kind eyes, penetrated to my soul. His quiet smile and gentle face made me long to hear his voice again. And at his breast, he bore a golden mark. Ellar's. The warrior was my brother Justice. The man who changed my life and the entire royal family. His legacy would last forever now. With eye catching strokes, I painted another figure a tall and beautiful woman. The woman who had, against all odds, brought her love and faith to her children. I could not bear to finish her painting for my tears would have washed it away. Dropping my paintbrush, I left my work and snuck into Justice and my old hideout. There I wept.

Hours later, I heard a knock on my door. Picking myself up from the ground, I left my hideout. Wiping my eyes quickly to make sure there were no remnant or escaping tears, I answered,

"Yes, who is it?"

"May I come in?"

It was Garcel.

"Y..yes," I said, shaky.

Quietly, he opened the door. His eyes caught the new colors and shapes I had painted. "Justice and Mother."

I nodded slightly, "They are incredible!"

I blushed and looked down.

"Mercy?"

"Yes?"

"He died."

I sighed. "Then you are king."

"Afraid so." Sighing he slumped down on a chair beside my bed. "Mercy?"

"Yes?"

"Can you do me a favor?"

"What is it?"

"Give this to Nadia and Armon if anything ever happens to me."

I look at the note he held out to me. Stamped in a red seal. I swallowed hard. "Garcel, what's wrong?"

"Everything Mercy but that's not the point."

I knelt down and took his hand.

"I love you Mercy. More than you could ever know. Hold onto Ellar. Do not depend on others to hold onto him for you."

"Of course, Garcel. What…"

He took my hands and lifted me up. His long powerful arms wrapped around me and he wept on me. I remained standing there offering whatever comfort I could. I did not know what this was about and I feared greatly to ask him.

# THE MERITS OF A GOOD DEED

**Raliph**

Bleeding and bound, I listened as they left for Whitestone. I struggled in the ropes but to no avail. Soon the camp was silent.

A few rays of the waning sunlight escaped through the trees and lent their warmth and light onto the roof of the tent. Larcos' extra weapons lay in piles on the floor. The hatchet he had used for my back lay, covered in blood, next to the chair I was bound to.

I was left alone. The only people here were a few guards to guard the new prisoners and a few drivers to train the young recruits.

"Ellar, spare me please," I pleaded.

I heard cries from the Blacksmithing tents. Cries like those one makes in battle.

"Go boys, hurry!" I hear.

A few seconds later, five boys enter the tent. I recognized them as the boys I had trained before Larcos had made me his shield bearer. I smiled at them, trying not to be intimidating.

"Untie him, quickly," the eldest ordered. The boys drew their knives and cut the ropes on my hands and feet. They surrounded me and pulled me up to my feet.

"Ow!" I groaned as I straightened.

"Now get out of here, Raliph!"

I smiled, touched by their kindness. "This will cost you boys your lives." I insisted, unmoving.

"Not if you kill Larcos." The looming figure of Marat shadowed the door. "He is out of control now. So power hungry and terrified of being denied it he'll do anything to be king. If you kill him, you will save Tarlen and become the rebel leader." He picked up Larcos' weapons on the floor to give to me. As he leant down, I noticed something shining underneath his shirt.

"Marat?"

He straightened and smiled. "Thank you, Raliph." He dropped the pile of weapons at my feet then left. That was the last time I ever saw that man. The boys busied themselves strapping the weapons onto me.

"Marat has a horse waiting outside for you packed with food for your journey."

I nod.

"Oh, and watch out for Caraph. He planned this."

My head is almost spinning with all my assignments. The boys practically dragged me to the horse and strapped me on. "Goodbye!" they say as I rein the horse forward.

"Thank you," I said to them. "I won't let anything happen to you boys, I promise."

I gallop into the woods until the path makes it impossible to do so. My mission is clear in my mind. Kill Larcos, save Tarlen. A better man could be chosen for such a task.

A smile creeps onto my face when I remember the five boys and soldier who came to my rescue. Perhaps, doing good things had its advantages not only to my conscience.

# A DARKER WAR

**Mercy**

"The rebels are in sight!" a guard said as he burst into the dinner hall.

Garcel stood to his feet. "Adann, take a quarter to the walls and ready the stones. Mercy, take care of the archers. Nadia, take the citizens to the heart of the city to protect them from fiery arrows."

"What will you do?" I asked.

"I will take care of the cavalry and the foot soldiers."

We scattered.

It had come at last. My first war.

---

**Raliph**

The sky was clouding over and it seemed as though night was coming on earlier than usual. I urged my horse to a gallop in the direction of Whitestone though it was a struggle in the thick forest. At a distance, I saw the many contraptions of war lined up against the city. The main attack was on the front gate. For the first time yet I questioned Larcos' military techniques.

The archers on the wall brought down any rebel attempting to get into Whitestone over the wall. The rebels also had a huge battering ram with thousands of men heaving it. Dead bodies fallen from the archers lay on the ground in blood like the grasses of the field. Men trampled on them as though they were exactly that.

Moans of the dying and battle cries rent the air. Catapults flung boulders at the walls of Whitestone but the walls were far too strong to cave to merely a few stones. Rocks and scalding water were thrown off the walls at those trying to climb into the city and those trying to climb into the city or break the gate with the battering ram. Arrows whizzed back and forth.

Bravely, I urged my horse on. Nearing the battle so close, I could smell the stench and feel my bones shudder every time the battering ram hit the gate.

The gates collapsed but soldiers on horseback plowed down the attackers with their horses. As I neared the scene, I saw Garcel was the leader swinging his sword mightily he cried for his men to follow him.

The sky darkened even more, my horse spooked and galloped into the fray. Darkness encompassed the scene and I felt a deep sense of evil. My memory went back to that day in Mercy's hideout when she told me of Morglin's shadow. I shuddered, couldn't be.

The cavalry hacked down on the rebels but the numbers never seemed to lessen.

Shadowy figures passed by around me, I felt my body weaken. My horse stepped over a moaning man, and then when I turned around, he was there no more.

I saw Larcos several yards away from me marked in black with the fire of Morglin's power in his eyes. I realized only I could see these shadowy figures I knew to be Morglin's servants. But all could see the shadow descending.

My horse reared and threw me off. My eyes scanned the walls for Mercy. Fighting ensued all around me, but no one laid a hand on me. I glanced over to see Adann wielding a battle-axe at a cloaked figure like he was a rebel. More surrounded him and he dropped his axe and fell to his knees. They grabbed him.

"Adann!" I shrieked. "Call to Ellar!"

Garcel heard my cry and turned to see me. I pointed through the fray and shadows towards Adann, helpless in their clutches. He reined his horse after them bellowing the same message as he plowed through the thick of the battle.

I watched the battle scene unfold. The cries around me seemed muted. I stared into the darkness terror in my every heartbeat. Out of the shadows, Garcel's dark horse emerged, his young brother limp in his arm. Terror was written on every face around me but Garcel's. He set Adann down on his feet, he was unsteady but regained his balance and strength in a moment.

"It is Morglin. He is here," he says gravely.

"People of Tarlen!" a young voice shrieks over the roar of battle. "Do not destroy one another! You are only being destroyed. Morglin is taking you one by one. Call Ellar!" I realized the young voice was Mercy's. I look up to see her jump down on the wall into the midst of the battle calling the name she loved the most. No one noticed, or cared. Too caught up in fighting each other.

I looked behind me to see Larcos. With the fire of Morglin in his eyes, he continued to hack down on his victims. His strength seemed almost supernatural. He roared for his soldiers to continue fighting, bellowing out curses and threats to those who did not obey him. In his fury, he saw Mercy as she bravely called out her message to bring peace and salvation for the people. Blind with inhuman rage, he came up behind her. I raced towards her, running into other fellow soldiers and tripping over dead bodies. Mercy turned around to see the fierce wrath of Larcos and Morglin combined. She was caught unprepared and he dealt her blow after blow. Garcel reached her first and knocked him down before he could brutally harm his beloved sister.

"Mercy, Raliph! Drive his servants away! I'll take care of

him," he said. Mercy met his eyes and nodded. Garcel drew his two mighty blades and stood ready, as Larcos stood back to his feet.

I forced my way through the fray of blurred blood and looming shapes in misery, calling out the message of the people's impeding fate and our only hope. Regardless of what I shrieked into the shadowy gray of death, no one heard me and the fighting continued.

I neared the bridge where Garcel and Larcos were fighting hard. The battle was a mighty one, one to be painted upon a wall or written in the great annals of kings. Garcel dealt upon Larcos powerful blows of all courage and valor. He fought strong. His dark hair glimmered and tossed in the light at his every move. His muscles bulging out of his armor. Sweat and blood marring his giant form of power. Larcos ground his teeth. His eyes were smoldering flames. He fought like a madman. Yet, a madman with unchecked power. His towering form made even Garcel seem small as he stood against him. He struck Garcel's helmet. It impacted him greatly as he staggered back but he regained his place and responded by attacking his opponent with his sword in the gut. The sword grazed Larcos' armor but did little else but draw a little blood. He roared in anger and with superhuman strength attempted a blow at Garcel's shoulders. Garcel blocked the hit with both his swords but the impact made both his knees buckle. They had been at it for only ten minutes and Garcel was already growing weak. He grappled at his deformed helmet and threw it into the moat. He then turned and ran into the city with Larcos behind him. He stopped when he was within the walls and attacked his opponent with the full force of his might. I followed forgetting all else. They fought hard. Garcel using desperate strength and Larcos, in mad and inhuman fury struck him, untiring with his sword. This battle was not between two men, it was man and a god, an evil god. Garcel defended himself and brought Larcos further from the gate, probably hoping that by taking this creature out of the main fray Mercy could more easily ward off the dark shadow enveloping the land. He was growing weak under this power that no mere human could defeat.

"You think you are a mighty man? You will fall!" I shuddered. That voice did not belong to Larcos. He dealt down on Garcel a mighty blow. Whether it was his words or his blow, I noticed Garcel was weakening. "You try to redeem yourself from all your bloody deeds by being what you think is a great king! But you are a failure. You will never escape your cowardly selfish heart. You are a monster, Garcel. A king of beasts!"

Garcel weakened and Larcos laid on him a crushing blow. He fell to the ground in blood and misery.

"No!" I shrieked and ran at Larcos in rage before he dealt upon my friend the crushing blow of death. Larcos was almost completely under the control of Morglin now. My anger boiled up at the creature as my love for my friend grew greater. He would not die a cruel death alone under the power of such a repulsive foe. I roared as I dealt the creature blow after mighty blow. With my foot, I kicked him down at my feet, my eyes red with rage. I stab him with my sword in the stomach and blood gushes out of him. He cries out in pain. I glance down to see his face, it was Larcos' again. He was covered in black marks and his huge form was writhing in agony. I step back. "Do not die in blood alone under the power of the dark one," I say to him, my anger subsiding when I see the terrified face of the proud man. "You yet have hope if you call to Ellar."

His face twists in anger and fear. "You worthless worm! You will pay for this! He'll get you! He'll get you all..." Blood continues to pour out of his body. I see him weaken. His eyes widen in fear. "I failed," he says hoarsely.

I turn for a moment to look at Garcel, when I turn again to him I see the dark mortifying shape of Morglin carrying him off. I ran to catch him, even save him if I could but it was too late. They disappeared and only the terrified wide and tortured eyes of a once mighty proud conqueror remained in my memory forever. He had chosen his fate, in life, as in death. I swallowed hard and turned to Garcel.

"My friend, do not allow these lies to penetrate your noble heart," I whisper kneeling down to him. "You must remember to whom you belong to."

I carefully take off his torn breastplate and uncover the golden letters on his heart. They shone still brightly and tears began to fill my eyes. "My friend, do not allow these lies to weaken you. There are no black marks upon your heart. It is but gold. Gilded gold and shining brighter than ever before."

Garcel turns to me, his face bloodied and battered. He takes my hand that is laid upon his breast. "I will not for you, my friend," he whispered. "How can I believe his words and die in that hopelessness when a man such as you has fought so bravely for me."

Tears overflow my eyes and smear my bloodstained cheeks. "My friend, my friend…" I simply whispered again and again.

He sat up, still clutching my hand next to his heart. I walked with him to the gate, supporting him with my waning strength. There we stood, looking over the shadowed scene of bloodshed, the dark shadow was becoming only a light mist now. "Larcos, lord of the Cansten rebels is now dead!" Garcel called out. Those near to him turned to repeat the message to the host behind him.

"As victor over Larcos, I command those under me to stop fighting their fellow men!" I call out to the crowd.

"As king over Tarlen, I command those under me to stop fighting their brothers!" Garcel calls out to the crowd.

Arm in arm, we stand as slowly the battle subsides and the day becomes bright over the crimson hills littered in dead bodies. Mercy smiles and comes to stand by my side. Adann stands beside her. Nadia appears from behind and stands by the side of her husband. The soldiers stare at us awed and blinking.

"Go to your homes! All of you!" says Mercy. But the men do not move. They stare at us as we stand together between the city and the battle. The sun begins to sink behind the hill that Whitestone is built upon. The light surrounded us and shone on us in its warmth but did not reach the fields of blood where the battle had ensued.

Overwhelming sorrow fills my heart when I see the horrors of the battle field as a still picture to be forever ingrained in my memory. I remembered the words of my brother, Justice, long ago when he told me to no longer crave a battle. I did not crave such horrors anymore. After staring at us as though trying to be sure that we are real, the soldiers slowly dispersed, the rebels disappeared over the hills all in different directions. I swallow hard when I hear the moaning of those left behind on the battle field. I turn to my side and watch Nadia and Adann carry my brother inside the gates. I knew what I must do.

# A BITTER VICTORY

**Mercy**

It was a dark day when peace was made. For over the hills lay hundreds and hundreds of dead. Those with the rebel mark and those without. Bitter enemies. Dead together. The women came out of the city in hopes of finding their sons and husbands still alive on the bloody fields. A few found some alive but most let out a cry that echoed all throughout the land of Tarlen. It was a bitter victory. Official peace had been made between the lords of Tarlen and the mighty captains of the Cansten rebels but peace between the hearts of the people was a lot harder to attain. The rebels slunk into the forest silently, afraid of the royal powers, and terrified of the thick shadow that had haunted the battle. The Tarlen soldiers slunk silently into the city dragging some of their surviving fellows with them, also terrified of the strange happenings of the battle. All homes were opened to the dying and Adann, who was acting king, decreed that the rebel soldiers who were still alive on the battlefield would be taken to the palace and tended to there. I watched as children as young as ten were carried into the palace and laid on mats on the floor among rows of other bloodied soldiers. I took off my royal robes and tended to the dying using the miraculous skills my mother had passed onto me. Raliph watched me silently for hours and would run to complete anything I asked him to do to help save as many lives as I could.

"I never thought we would be here again," he whispered as he stared at my hands bandaging a man's bloody side.

"In the palace?"

"Yes."

"Nothing is at all as I had imagined it," I said softly.

"War?"

"And saving Tarlen. And loving you. And serving Ellar." I move on to the next man leaving a servant girl with my last patient.

Raliph sighed. "You should rest."

"I will when this is over," I respond inspecting the next man. He was older than most. His leg had been brutally hacked by a battle-axe which had shattered his knee and left pieces of itself inside the wound. He was passing in and out of consciousness. I swallow hard and thank Ellar that I have a good stomach.

"Caraph?" said Raliph behind me.

"You know this man?" I ask him.

"He was my captain and my friend. I saved his life in a battle," he responded. "He is still alive."

"He will probably lose his leg and his loss of blood has put him in danger but I will be able to save him."

"Mercy, you are incredible."

I cannot help but smile a little bit at his admiration. It had been a long time since I had heard that admiration and love in his voice towards me. It had been a long hard time of attempting to be strong and brave with no one to be strong for me when I could no longer stand. Tears filled my eyes suddenly. "Oh Raliph, it's so hard."

He takes me in his arms and holds me for a moment before I go back to my work.

Adann appeared behind us with some soldiers. "I'm sending Raliph into the forest to bring the people of Tarlen back to their homes."

"He must leave already?"

"We need to disband the army before they find a new leader. Raliph is officially their leader because he defeated Larcos. He must take command or we will have another revolt on our hands."

I sighed.

"Sunfare will help you here," said Adann.

"What about the slaves at the mines?" I ask.

"I have sent a cohort of trusted men with food and water to the mines with signed orders to release and care for the men in the Pits."

I stand up and look Adann in the eyes. He suddenly seems taller to me. His shoulders are not slumped and his expression no longer timid. "My brother you are wise. Garcel will be proud when he awakes," I say quietly.

He smiles a little. "I'm just trying to do what Justice and Garcel would do."

The mention of Garcel evokes fresh tears in my eyes and I turn back to my work before I waste more time on tears. I am afraid for him but cannot leave the side of the dying to tend him. Raliph leaves with Adann and I am left alone with the servants and hundreds of wounded dying men in the great hall.

"You…are the princess…Raliph loves, are you not?"

I jump, surprised to hear my patient speak. "Yes," I reply.

"He did it… didn't he?" the man said slowly.

"Did what?"

"Defeated Larcos and ended the war?"

"Yes, he and my brother." I wet a cloth and began to cleanse his wound. "Hold still."

"You have that mark on you, don't you?"

"Yes, I do, but be quiet, you must save your strength."

"Tell Raliph when he gets back that I…want to talk to him

about getting one too."

I smile. "I will. But hold still now, you are not out of danger and I would like to see if I can save your leg." I gave him some strong liquor to numb his body and make him pass out. We had run out of any more sedatives in the city. I took a swig of a strong unpleasant drink used in Tarlen to keep soldiers awake and alert. When one is in the business of saving lives, they must be as intent upon their task as humanly possible.

I bent over my patients using the healing hands I had and whispered a prayer for every soldier to Ellar. I saved many. But some did not make it. So this was victory? Hundreds of dying men in the great royal hall lined up on mats drifting in and out of consciousness. So this was victory? Hundreds of dead men lying on the fields before the city. Many children. Hot anger rose in me against the injustice of it all. I had done as my mother had prophesied. I, with the help of my brothers and Raliph, had ended the war and saved thousands of innocent lives in Tarlen. I had taken Ellar's mark and used that power to save many lives from the power of Morglin. Why did I feel so discouraged? Why did I feel so useless, so incapable, and so helpless? I'm a royal! A princess. This was victory. The dream I had so held onto for years. I glance down the hall, hearing the sounds of the moaning and dying. This is sorrow. This is heartbreak. This is shadow, and coldness, and anger, and hate. Victory? Yes. But what am I left with?

"Nothing but a bitter victory," I whisper and wipe a tear off my cheek.

# THE END OF A LOVE STORY

There is a story that has been left off. A story that is told little of but had the greatest impact upon all of Tarlen. The story of Garcel and Nadia.

After the men dispersed and the war ended, people were freed from oppression and the whole kingdom went in an uproar and complete offset in the balance of power. Prince Garcel was taken to his quarters. There tended by the faithful hands of his wife. She did not leave his side. Adann would come in between the affairs of state and speak in low tones to his beloved brother. I would kneel down and weep and beg to him to stay with us for his strength was waning away. But Nadia never left. At night, I would sneak down the stairs to catch a glimpse of Nadia sleeping beside him. My heart would pound. There seemed to be something strangely sacred about their love. I feared to enter. Nadia had what seemed like a great weight upon her shoulders. The weight of her dying husband. For Garcel was dying. And no one, not even I nor Adann felt the pain of it stronger than Nadia.

I watch her weep beside the bed, holding his colorless fingers with a trembling hand. Sometimes, I would listen through the door, just to hear what they would say in low voices when he was conscious.

"I wish you never had to bear this. I wish you could but leave and forget you ever loved me. But with all my heart, I long for you to stay…"

She does not speak only takes his hand and holds it. "My husband…" she whispers.

"Come up beside me, child," he whispered.

Obediently, Nadia crawled into his bed underneath the covers. She put his arms around herself and laid there in silence.

"You are trembling," he whispered.

"And so I will tremble, my love, until the day in which you stand once again to your feet."

"My heart burns within me to know that that day will never come."

"No!" she wept. "You must not say that."

"The wound to my head is fatal indeed. Though my heart is not pierced by Morglin's power, my body is bearing the mark of it."

My heart stopped at such words.

Nadia weeps.

"Do not weep, child. You will find another. But stay with me tonight. Stay with me until I pass."

"I shall weep my lord, for I will never find another. But I do not regret loving you. Not for a thousand years with anyone else. Not for a thousand years of happiness."

I weep silently as I hear the two great lovers profess their undying devotion. In the shadows of the dimly lit room another appears. My heart leaps when I recognize the presence of him. In a deep red cowl and with gentle hands, he approaches the bed of the two greatest lovers known to man. Nadia embraces him in ardent love and devotion but releases him quickly, knowing that she is not his sole purpose for approaching. He kneels down to Garcel. In weak effort, Garcel lifts his body up to touch the face of his great lord.

"Lay down your burden, my son," said Ellar. "You will be free."

And so I watched as Nadia tenderly kissed the lips of her one and only love and Garcel embraced the trembling form of his devoted and pure wife and it was over. Over. I blink trying to convince myself that I was mistaken. There is only one in the room now. Both left. Not in a flash of light, or a swirl of colors, or even the sound of fading footsteps. They left. And I sat baffled, wondering what had become of my brother and his lord. Nadia let out a cry. A cry that no one could recognize as anything but the cry of pure anguish, pain, and despair. She lost her love. She lost her husband. Not even Nadia could be strong enough to bear up under that pain. I weep, unable to move to help her. I weep in grief but a strange peace is yet instilled upon my heart.

Nadia wipes her eyes and whispers between sobs, "Lay down your burden, my husband. Be free from guilt and shame."

And that is the end of their love story.

# THE END OF NADIA'S STRENGTH

I stared up at the roof. Adann was king now. He set a marriage date for his queen. Said the kingdom needed a queen and Sunfare being a common girl would hopefully bring down some of the resentment the lower classes had of the royal family. Raliph and I were just so relieved we could be seen together we didn't even think of marriage. He became a general in the Tarlen army. Went around trying to disband the rebel army and dispel any uprisings that would happen in a country constantly full of war. He was away in the region of Nahon Valley trying to make peace with the lords and people of the region. I was alone in my room. Finally allowed to process everything I just went through. I'd been trying to stay busy in order to avoid that.

Everything that had happened over the past few years came upon me at once. Who was the strange princess who was staring up at her brilliantly painted roof? Was she even the same person as the sixteen year old girl who dreamt of battles and adventures? I thought of my family. Mother, the brave woman who had brought her faith into the royal family and changed their lives forever. Justice, a great prince whose honor and great character had changed the life of his little sister and left the brand of his faith on her heart. Father, the cruel man who had done all but harm until his death where he accepted forgiveness from Garcel. Garcel, the greatest king to ever live in Tarlen. The greatest man I had ever known. The man who stood between war and peace and brought peace. Who would willingly give his life up for those he loved. Whose passion and strength were a force to be reckoned with. Garcel. My brother. Tears filled my eyes again. Getting up, I go underneath my bed and procure a large chest of which I place upon my bed. There I stood as I, with wide strokes, paint white over the bloody battle scenes. Then, I began on a new figure. In swirling colors, I painted the mighty man who changed Tarlen because of his devoted obedience to Ellar. My tears flowed freely as I colored every shade of his clothes and every feature of his face. A knock sounded on my door.

"May I come in?"

It was Nadia.

"Yes," I said stepping down from the chest and down onto the floor from my bed.

"I read his letter." She held out the note with Garcel's final words scribbled out.

"May I read it?" I asked hoarsely.

"Yes," she said, her voice barely audible.

*"My Dearest Nadia,*

*When you get this letter I will be gone. This is the hardest thing I have ever done and it is even harder knowing how much love we have shared and could have shared with our beautiful son. I know you know the pain that I bear because of the man that I once was and know now that I am free from that and those scars I bear from my own cruelty, I will never have to bear again. Ellar chose me, Nadia. He chose me from that dark wreck that I was and gave me you, he gave me Armon, though only for a little while. More than that, he gave me himself and his name. I'd rather bear his name for a day than live a thousand years without it. I know you understand this. You probably understand it better than I do. I don't. I wish I did. It's hard, Nadia to say goodbye. I can't bear to say goodbye because you have been a beacon of pure light to me in the dark hopelessness of my ugly world. You have been the grace that gave me eyes to see a world I never would have known had you not, in your gentle way, opened my eyes to kindness and love. You taught me strength. You gave me a reason to fight for everything good. For some people when they fight for the cause of good, they get to live in the world they fought for. Some don't. I am one of them but I am glad to have fought for it all the same. I'm glad that you taught me of the strength and fortitude it takes to fight. Don't lose hold of Ellar, my love. Don't give up. Never stop using those beautiful eyes of yours that can see things that no one else but Ellar can see. I am proud to call you my wife. Proud to have shared with you the little time we had together. You are a treasure. A beautiful, perfect, unstained treasure of unmatchable purity. You changed my life, you saved my life. I love you. Tell Armon I'm sorry I couldn't be there for him as he grew up. I love him all the same and am proud to have been the father of him for as long as I had. Tell him of Ellar and tell him how much his father loved him though he won't remember me. He is a gift. A wonderful gift. For Mercy, please watch out for her. She needs it and she'll take it hard. Tell her I love her and Ellar loves her more. She saved Tarlen that girl did. She saved me too. I love her. I love her so much.*

*Goodbye my dearest Nadia.*

*With all my love. Garcel."*

Nadia's eyes filled with tears and she let out a heartrending cry of grief. She had lost her love. She had lost her husband. I had lost my brother but I had had years with him. She had so little time with him and had such great love for him. Love I could never imagine.

"He's gone!" she cried. "I keep wishing he would return somehow but he's gone! I wish that I could go with him." She sank to the floor and sobbed in utter despair. Her body shook uncontrollably in desperate anguish. "He's gone," she whispered her voice like a fragile thread when all her strength was spent.

I wrapped my arms around her slight form and she trembled in my arms. My heart broke for her. She was always the strong one; the one who could withstand anything. Never had I seen Nadia so desperate, so hurt, so broken, as the day she knelt on my floor in a puddle of tears.

"Thank you, Mercy," she said, her voice stronger now. "It will not be long before you find me crying again."

I hug her. "I can always be here to cry with you."

She drew a deep shuddered sigh. "Come, Mercy," she said. "He made me promise never to lose my eyes to the pain around me, however much pain is inside my heart." She stood up and took my hand. "So I won't."

"Where are we going?"

"To the darkest street in Whitestone of course," she replied. "Tarlen will always have oppression, injustice, poverty and pain, so we must keep fighting it. Until the day Ellar deems it right for us to stop, we must keep fighting."

I follow her as she leads me down the stairs, out into the night, through the city until the shining white stones darken into dull grey rocks in the darkest street in Whitestone.

"I pass by the darkest street in Whitestone

An old man lies dying at my feet

Three dirty children pass by in a hurry

And harlots cry in the street.

I hear the drunken calls from the tavern

I smell their puke and I see

A young child begging in raggedy clothes

In Whitestone in the darkest street.

In a house by the corner a woman's shrieking

A child cries from her wrath

My eyes are adjusted, now to the dim light

As I continue to pick out my path.

Dust rises with every step I take

Dust covering the beggar I see

It all isn't right; I wonder how I can live my life

When I know of this place and this street."

It all isn't right; I wonder how I can live my life

When I know of this place and this street."


## THE END

CPSIA information can be obtained
at www.ICGtesting.com
Printed in the USA
LVOW13s1807220517
535421LV00036B/1510/P